I0563230

The Murdered Matron

Matron

A Doro Banyon Historical Mystery-Book Two

D.S. Lang

Copyright ©December 2023 by Debra Sue Lang

All rights reserved.

No part of this publication may be reproduced, distributed, or transmitted in any form or by any means, including photocopying, recording, or other electronic or mechanical methods, without the prior written permission of the publisher, except as permitted by U.S. copyright law. For permission requests, contact [include publisher/author contact info].

The story, all names, characters, and incidents portrayed in this production are fictitious. No identification with actual persons (living or deceased), places, buildings, and products is intended or should be inferred.

Book Cover by Karen Phillips

Editing by Alyssa Colton

ISBN paperback: 978-1-962039-06-2

ISBN ebook: 978-1-962039-05-5

Chapter One

Friday signaled the end of the school week, but not the conclusion of the work week for Dorothea Banyon. As a college librarian, she often put in a few hours on Saturday, especially as a term concluded. Although the holiday break lay ahead, her duties as a member of the Christmas festival committee added to her burden. Despite loving her job and the annual celebration, Doro would have enjoyed snuggling under the covers for another hour—or longer.

With grim resignation, she climbed out of her warm bed, hurriedly dressed, and consumed a cup of coffee with a roll before leaving the cozy confines of Wheaton Hall, the residence for women faculty members. As soon as she stepped outside, a blast of cold air hit her. Only a light coat of snow dusted the ground, but gun-metal gray clouds hinted at more falling. How lovely it would be to curl up in an easy chair by her fireplace with a book and coffee. Such a respite would not happen today.

This morning, ambivalent feelings filled Doro as she scurried toward the auditorium for another planning meeting. As far back as she could remember, the annual Christmas event had been a major occasion in Michaw, her hometown. Everyone—residents and students—eagerly anticipated the weekend. This year was no exception, although the celebration had dwindled down from three days of fun to only a party, mostly because fewer and fewer people volunteered to assist. Even so, folks were looking forward to it more than ever. Doro certainly was. A period of uneasiness had followed the murder of a professor in October. Although the case had quickly been solved, shock about such an awful crime occurring in their peaceful village had rattled folks. Now, they were ready for a return to normalcy. The coming revelry would help.

As a member of the committee, Doro felt excited about instituting new touches: electric lights on the tree, boughs of mistletoe in the archways, and a phonograph for the latest music. All were among her suggestions. At the last meeting, most of the committeewomen had been enthusiastic. Today, a final decision would be made—and the possibility that her ideas would be dismissed by the person in charge kept Doro's spirits contained.

Upon arriving at the meeting site, Doro found several ladies gathered at a table in the far corner of the room. With a smile on her face, she rushed to join them. "Hello."

"You're late, Dorothea." An imposing woman in her sixties commented from the head of the table.

Doro's enthusiasm ebbed. Why-oh-why was Mrs. Frotis still chairwoman of the event? Twenty years was too long, especially when the matron ruled with an iron-hand, albeit one clad in a pristine white glove. She had not yet commented on Doro's recommendations. Would she object? Probably. If so, would the others support Doro, or would they give in to the imposing matron?

Since she was right on time, Doro did not reply. Instead, she took the only empty seat, which was unfortunately next to Mrs. Frotis. As she glanced around the group, Doro noted the sympathetic expressions on two faces. Irma Green, whose husband was an area farmer, and Magenta Silven, whose spouse was the town doctor, smiled at her. Both women had endeavored to modify party plans over the past several years, but Mrs. Frotis had held sway. When Doro had met with the pair on Wednesday, both women had agreed to support changes. But neither was a fighter. A struggle might occur, because power was rarely ceded, especially by someone like Hortense Frotis. While the chairwoman's narrowed gaze remained on her, Doro pulled off her mittens and took off her wool cloak.

"Dorothea, a lady wears gloves. Mittens are for children and laborers." The stinging criticism again came from the chairwoman.

Instead of tucking the mittens into her coat pockets as she had been about to do, Doro laid them on the table. For a long moment, she studied the beautiful craftsmanship and considered how many hours her mother had dedicated to knitting the gift. The mittens not only protected Doro's hands during winter walks across campus, they warmed her heart. Like the locket at her neck, a family heirloom from her mother, the apparel was a physical connection to her parents, who now lived hundreds of miles away in Colorado.

"I'm sure they do a better job of keeping your fingers toasty than gloves would," Magenta Silven said. "And they're pretty, too."

Doro turned to the doctor's wife, who offered a smile along with her kind words. "You're right about them providing warmth. They do." She fingered the zig-zag pattern, knit in shades of blue, as she spoke. According to her mother, the dominant color—a soft blue—exactly matched Doro's eyes.

A harrumph left Mrs. Frotis but, before she could say more, barking erupted. Doro grinned as she turned toward the door. The campus security officer, Everett Mallow, was making his rounds with little Agatha Christie in tow. When they had adopted the stray in October, Doro and Ev had chosen the name because both loved the mystery writer's work.

Tee, the puppy's nickname, was yapping wildly and pulling hard on her lead. After Ev petted the little ball of fur and whispered to her, she quieted, and he moved forward. This time, Tee was not as wild, but she danced toward the group of women like a prima ballerina. When the pair reached Doro, the dog fell to her side and showed her belly. Doro could not help but laugh as she stooped to stroke Tee's warm tummy.

"That little yapper should not be inside this building. She'll spread her fleas everywhere." The complaint came from Mrs. Frotis, who shot a scowl at the dog and then, at the security officer.

"She doesn't have fleas, ma'am." As he took off his gray uniform cap, Ev replied in a respectful tone, but annoyance flickered in his silver gaze.

A harrumph left Mrs. Frotis. "All curs have fleas."

"Tee is a pet." Doro gently stroked the pup while avoiding the matriarch's censorial gaze. "Officer Mallow takes good care of her. I'm sure if a flea gets on Tee, he removes it quickly. I've seen no sign of any when she's with me."

The older woman's scowl deepened. "Letting that filthy thing stay in campus housing is abominable."

When Doro glanced at Ev, she saw his jaw tighten. "The rules are made by the college administration," he said in an arctic tone.

"That's right," Doro agreed. "Besides, Officer Mallow lives in the attic apartment above the president's garage, not in actual campus housing."

"The mutt has been in your apartment, hasn't she, Dorothea?" the older woman asked.

"Tee has only stayed with me two nights, when Officer Mallow was out-of-town," Doro replied.

Mrs. Frotis lifted her chin and stared down her formidable nose at Doro. "She could spread her fleas in two minutes. Besides, she's unruly. Get her off me right now."

Tee, while within two feet of the chairwoman, was not touching her. Even so, Ev reached down and swept the puppy into his arms.

"She always seems well-behaved," Mrs. Silven put in, a grin on her pretty face.

"She is, ma'am," Ev added.

Doro smiled. "Officer Mallow has done a great job of training her."

"Ha! Dogs do not belong inside." Mrs. Frotis made the statement as she looked straight at Ev. "You should leave it at home, not bring it to work."

Annoyance overcame Doro's usual restraint when dealing with the matron. "Tee is a *she*, not an *it*," Doro said.

Mrs. Frotis, an angry flush on her angular face, turned to Doro. "I plan to talk with the trustees about allowing a mutt on campus."

"I doubt if any of them is as starched up and small-minded as you." The statement came from a newcomer, a lithe blonde in her thirties. She bent to pet Tee before greeting Officer Mallow. "Hello, Ev. How nice to see you again."

"Good day, Mrs. Parson," he said with a slight lift of his chin. Clad in a gray, hip-length, fitted uniform jacket and matching pants, the campus security officer looked much like any small-town constable but with an added aura of authority that probably came from his time as a Prohibition agent.

"I've told you to call me Veronica." As she spoke, the woman gestured toward a chair sitting against the wall. "Would you mind getting that for me, Ev?"

"Of course not." Ev handed the leash grip to Doro. He patted Tee's head and murmured, "Stay with Doro."

"Here you go, ma'am," he said, setting the chair down for the woman. Once again, his tone was clipped.

Mrs. Parson laid a gloved hand on his arm. "Thank you, Ev."

"You're welcome," he replied.

When he stepped farther away, she smiled at him again. "Would you help me with my coat?"

"Sure thing." Again, neither his expression nor tone held any enthusiasm. After assisting the woman, he hung the garment over an extra chair by the wall.

"Thank you again, Ev," Veronica murmured with a level of sweetness that didn't match his simple courtesy.

The exchange hit a sour note with Doro. In the weeks since she had helped Officer Mallow solve a murder, Doro had gotten to know him better. At their first meeting, he had seemed officious and overbearing, but first impressions were not always right—and that was true in his case. Sometimes, he was reserved and serious but, more and more often, he was open, amusing, and fun. And always, he was handsome. His face had an appealing symmetry, while his dark brown hair was thick and glossy. But his eyes were his most striking feature. Fringed in black lashes, they reminded her of polished silver, but now they more closely resembled river ice.

When his gaze met hers, Doro inwardly chastised herself for her mental meandering and focused on the meeting. She glanced around the table. "I start work at noon today, so maybe we could begin."

Another harrumph left Mrs. Frotis. "We cannot commence in a timely manner when committeewomen are late." She glared at Doro and then, at Mrs. Parson.

"Since you make all the plans yourself and dictate to the rest of us," Mrs. Parson said, "I don't know why we meet at all. Why not make lists and give them to us? It would save time."

"Why I never," Mrs. Frotis barked out.

"No, you never listen to anyone," Mrs. Parson said with a laugh.

Several moments of uncomfortable silence passed before Ev spoke. "Excuse me, ladies. I need to check the other buildings and such." He extended his hand and took the leash from Doro.

When he turned toward the door, Doro wished she could leave with him and Tee. They could play with the pup and laugh together. Instead, she braced herself for another tedious meeting, which turned out to be as miserable as she feared.

As soon as the officer was gone, Mrs. Frotis wasted no time in grabbing her gavel and pounding the table. "We need to come to order." She immediately called for the secretary, Eloise Vining, to read the previous minutes.

As the chairwoman followed Robert's Rules of Order to a fine point, Doro remembered her first committee meeting—twenty years ago—when she had come with her mother. They had not stayed long due to Mrs. Frotis' objection to a child being in attendance. At age five, Doro hadn't heard of meeting rules. Now, she knew them like the back of her hand, mostly due to Mrs. Frotis and her insistence on proper parliamentary procedure. More than once, other committee women had suggested dropping the formality, but to no avail. Majority rule wasn't on Mrs. Frotis' agenda. Criticism and domination were.

After Miss Vining finished reading the minutes, the chairwoman spoke again. "You missed some details, Eloise, but you always do."

Eloise Vining, a raw-boned woman in her forties, offered a faint smile. "I get all the crucial details, Hortense, just not every syllable of your meanderings."

Was there a slight edge in Eloise's tone? The spinster seldom spoke up at the meetings or elsewhere. She was a native

Michawan, who still lived in her family's cottage on the edge of town. And on the edge of life, in general. Scarecrow-thin with a gaunt countenance and wiry gray hair, Eloise was plain. Mousy was how townsfolk described her, which Doro found rude. But the woman did not try to look pretty or dress well.

Scarlet formed twin splotches on Mrs. Frotis' lean cheeks. "You are impertinent, Eloise. We should never have allowed you to take your mother's place as the committee secretary."

Veronica Parson chuckled. "We don't need officers. The mayor's clerk handles the money, which is most important. If you weren't so starched up, Hortense, you'd get a few people to take care of the various tasks and let them do it. Instead, you race around checking up on everyone, which is why the committee gets smaller every year. You're running out of ladies who will put up with your nit-picking. If you keep antagonizing people, you'll be all alone. Or maybe you'll be replaced."

Mrs. Frotis snorted derisively. "You won't be put in charge, in any case. You can't even control those mutts of yours."

After staring daggers at the chairwoman, Mrs. Parson lifted her chin. "Duke and Duchess are pure-bred Airedales, not mutts."

"Ha. They're nuisances, running loose and digging everywhere," Mrs. Frotis shot back. "And you're responsible for their damage to my flower beds."

"Ralphie replanted your chrysanthemums two months ago. They'll bloom next year," the other woman said.

Ralph Bolt had worked for the Frotis family since boyhood, which was long before Doro was born. He lived above the garage and served as gardener, handyman, and errand boy.

"And your mutts will dig them up again," Mrs. Frotis said. "Those two beasts should be put down."

All casualness left Mrs. Parson's expression, and red-hot anger replaced it. "If something happens to either Duke or Duchess, you will live to regret it...but you won't live long."

The outburst surprised Doro. As she glanced around the table, she noted the others had similar reactions.

Color surged into the chairwoman's face. "Do not threaten me, or I shall go to Constable Lammers. Then, we'll see about getting rid of your mutts permanently." She looked at Doro. "And that little flea bait of yours, too. All the troublemakers should go."

Before Doro could respond, Veronica spoke again. "If that's the case, you should be at the top of the list, since your bullying upsets half the town. Maybe more."

Something between a chuckle and a chortle left Eloise before the spinster clapped a hand over her mouth and focused on her notepad. Seconds of silence passed as everyone else appeared to be held mute.

Then, Mrs. Silven raised one hand. "We're here to discuss the annual Christmas party. Some of us have other obligations, so it'd be best if the meeting continues without side conversations."

"Yes," Irma Green added. "I have to take our littlest one to the doctor this afternoon."

Mrs. Frotis continued to scowl but nodded. "All right."

From that point on, the group covered the various tasks ahead of them. Although the remaining path wasn't entirely smooth, it was not as rocky as the beginning had been. Unfortunately, when Doro's suggestions came up for review, Mrs. Frotis rejected most of them.

"We'll have the church choir, as usual, to provide music," the chairwoman observed.

"People enjoy dancing," Veronica put in. "They can still sing along with the choir for a time, but a phonograph would be better for kicking up our heels."

"I'm sure you'd love to prance around." Mrs. Frotis scowled again. "Some folks dance when the singing goes on. Improper and rude, but I cannot control everything."

"But you would if you could," Veronica sniped.

Eloise snickered before again bowing her head. Since Doro still hoped to see her other ideas implemented, she ignored the remarks and posed a question. "What about the mistletoe and electric lights?"

The chairwoman took a sidelong glance at Doro. "Mistletoe is unseemly, but the lights will be fine. I assume you know where to purchase them."

Winning on one count was better than none, so Doro nodded. "The hardware store in Sylvania just started stocking them. I'll call this morning."

"Fine. You can fetch them," Mrs. Frotis said.

Despite her busy schedule, Doro wanted the glittering lights, which remained a novelty, on the tree. "Of course. I can drive over tomorrow." Perhaps, she and her grandmother, who lived in Sylvania on Summit Street near uptown, could have lunch together. "We haven't discussed refreshments. I know we'll meet again, but what time will the Adlers deliver everything?"

"They won't," Mrs. Frotis said. "I'll speak with them later today, but I've hired a bakery in Toledo to supply the event. It's near my new attorney's office, and they do a splendid job."

Gasps escaped the other women. Eloise was the first to find her voice. "The Adlers have always made the party treats. By now, they've probably started work."

"I'm sure they have, which means they may be stuck with baked goods," Irma Green added. "We should at least buy what they have on hand."

"The decision is made, and I must be on my way." Mrs. Frotis banged her gavel again, ended the meeting, and hurried out.

In the aftermath of her departure, the other women chattered among themselves about the Adlers being dropped. Although Doro wanted to voice her perspective, she had to get to the library before her shift started. A few quiet moments in her little office would provide a chance to review plans for her mystery class's final meeting. Thinking about all her duties—as a librarian, a professor, and a volunteer—weighed on Doro. But teaching a course on the mystery novel played into one of her lifelong pastimes—that of playing armchair detective. A smile touched her lips. Weeks ago, Ev had crowned her as an amateur sleuth, steps above an armchair detective.

As Doro left the building, Irma caught up with her. "That was the worst meeting yet," the other woman, a petite blonde in her early thirties, said. "Rejecting the victrola and mistletoe was foolish, and dropping the Adlers. Just awful." She shook her head. "The worst thing was Mrs. Frotis threatening Veronica's dogs. I don't blame Veronica for being upset, but she sounded furious in response."

"It was an ugly exchange." Doro didn't want to admit her genuine reaction, because Irma's effervescence often made her too chatty. Going over all the issues in detail would take too much time, time Doro did not have. "We don't need to tell people, though. Harmful gossip hurts everyone, and I'm sure neither will act on their threats."

"Of course not. I hope the next meeting goes better." Irma wrung her hands. "I'm nervous about the decorations. We have beautiful trees on the farm, and my husband and his brothers will cut one down and bring it to town. The children and I can gather greens, but putting ornaments on the tree will be tricky. The same with lights. We've never used electric ones."

When Doro shot a sidelong glance at the other woman, she saw anxiety in the dark eyes. "You'll do a wonderful job, and we'll all pitch in."

Irma bit her lower lip. "Hortense is so particular. Remember last year when she went to check the decorations the morning of the party and didn't like how Anna Orvis did the ones on the tree? Hortense got on the ladder and changed them all around. Two of us had to hold it for her, and the job took forever. Afterward, Anna left the committee."

The memory of last year's quarrels rose in Doro's mind. "I recall the incident. I was sorry Anna quit, but it's understandable."

"It certainly is," Irma agreed. "I saw her right after Hortense gave her what-for. Anna was beside herself."

"When are you bringing the tree?" Doro asked in an attempt to move away from old difficulties.

"Most likely, we'll bring the tree on Wednesday, but when it gets decorated will be up to Hortense."

Doro nodded. "Whenever she wants it done, we'll do it. Now, I need to go, or I'll be late to work."

"I'll see you at the next meeting." Irma Green offered a faint smile and moved on.

As Doro turned toward the library, she fought the gusty wind. Most of the college's buildings, constructed of red brick with white wood trim, were grouped in a u-shape around College Commons. Benches sat every thirty feet along the paths, and they were usually filled during spring and fall. Winter was a different story. No one would sit out in today's blustery weather.

Although the holiday season was always fun, the wintry weather that usually accompanied it was not. Despite her wool mittens, Doro's hands were icy, so she shoved them into her pockets and rushed on. In her haste, she nearly collided with another person. "Sorry." Surprise hit her when she saw Eloise Vining. "Are you heading home?" Doro aimed for a friendly tone. Although she was in a hurry, Doro could talk an extra moment or two.

Eloise lifted her chin. "I have a few errands to run, but Veronica and I chatted for a bit. Both of us are appalled by Mrs. Frotis picking on the doggies. Surely, you agree. She threatened sweet little Tee, too."

A long breath escaped Doro. "President Adams approved Tee living in college housing, so Mrs. Frotis won't get her removed."

"She might mean to have them put down, not just taken away."

"I think it was bluster." That was typical of the matron.

Eloise shook her head. "You're naïve, but that's to be expected, since you have little experience outside school."

Several harsh retorts came to the tip of Doro's tongue as she stared at the spinster. The woman had never lived away from her family home, so she was in no position to judge others. Doro's ingrained courtesy kept her from being snide. So did the knowledge that she had spent most of her life in school as a student, teacher, and librarian. But she had lived in Ann Arbor, while attending school there, and she'd traveled to Colorado—alone—several times, which made her far worldlier than Eloise Vining. Finally, Doro managed a reply. "Mrs. Frotis is dramatic, but she wouldn't kill any pets."

"She might pressure Ralphie to do it. Or some vagabond."

Ralphie was a gentle soul who wouldn't harm any critter. As for the other suggestion, it was ludicrous. "Vagabond?"

Eloise tsked-tsked. "You really are in your little world on this campus. Vagabonds ride the rails. They stop in little towns like ours to steal or earn a few dollars before moving on. You think you know so much, but what about the rest of Tee's litter? What about her mother? Did you know they were hiding in the Frotis' shed, and that miserable woman wanted them gone?" The words tumbled out like rocks sliding down a mountain.

"How do you know that?"

"I hear things."

Doro's heart hammered against her ribs. "Did someone kill the others?" Surely not.

"I don't know," Eloise replied before turning on her heel and striding off.

Doro stared at the older woman's retreating figure in stunned amazement. Was Eloise right, or was she sharing a tall tale to make trouble?

؏ﻮﻤﻌ

Later that day, Doro looked up from her desk to see Ev Mallow talking with her boss, Floyd Quartine, the library director. For a moment, she dithered about joining the two men. Doro wanted to reassure Ev about keeping Tee in his quarters. Despite Mrs. Frotis' threats, the little dog was welcome in all college residences. The interim president, Miles Adams, had promised as much, and the man always stood by his word.

When Floyd turned toward the bookcases, Ev headed toward Doro's office. As soon as he stepped inside her tiny quarters, she gestured to a chair. "Sit down."

"Thanks."

"Where is Tee? You didn't take her to your place because of what Mrs. Frotis said, did you?"

He shook his head. "I needed to talk to Mr. Quartine about security for a big meeting coming up. Since he's allergic to dogs, I dropped her off at my apartment." A grin curved his lips. "She was tired after making the rounds with me. Most of the students lavish her with attention, which she loves. But she's still a puppy and tires quickly. I'll give her time for a nap and take her along later today."

Relief filled Doro, who had worried about Ev not wanting to cause commotion by keeping the pup with him. "Tee has

President Adams' support, so Mrs. Frotis won't be successful in her machinations."

"I figured as much, but I didn't want to argue with the woman. She seems like a formidable force."

Doro rolled her eyes. "She is. I'm sorry she got abrupt with you, but she's like that with almost everyone."

Ev leaned forward and braced his elbows on his knees. "How was she chosen to be the committee chairwoman?"

"She wasn't chosen," Doro replied. "She appointed herself years ago when the last committee head stepped down. No one else came forward, from what I know. Mrs. Frotis volunteered to take charge, and she's held the reins ever since. My mother said the woman wasn't as bad at first, although Mrs. Frotis has long been a stickler for proper protocol. Now, it's not just that. She wants every little thing done a certain way. Her way."

His lips quirked. "Working with her can't be easy."

"It isn't, which is why the group has dwindled from twenty to six over the past few years." Doro rested her elbows on the desk edge.

"That's quite a drop," Ev commented.

Doro was about to recap some of the morning meeting's low lights when a student appeared at her office door.

"I'm sorry to bother you, Miss Banyon, but we're supposed to talk about the last mystery book club meeting next week." The girl's gaze flitted to Ev and back to Doro.

Without hesitation, Ev stood up and addressed the young student. "I was about to leave." He glanced at Doro. "If you want to walk with Tee and me later, we're taking our usual jaunt around campus at five-thirty."

Disappointment hit Doro hard. She loved walking with them. "I'm working until eight, since it's the end of classes and the library will stay open late. Plus, there's the Christmas party committee and preparation for my last classes."

"Tee will miss your company." He gave a nod before bidding Doro and the student farewell.

Doro would miss Tee, too. And Ev. But she quashed the latter thought immediately.

Chapter Two

The next days passed in a blur. Sunday should have been restful, but her various duties combined to give Doro no free time, so she ended up grading papers after church. The following morning, Doro saw Ev and Tee in passing. The little dog was excited, and Ev was friendly. He asked about plans for the big party, and Doro provided cheery updates despite feeling on edge. At the Monday meeting, Mrs. Frotis barked orders, Veronica interjected an occasional snide remark, and Eloise snickered intermittently. The other two members listened with grim expressions, and Doro was constantly braced for them to quit. How would everything get done if that happened?

She arrived at Tuesday morning's meeting to see a newcomer. Seated at the table with Mrs. Frotis, the slender woman wore a green wool frock that had been in fashion early in the decade. Her matching cloche, sporting an ostrich feather, was slightly faded, and the woman's bob needed a trim, but she was pretty. A few strands of gray were visible in otherwise brunette hair, but her eyes shone brightly. "Good day," Doro said, looking from the chairwoman to the stranger, who smiled in response.

"This is my sister, Mrs. Loretta Hood," Mrs. Frotis said as Doro took her seat. "She came from her home near Bowling Green to visit. Loretta, this is Dorothea Banyon."

Doro smiled at the woman, who appeared to be a decade younger than her sibling. "How lovely to meet you, Mrs. Hood."

"I'm pleased to meet you, Dorothea, but please call me Retty," the other woman said.

"I go by Doro."

A harrumph left Mrs. Frotis. "Such informality is unseemly." Her gaze narrowed on her sister. "But your attire is unseemly, as well. A widow dresses in black for a year after her husband's death."

Retty stiffened before visibly fighting down some emotion. "Times have changed, Hortie. We need to change with them."

Mrs. Frotis sputtered with indignation. "I have told you many times not to call me that. In private, you may use my given name—my full given name. But do not use it in public."

Mrs. Silven, Mrs. Green, Miss Vining, and Mrs. Parson entered the auditorium during the exchange. The chairwoman introduced them to her sister, before calling the meeting to order. "We have much left to do," she said after banging her gavel on the table.

"Will you be assisting, Retty?" Mrs. Parson asked. Clearly, she had heard most of the conversation.

"As I can," the other woman replied. "I'd planned to visit friends in the Toledo area but stopped to see my sister on my way. I'm happy to pitch in before and after my trip to the city. It's been years and years since I've been in Michaw to enjoy the holiday festivities."

Mrs. Frotis scowled at Mrs. Hood. "You're attending a tea tomorrow afternoon, aren't you?"

A smile curved the younger sibling's bow-shaped lips. "I am, but I can lend my party planning expertise today. Although I've promised to go to a concert on Thursday night, I'll return on Friday."

"That isn't necessary," her sister said.

"Nonsense," Veronica put in. "We need all the help we can get."

"That's true," Eloise added. "I've worried about how we'll manage with so few of us."

The chairwoman again hammered her gavel on the table. "You are all out of order."

Veronica chuckled. "That's the least of our worries. I, for one, am happy your sister will pitch in, and I'm interested in her ideas, although it may be too late this year." She turned to Retty. "We've tried and tried to convince Hortie about making changes. She hasn't listened."

A snort left Mrs. Frotis, who went red in the face. "Do not use that awful nickname."

"It's cute," Veronica replied.

Retty Hood grinned. "I'm glad someone agrees with me."

"I agree, too," Eloise commented. "We don't need to use titles among us."

Mrs. Silven, always the voice of reason, cleared her throat. "I don't mind being called Magenta, but we should respect Mrs. Frotis' wishes."

"Yes, we should," Mrs. Green added. "Feel free to call me Irma, though."

"Almost everyone calls me Doro, which I prefer to Dorothea or Miss Banyon." With effort, she did not look at the chairwoman, who persisted in using Doro's full given name. "I definitely side with those who believe we should all choose how we want to be addressed, and our choices should be honored."

Veronica waved one well-manicured hand in the air. "Fine. Anyone else insist on being addressed with a title?"

Every woman, except Mrs. Frotis, shook her head. A harrumph left the matron. "Let us get down to business, since we've wasted enough time." She went through the list of tasks left to complete and reviewed the schedule.

"You don't have sleigh rides as part of the celebration any longer?" Retty asked. "Or caroling around town on Friday night? What about ice skating? The creek is frozen, and it was always fun to spend part of Saturday there."

"Everyone was terribly disappointed when all that ended," Eloise said.

"Why stop having them?" Retty asked.

"The sleigh rides ended because your sister refused to allow Anita Ressiger on our committee," Veronica replied. "Her family provided the sleigh and horses at no cost to the town. It's not hard to understand why they quit doing so after Anita was belittled."

Retty's ebony eyebrows shot up. "Why would you belittle her, Hortie?"

Color made splotches on Mrs. Frotis' wide face. "We can't let just anyone on this committee."

"What do you mean?" Retty asked. "The whole town was involved when we first moved here."

"Circumstances have changed since you took off." Mrs. Frotis' lips pursed as if she was tasting something unpalatable. "Anita Ressiger is a former maid, who married a farmer. She had nerve asking to be a committeewoman."

"I'm a farmer's wife," Irma Green said in a small voice.

Hortense Frotis immediately turned to her. "But your father and your uncle were teachers. You're from good stock. Mrs. Ressiger originally came from the city to work for Mrs. Parson, who has shared nothing of the girl's background. That tells me all I need to know."

Her haughty tone revealed as much as her words. As Doro looked from one sister to the other, she wondered why they were so different.

"That's ridiculous," Retty said. "You've always been snooty, but you've evidently gotten worse since Roderick died. I suppose you'd prefer I call him Dr. Frotis, but he didn't mind informality. You shouldn't, either."

"I have standards," her sister shot back, "something that you do not, and neither did your husband. Both of you lacked morals and sense. Now, your poor decisions are coming home to roost, which is most likely why you're here."

Color rose in Retty's cheeks. "I came hoping to get past old grievances, since you and I are both widows now." Her tone, while subdued, held an edge. "And we'll always be sisters. It's only the two of us left."

A stricken expression blanketed the older sibling's face. "You're right. Being a widow is hard, and we have no other family." She glanced around the group. "Our meeting time should focus on business, so let's return to that."

"Good idea," her sister said as she patted the chairwoman's hand. "You and I will have plenty of time to have a heart-to-heart chat in private."

Although talk went back to the following Saturday's festivities, Doro wondered what Mrs. Frotis meant by poor decisions, and why would they cause Retty to visit? Despite spending almost all of her life in Michaw, Doro did not recall ever seeing the younger woman before, but Retty Hood had made a wonderful first impression, and Doro liked her. Perhaps, they could chat briefly after the meeting. Then, Doro might learn more about both sisters.

۔عیم

When the group broke up, Retty stood immediately. "I want to stop in a few stores uptown and see some folks," she said to her sister. "I'll be back at your house in a couple of hours."

Mrs. Frotis hesitated a moment before nodding in response.

Doro grabbed her cloak and hurried to catch Retty, but the chairwoman stopped her. "I need a copy of the receipt for the lights, Dorothea. You got them, didn't you?"

Annoyance flickered through Doro. "Of course, and I'll bring the receipt to the next meeting." Before the older woman could say more, Doro darted out of the auditorium. By the time, she got outside, Retty Hood was well ahead of her, so Doro picked up her pace. Within moments, she caught up.

"Hello, Doro." Retty turned toward her with a smile. "Are you going uptown before you begin work?"

Although she had little time, Doro nodded. "I want to stop at the bakery for some cookies to take to my class." That had not been her original intention, but she wanted to speak with the visitor.

"How kind of you. I want to go there, too. The Adlers were always nice to me. They still own the place, don't they? I'd be disappointed, if they don't."

"They do." Should Doro mention Mrs. Frotis dropping the local bakery for the party? Not yet, she decided.

"Good. I always loved their muffins."

"They still have a wonderful selection," Doro replied, "so you won't be disappointed."

"Perfect. Ralphie is meeting me there."

The comment provoked curiosity in Doro. "Did you know him when you lived here?"

"I did. My brother-in-law's family gave him a place to live when his folks died, which was a few years before Hortie married Roderick. Ralphie is close to my age, but had already quit school." Sadness clouded her eyes. "Some kids teased him terribly, because he had trouble learning. I made sure he got basic ciphering down and was able to read a little."

Warmth spread through Doro. "That was nice of you."

"I enjoyed helping. He was a good boy, and he's a good man. But lonely. It's hard since he's so much slower than most folks.

He loves sweets, so I suggested we meet at the bakery this morning."

"I bet he was excited," Doro commented. "He stops there a few times a week, but he seldom has anyone to share a treat with him."

"The housekeeper mentioned as much to me. I'll see that he has company while I'm here, although that won't be for long." A note of melancholy tinged her voice.

"There's no chance of you staying on?"

A soft sigh left the other woman. "I doubt that will happen."

Before more could be said, the conversation was interrupted by Ralphie Bolt loping toward them. A bright smile lit his weathered face. "Hullo, Miss Retty, Miss Doro," he said as he stopped beside the women.

"Good morning, Ralphie," Doro said. "I hear you're going to the bakery for a snack."

When his head bobbed up and down in answer, locks of dark hair fell across his thin face. Although the man-child loved sweets, he was lean. "Yep. Miss Retty is buying. We're gonna sit at one of the little tables inside, too."

Usually, Ralphie got a small bag of day-old sweets from Mrs. Adler and ate them elsewhere, so being a regular customer with a companion had to be special for him. "How lovely," Doro replied with a smile. Although she wanted to chat more with Mrs. Frotis' sister, Doro did not want to intrude on their outing. "I need to get to work, so I'll let you two be on your way."

Retty frowned. "Weren't you getting cookies?"

While that had been an excuse to walk with Retty, Doro needed to follow-through on it or evoke curiosity. "Of course."

Although she had little time, Doro went in and bought three dozen. Although Mrs. Adler chattered, as usual, Doro escaped quickly.

༄

Once she got to her classroom, Doro set aside all thoughts of the meeting and the sisters. With the semester coming to a close, her students handed in their final essays, ate cookies, and said their farewells. Although most would be at the Christmas party on Saturday night, they wouldn't meet as a group again. The end of a term was always bittersweet. While they would see one another on campus, the community established in class would vanish shortly.

After wrapping up, Doro gathered her students' papers and headed to the library. For the first few hours of her shift, she kept busy answering research questions and finding materials. A lull hit late in the day, and she sought out her boss, who was having a cup of tea in his office.

"Sit down," he said. "It's been a hectic day. Far too many students waited until the end of the term to work on their papers."

Doro slipped into the chair nearest the door. "Mine turned theirs in, which means I have plenty of grading to do. Sometimes, I think I should assign fewer papers."

"Teaching a course is extra work," her boss said.

"It is, but I love teaching, especially about mysteries."

The older man nodded. "From what your students say, you excel at making the books come alive. Not that I'm surprised.

You're an extraordinary librarian. Knowledgeable and helpful and patient."

The praise pleased Doro. "Thanks. You set an inspiring example."

"I try," he replied. His expression grew thoughtful. "You'd make a fine head librarian. When it comes time for me to retire, I'll recommend you as my replacement."

"I appreciate that." Ever since her father had brought her to the Michaw College library as a little girl, Doro had been enthralled with the place. Her love of books, combined with her affection for the campus, had motivated Doro to become a librarian. Her fondest dream was to take Mr. Quartine's place someday. "You aren't still thinking about retiring at the end of this school year, are you? I thought President Adams' return would change your mind."

A smile touched the older man's mouth. "It has, so I'll stay on for another year or two. Perhaps a little longer."

"Longer would be better for me," Doro said, "because I'd have more time to prove myself." And to achieve tenure, which was a requirement for the library director.

"My thoughts, too." He picked a pen up from his desk and rolled it between his hands. "You and Officer Mallow have gotten friendly, what with sharing the puppy and all."

Unsure what he meant by *and all*, Doro formed her response with care. "We both love dogs, and he enjoys reading mysteries, too."

Mr. Quartine nodded. "Nice to have things in common."

Uncertainty continued to plague Doro. What was her boss wanting to say? Did he, like a few others around town, think she and the campus security officer were interested in more than collegiality? Refuting the assumption usually led to people smirking, so Doro made a benign reply. "Yes, it is," she murmured before getting to her questions. "This morning, the Christmas party planning committee met again, which we're doing every day this week."

"It has to be hard, since you've lost so many members."

"Being short-handed is challenging, but we had an extra person this morning."

His gray brows rose a fraction. "Who was that?"

"Loretta Hood, Mrs. Frotis' younger sister."

Surprise slackened his jaw. "I remember her as Retty Bottoms. That was their maiden name. When Rod Frotis married, his missus brought her younger sister along. Their parents were gone, so the girl lived with them for a few years."

"I don't recall ever seeing her."

"You probably never did," Floyd replied. "After high school, Retty left to take a job in the city. She wed within a year or two and never came back."

"Not even to visit?"

Floyd shook his head. "Mrs. Frotis didn't approve of Retty leaving or marrying. The boy came from a wealthy family from down around Bowling Green, but he didn't have a good head on his shoulders. Although he could've taken a job with his father, he went out West for some get rich quick scheme. It didn't pan out. Rod and I were good friends, so he confided in me about staying in touch with Retty over the years. He tried to get his wife to relent, but she never did. Retty leaving and marrying without her approval was bad enough for her, but when the young couple went into vaudeville, Hortense was livid. Rod said the husband was a talented musician, and Retty had a lovely voice, so I imagine they were a popular act. Rod wanted to see them when they were in Toledo one time, but Hortense was irate. Due to her objections, he asked me not to tell anyone about Retty being on the stage."

"I see." Doro found nothing wrong with the stage shows. Some of the women's costumes were skimpy but not indecent, although Mrs. Frotis would have seen them that way. "Mrs. Hood has been living near Bowling Green, so they quit vaude-ville, I suppose."

"She and her husband might've inherited his family's house."

"He passed away within the last year, from what I under-stand." Doro thought back to the exchange between the sisters. Wearing black for a year after the death of a close relative was standard. Did Retty ignore the custom out of rebelliousness or disinterest or penury? Her suit was well-cut, but far from new. Perhaps she had, as the old saying went, married in haste and repented at leisure.

"Sorry to hear that," Floyd murmured. "I hope Retty's visit here means she and her sister are reconciling."

Doro chewed on her lip. "Retty expressed hope that they will, but they seem at odds in a lot of ways. She's going to see a friend in Toledo tomorrow but will be back Friday." A tap on the door interrupted, and Doro swiveled to see one of her students waiting. Briefly, she turned back to her boss. "I need to return to work."

For the rest of the day, Doro remained busy and, by the time she got to her apartment, exhaustion laid on her like a heavy weight. A hot meal by her little fireplace sounded heavenly. So did quiet solitude, but that was interrupted by a knock as she took off her cloak. Wearily, Doro opened the door to find her best friend, Agatha Darwine, in the hall. "Come in."

After Doro stepped back, Aggie—a basket over her arm—entered and stopped. "You look drained. I brought some cookies from the bakery, since I stopped earlier today. I thought we could have them with tea. But I can leave the basket, if you'd rather not have company."

If anyone other than her best friend had come calling, Doro would have used grading papers as an excuse to be alone. While she had a lot to do, a friendly chat over supper was welcome. "Your company is always a treat. I'm going to fix a sandwich. Do you want one?"

Aggie crossed to the small table and put the basket down. "I ate downstairs. Mrs. Farmer sent a family-style meal over for us. Fried chicken, mashed potatoes, snap beans, and biscuits. I would've saved some for you, but barely a nibble was left."

"I can understand why. Mrs. Farmer puts out wonderful food, and her chicken dinners rank very high in my estimation." The woman had served as the cook in the girls' dormitory for many years. At the end of each term, she also provided dinners for the female faculty living in Wheaton Hall.

"They always did," Aggie said with a smile. "Back when we were students, you often asked when she planned to fry chicken again."

The memory made Doro smile. "And she always did within a few days. I'm sorry I missed tonight's treat, but the library is busy, so I stayed late. Let me make tea and a sandwich. Then, we can sit and chat."

"I'll start a fire to take the chill off," her friend said.

"Thank you."

Within a few minutes, Doro returned with a tray. After Aggie made space on the low table, both young women sat down. Following several bites of her sandwich and a long swallow of tea, Doro leaned back in her chair. "This is wonderful."

"It is," Aggie agreed as she glanced around. "Your apartment feels a lot like your parents' home."

Her friend's observation rang true. The two overstuffed chairs had been in the Banyons' front parlor, as had the little table now sitting between the matching pair. On the far wall was a keyhole desk, once used by Doro's mother. Next to the front door stood a tall umbrella stand with hooks and a long mirror. At one time, the hooks had held the family's hats and coats. Three umbrellas had rested in the open bin on the left side, while Doro's school books had often sat on the right-side shelf. Now, only her winter cloak, a wool cloche, and a single parasol were in the rack. "It feels like a small part, at least." A soft sigh escaped her. "I should probably give away everything my grandmother is storing in her attic. I'll never have room for a whole dining set, two sofas, more chairs, and all. I looked at all of it when I went to town for the Christmas tree lights and stopped to visit with Gramma." Since her parents had taken only a few items to Colorado, they had left the rest for Doro.

"When you have your own home, you'll need more furniture."

Doro grimaced. She and Aggie had discussed this topic in the past and more than once, so Doro need not repeat why she did not plan on having a house of her own with a family to fill it. "Mr. Quartine mentioned staying a few more years, which would give me a chance to earn tenure and become a serious candidate for library director when he retires."

Aggie sat back and met Doro's gaze. "The college may change its policy about employing married women. The proposal only fell one vote short last time."

Her friend's observation struck at the core of Doro's dilemma. "True, but the board won't change enough in the next couple of years to make a difference, and a few male faculty members are opposed, too," she pointed out. "Besides, I'm not stepping out with anyone. I never have. Not steadily."

A broad grin formed on Aggie's face. "That could change."

Mr. Quartine's observations returned, but Doro brushed them back, as she did her friend's teasing. "I have plenty to do right now. A stack of papers to grade and more committee work before Saturday. I just hope things run smoothly until then."

Aggie's amusement disappeared. "I do, too."

Something in her friend's voice disturbed Doro, who studied Aggie's expression. "What's wrong?"

After putting her cup and saucer aside, Aggie met her friend's gaze. "I mentioned being in the bakery earlier."

Doro nodded. "What about it?" A niggling sense of unease shimmered through her. "Did you see Mr. Adler? I was there, but he wasn't." Mrs. Frotis' decision to change bakeries surfaced. Mrs. Adler had not mentioned it, but Doro had been in a hurry.

"Unfortunately, I did. You'd already told me about Mrs. Frotis changing bakers at the last minute, and we both figured the Adlers were upset. But he's beyond that. He's irate. As soon as he saw me, he began ranting and raving about Mrs. Frotis. Mrs. Adler tried to calm him down. Finally, he stomped into the back room. Before that, he threatened to make Mrs. Frotis pay for trying to bankrupt them." Little color remained on Aggie's freckled face. "It was unsettling."

Her friend was a sensitive soul, so a tirade would unnerve her. "I'm sorry you had to hear his outburst, but why did he complain to you?"

One of Aggie's shoulders rose and fell. "After he left, Mrs. Adler said he's been complaining to everyone he sees. She's afraid he'll drive away more business, which they can't afford since they aren't providing baked goods for Saturday."

"I should stop and see them, if only to say the rest of the committee didn't know until last Friday, and no one agreed." And she shouldn't have rushed off earlier without mentioning that. But she had been pressed for time.

Aggie hesitated before responding. "You won't be able to reason with him, and you don't need to listen to his diatribe. Why not wait until after this weekend? You won't be so busy, and he might calm down."

"Probably a good idea," Doro replied, but she tucked the idea into the back of her mind. "Did he say how he planned to get even? I hope it isn't by ruining the party, because that would hurt everyone."

"Mrs. Adler shushed him up when he started talking about retaliation."

"I understand why he's upset, but him losing his temper surprises me." Doro took another bite of her sandwich and considered what she knew about the baker. "The Adlers have owned the bakery ever since I can remember. He's seldom in the shop, since he bakes early and delivers their products. He seems reserved, so I've always thought of him as calm. The two don't necessarily go together, though."

"No, they don't," Aggie agreed. "Maybe he's blowing off steam by berating Mrs. Frotis."

Despite the warmth from the fire, Doro felt chilled by the dissension in her hometown. The holidays should be a time of peace and joy. "He's not the only one who's voicing displeasure. Veronica Parson has been, too." Since Doro had not told Aggie about Retty Hood being in town, she supplied the details—including Floyd Quartine's comments.

"The split between the sisters is sad, but Mrs. Hood wanting to reconcile seems like a good sign," Aggie observed.

"It does, but Mrs. Frotis said her sister had made mistakes, which were coming home to roost. I'm not sure what that means."

Before replying, Aggie gazed into her teacup for a moment. "It's an odd comment, but Mrs. Frotis is starched up, and it sounds like her sister isn't."

"Not at all," Doro replied before adding her boss' revelations about the Hoods being on the vaudeville circuit.

Aggie's auburn eyebrows rose a fraction. "I'm sure Mrs. Frotis didn't approve of that."

"True, which is probably why Retty didn't mention it. She wanted to smooth things over," Doro remarked.

After breaking a cookie in half and taking a bite, Aggie again met Doro's gaze. "While I was uptown, I also went into the dry goods store for a few items. Veronica and Eloise were talking with some other ladies and telling tales about Mrs. Frotis and how awful she is. The dogs were mentioned, and everyone was in a dither over them being threatened. Veronica vowed to take care of Mrs. Frotis if either Duke or Duchess is ever hurt. Eloise didn't say much, but she nodded a few times, especially when Veronica said someone should see to Mrs. Frotis first."

Anxiety and fatigue combined to overcome Doro, who laid her head back and let her eyes close. "They must've gone uptown from the meeting," Doro said. "I don't believe Mrs. Frotis would harm the dogs, despite what Eloise told me the other morning." Doro shared the exchange.

"Ralphie would never hurt an animal," Aggie said. "As for vagabonds, Eloise's imagination is running away with her."

Doro figured her friend was right, but she couldn't dismiss the idea of something bad occurring. To what or whom, she did not know.

Chapter Three

Wednesday morning, the committee assembled again, but without Retty Hood, who had left for Toledo. Both Veronica and Eloise expressed their disappointment over the woman's absence and talked about what good ideas she had for the celebration, since the trio had chatted the previous day when Retty returned from her foray uptown. Why and where was not mentioned.

As Mrs. Frotis listened, her face got beet red. After a couple of minutes, she banged down her gavel and shouted, "We need to come to order and get down to business. Time is wasting."

When quiet reigned, the group discussed their final plans for decorating the auditorium.

"My husband and his brothers plan to bring the tree after supper tonight," Irma Green said. "My boys will come with me to help decorate. They can fetch and carry, as well."

"How wonderful," Mrs. Silven said with her typical warm-heartedness. "Your family's trees are always beautiful."

A harrumph left Mrs. Frotis. "The ornaments make the tree look pretty. Please ensure your menfolk are at the auditorium no later than six-thirty. The committee can convene at that time. With all six of us working, we'll get it done tonight."

"I'm going to Toledo to meet friends for supper," Veronica Parson put in. "I've invited Eloise to join us, so we'll both be late."

Mrs. Frotis scowled at each woman in turn. "How late?"

A smile curved Veronica's lips. "When girls get to talking, it's hard to say." She winked at Eloise, who offered a wobbly grin.

"It will be fun," the spinster said.

The chairwoman showed no amusement as she gazed steadily at Eloise. Her chin lifted and her eyes narrowed before she spoke. "Being a committeewoman, especially for the town's Christmas party, is a solemn responsibility. You need to be here. Both of you." Mrs. Frotis' attention went from Eloise to Veronica.

If Hortense Frotis had been an army sergeant, she could not have sounded any sterner or more officious. When Doro saw Veronica's expression grow grim, she struggled for some way to stem what was sure to be another angry exchange. Before anyone could intervene, Veronica stood up.

"I've had enough of your dictatorial ways, rude remarks, and veiled threats. I'm done with this committee." Veronica looked at Eloise. "And you should be, too."

After a slight hesitation, the other woman got to her feet. "I am." She snapped her notepad shut and plunked it on the table. "Here are my notes from the meetings."

Satisfaction lit Veronica Parson's features. "Good luck to the rest of you." The lilt of amusement echoed in her voice as she sashayed out the door with Eloise in her wake.

The others stared at the retreating figures. Even Mrs. Frotis appeared to be stunned. After several moments passed, the chairwoman found her voice. "We have a stronger group without the complainers. Dorothea, please take notes."

Although she wanted to object, with only four members remaining, Doro shouldered the responsibility. Her excitement about the annual party reached an all-time low as she picked up the writing supplies. Only a few days more, and the event would be over. Next year, if Mrs. Frotis was still in charge, Doro would not be involved. If the remaining members felt the same way, a new committee might be formed.

꙳

That evening, Doro headed to the college auditorium, where the enormous tree was already in place. Irma Green, her husband, and her two brothers-in-law had gotten the Fraser fir set up. By the time Doro arrived, the men were gone, but Irma and her twins—David and Daniel—were pulling decorations out of boxes. One of them grabbed a handful and headed to the tall ladder next to the tree. Before the boy had gotten both feet on rungs, Mrs. Frotis shouted at him. "Get down right now. It's dangerous to be climbing up with no one holding the ladder for you."

All color drained from the child's face. "I'm careful," he said.

"Get off the ladder." The chairwoman's voice was shrill and cutting.

"Do as you're told," their mother said in a calmer tone.

When the boy was down, he joined his brother. Mrs. Frotis, who stood to one side, snapped out orders. "No one goes on a ladder without proper precautions, and don't forget it. Not ever."

Although this was not the first time Mrs. Frotis had gotten upset over the use of a ladder, Doro thought she was being too hard on the boys. A glance at Irma Green revealed she felt much the same way.

"Boys, help me get all the decorations out of boxes," their mother said.

Eventually, Irma assisted Doro in extracting the electric lights from their crate, leaving the twins to put out ornaments. As they did, the eleven-year-olds were called to account for minute issues with every other sentence. When one of them broke down in tears, Irma interceded.

"That's enough, Mrs. Frotis," the mother said. "My young ones are helping when they could play, and they don't deserve to be berated. If you weren't so bossy with everyone, the committee would still have plenty of members, and my boys wouldn't need to pitch in. Now, you'll be lucky if you don't drive the rest of us away."

As surprise hit her, Doro stopped in her tracks. Mild-mannered and self-effacing described Irma Green, who never spoke up to anyone on any topic. Clearly, she made an exception when her children were being bullied, and Doro did not blame her.

Maybe the chairwoman would apologize. Getting every-thing done would be impossible if Irma quit.

A harrumph left Mrs. Frotis. "Your bratty boys are mis-handling the ornaments. If half of the items survive their pawing, I'll be surprised." She turned to the twins. "I'll expect you two to work off any damage you've done. Deco-rations are not free."

Those statements had both twins in tears, and Irma in high dudgeon. "Get your coats, boys. Wait in the hallway; I'll be out in a moment." They nodded and rushed to the cloakroom without a backward glance.

"When you get back," Mrs. Frotis began, "we'll get this tree decorated."

Irma, her eyes narrowed to slits, lifted her chin, and squared her shoulders. "I won't be coming back. Not to decorate and not to meet. My family and I will be at the party, and I'll expect to see us credited with donating the tree. Now, I'll bid you a good evening." As she brushed past Doro, Irma's expression softened. "I'm sorry to leave you alone with the tyrant, but I cannot stand another moment of her bossiness and bullying. Maybe Mrs. Parson had the right idea." She rushed out before saying more.

Doro wondered if the woman had referred to Veronica's threats to see Mrs. Frotis got what was coming to her. Surely not.

Mrs. Frotis' voice cut into Doro's reverie. "Don't just stand there. We need to get to work. This entire room must be deco-rated, along with the tree. Plenty to do. I'll place a call to Mrs. Silven and see why she's late. In the meantime, start looking through those boxes." She thrust a hand toward the crates by the tree. "I hope those awful brats didn't break all of them."

For the next ten minutes, Doro sorted through the boxes. Nothing had been broken, which came as no surprise. The Green boys were better behaved than many of their buddies. If only they were still here to help. Doro allowed a sprig of optimism to bud. Perhaps Magenta Silven would bring her husband and children along. More hands would make the work go faster. When she heard the door open, Doro looked at Mrs. Frotis with banked hope.

The scowl on the chairwoman's face sent Doro's spirits plummeting. Despite her gloom, she tried for a perky tone when she spoke. "When will Magenta be here?"

"She won't. Both of the children are down with colds, and Doc is out on house calls. You and I are the mainstays now. Let's not waste time. There's much to be done."

Despite the chairwoman's commands, Doro didn't move. "We need more help. You and I can't accomplish every task this evening, and I have to work late tomorrow." She didn't add that the chairwoman hardly helped at all. Instead, she ordered people around, so Doro would be the one doing everything.

"We won't get anything done if you keep chattering, so let's work instead."

Briefly, Doro considered walking out and not coming back. Only community pride and obligation held her back. Many people looked forward to the holiday soiree, and Doro did not want them to be disappointed. Not when it had dwindled down to a single event.

During the next two-and-a-half-hours, Doro worked while Mrs. Frotis directed her here-and-there. Although the room wasn't heated, sweat dampened the back of Doro's blouse and beaded her brow. She was about to again suggest enlisting more help when the door opened, and Ev stepped inside.

He looked around the space before focusing on Doro. "I saw the lights still on and wondered if someone forgot to turn them off. I didn't figure you'd be working so late. Did everyone else leave already?"

"We've been working all alone," Mrs. Frotis said.

Not completely true, since Doro had been doing most of the actual work. Doro faced Ev and rolled her eyes. When his lips twitched, she knew he got the message.

"A big job," he replied, "but it's getting late. Maybe you ought to wrap up and come back tomorrow."

Relief spiraled through Doro. If she had to work another hour, she might drop in her tracks. "Good idea."

Mrs. Frotis scowled at Ev and then, at Doro. "I thought you were busy with work tomorrow."

The statement rang with accusation and censure. Only the greatest self-discipline kept Doro from responding in kind. "I have to work late, but I can come here early and help. How about seven-thirty? That would give me several hours before I need to be at the library." If she got as sweaty and dirty as she was now, Doro would have to clean up afterward. "And time to change clothes and such before my shift."

"I could assist the two of you from seven-thirty to nine," Ev offered. "I need to make my campus rounds then."

"An extra pair of hands would be wonderful," Doro said with genuine enthusiasm.

"As long as you don't bring the mutt," Mrs. Frotis put in.

When Doro glanced at Ev, she saw anger flash in his eyes, but he kept his features carefully schooled. "Tee will appreciate going back to bed after her early morning walk, so I'll be alone."

Before Mrs. Frotis could make another cutting remark, Doro spoke. "We should be able to get most of the decorations in place tomorrow morning. I'll be here by seven-thirty."

"All right," Mrs. Frotis said. Her gaze went to the tree. "I want everything just so, not like last year when the topper was listing to one side." She shook her head, as if in disgust.

"We'll make sure everything is perfect," Doro assured her. "Now, I better get home. I'll see you tomorrow." She grabbed her coat and headed to the door.

"Will you lock up, ma'am?" Ev asked the chairwoman, "or should I?"

A harrumph left Mrs. Frotis. "I've been securing the place long before you came. Probably since before you were born."

Ev nodded. "Then, I'll say good night," the officer replied before following Doro outside, where he spoke again. "How do you put up with her? And why? I'd let her do it all herself."

Doro shoved her hands into her coat pockets. "I'm doing it for the townsfolk and students, who look forward to the celebration. Mrs. Frotis can't get everything completed alone."

His nostrils flared with a sharp intake of breath. "No, I suppose not. Has she run off the entire committee with her nonsense? You said it was only the two of you working tonight."

After revealing why Mrs. Parson, Miss Vining, and Mrs. Green had quit, Doro ran one hand over her face. "I can't blame any of them. Mrs. Silven is left, but her children have colds, and Doc is visiting patients this evening. Under the circumstances, she may not be able to help anymore this week, since the kids won't go to school tomorrow. Even if they could, Magenta helps Doc in the office. She has her hands full."

His gaze scanned her face. "So do you. Like I said, I can pitch in early tomorrow. If we don't finish, I'm happy to come back in the evening, too."

The offer lifted Doro's spirits. "That'd be wonderful, but I don't want to impose. You're busy, too. Besides, I won't be able to leave the library until late." In the faint light from the outside door sconces, his features were not clear, but his smile was.

"As long as I'm not working alongside Mrs. Frotis, I'm happy to help. How about if I come around quarter to seven? You and I can get mostly done before the dragon lady comes, don't you think?"

His characterization of the chairwoman made Doro smile. "That would be perfect. Even though Mrs. Frotis says she'll be here early, she won't. At least she rarely has been in the past. Our committee meetings are always after ten in the morning or evenings because she's not an early riser. Not that she would admit to such a shortcoming."

A chuckle rumbled out of Ev. "Does she admit to any shortcomings?"

Doro grimaced. "No, but she's quick to point out deficiencies in others."

His brow furrowed. "She can't find many in you."

The comment had warmth invading Doro's face. "She chastises me often enough."

"I hope you ignore her."

"I do, but it's wearisome to work with the woman."

"I can only imagine." His gaze narrowed on her face. "Let me walk you home. Morning comes early."

When she awoke before six o'clock, Doro remembered Ev's observation and silently agreed. Morning came very early, especially when she had sat up until midnight grading some essays. A yawn escaped her. At this time of year, rising early meant dawn was yet to come.

Hours of light were at a low ebb during an Ohio winter, so she'd have little opportunity to enjoy sunshine. If there was any. But one bright spot was on the horizon: Ev would help her this morning. The thought had her tossing back the covers and getting ready.

Thirty minutes later, she was on her way. When the brisk wind hit her, Doro looped her scarf more tightly around her neck. Winter was not her favorite season, but she loved walking the Michaw campus and had, ever since she was first able to toddle alongside her father on the way to his office. As her attention went to College Hall, she felt bittersweet memories rise in her mind. Several years had passed since she'd been able to visit the history department and her dad, but she still thought of him every time she entered the school's main building. He would never teach at Michaw again because her mother's health was better in Colorado.

The recollections had Doro thinking back to Eloise's comments about her being naïve and sheltered. Briefly, she looked around the campus, which was as familiar to her as the back of her hands. If Michaw College had offered a master's degree in library science, Doro would never have left her hometown. But it didn't, and she had gone away for her graduate studies. Not far and only for the academic year, but away. Every summer and every holiday, she had come home. Maybe she wasn't as independent and mature as she liked to think. Maybe she was shielded too much. The niggling doubt disturbed Doro, but she brushed it away and returned her attention to her surroundings.

The elms, oaks, and maples that provided much-needed shade in the summer now stood bare, and the evergreens dotting College Commons did little to break the wind sweeping across the adjacent farmland and lawn. At least, no snow was falling, although the leaden sky suggested more was on its way. With several inches already on the ground, getting about could become difficult. Luckily, she had dressed warmly—mittens, included. Fancy gloves might be a hallmark of ladylike gentility, but warm hands were more important.

After she entered the auditorium, Doro gave a sigh of relief. For a moment, she savored being out of the frigid gusts. But only for a moment. Doro wanted to get as much done as possible before Mrs. Frotis arrived. She rushed toward the double doors and inside the spacious room before stopping dead in her tracks. The chairwoman was on the floor with a tall folding ladder on top of her and her legs tangled in the rungs. Shock and horror warred within Doro. Was the older woman badly hurt?

After dashing to the woman's side, Doro dropped to her knees. The closer vantage point revealed an odd angle to Mrs. Frotis' neck. Doro put her shaking hands to the woman's face. "Mrs. Frotis?" She whispered the name, not expecting a reply. Doro wasn't sure how long she kneeled there, perhaps one minute or maybe five. She only realized time had passed when Ev's voice sliced into her distress.

"Doro, what's wrong?" The query was followed by him squatting beside her and putting one hand to the older woman's neck. After several moments, he spoke in a hushed tone. "She's gone."

His voice seemed to come from far away. When she finally absorbed his words, she spoke again. "I figured as much." Doro's voice came out as a hoarse whisper. Ev's verdict hadn't stunned her; finding the dead body had.

Ev took her elbow, stood, and pulled Doro up beside him. "Take a few deep breaths." Concern darkened his silver eyes to storm cloud gray.

When his arm went around her shoulders, Doro let herself lean against him and followed his suggestion. After regaining her emotional equilibrium, she murmured, "I didn't expect her here so early. She must've been putting decorations on the tree." Her rough, ragged voice sounded alien, like it belonged to a stranger. "She shouldn't have gotten on the ladder. She never has in the past. She usually orders someone else on how to arrange the ornaments. And she doesn't come early, as a rule." Realizing she was babbling, Doro snapped her mouth shut.

One of Ev's shoulders lifted in a half-shrug. "I get the idea, but she was on the ladder."

Unable to deny the obvious, Doro nodded. "What I wonder is why she did that when no one else was around. She was always cautioning the rest of us to use the ladder, not a chair or table, and to never climb on it without someone holding the base."

Ev moved back far enough to meet Doro's gaze. "She was strict about having another person at hand?"

"Absolutely. She was a stickler for all of us being careful, and I can't believe she got on the ladder alone. Just last night, she scolded one of the Green twins for climbing one rung with no one nearby."

Silence stretched out as both Doro and Ev studied the toppled ladder and the prone body. She watched his expression and knew his mind was working to put bits of information, supplied by Doro and by the scene, together.

"What's your gut feeling?" Ev asked when he turned back to Doro.

For a long moment, she pondered the question. As the shock slowly receded, Doro's intuition surged forth. "I'm not sure what happened, but I'm not ready to believe it was an accident. For the reasons I already mentioned and because she was at odds with more than a few folks."

"I heard Veronica Parson get snippy with her the other day."

"That was only a prelude," Doro said before filling in details, including the dog issues, Veronica and Eloise leaving the committee, and their airing of grievances in town the previous day.

"It's all troubling, but how would Mrs. Parson know Mrs. Frotis was here early and alone?"

"They're next-door neighbors," Doro replied. "Veronica might've seen her leave and followed her here."

"It's possible."

The brief reply increased Doro's uneasiness, and she wondered what he was thinking. "Do you believe it was an accident?"

His shoulders lifted and fell. "Her penchant for not letting anyone on the ladder without another person holding it gives me pause. People don't usually alter their habits, especially not someone her age. Not only that, they often get more, not less, cautious. And she has got on a lot of nerves."

"That includes the Adlers." Doro revealed Mr. Adler's angry outburst when Aggie was in the bakery.

Ev ran a hand over his clean-shaven face. "Also, disturbing."

Doro was not surprised when Ev offered no conclusions. A good detective gathered detailed evidence first. She looked back at the body. Dismay hit her when she noticed the woman's footwear. "She's wearing high heels."

"Yep," Ev agreed. "Didn't she usually?"

"She did," Doro replied, "but we weren't allowed to get on a ladder in heels, even with someone watching."

His expression darkened. "Which tips the balance toward foul play, although an accident is still possible. In any case, I need to call Wade and get him over here."

Doro nodded. Wade Lammers was the Michaw town constable and, although Ev had special deputy status, the other man was in charge. "Can you get into the office here to use the telephone?"

"I can, but I'd rather not disturb things in this building any more than we already have. I'll lock up, so no one else gets in." Ev turned back to Doro. "My office isn't far, so I can call from there. Although President Adams isn't apt to be in yet, I'll call him at home. Why don't you come with me? I'm sure Wade will want to talk with you, too."

"Of course," she agreed before preceding him out of the auditorium and on to College Hall.

Chapter Four

Neither spoke until after they reached his office, and he placed the calls. Then, Ev pulled out a notepad and pencil. "I want to get some details down before Wade comes over. The three of us can discuss the situation before heading back to the auditorium."

Did his statements mean he planned to include her as part of the team? Doro hoped so, but she replied with care. "I'm happy to help."

A grin lit his handsome face. "I thought you might be."

Doro refrained from reacting to his amusement. "I could jot down notes for you."

The humor didn't leave Ev's expression as he handed the writing materials to her. "If you start with your observations, that would give us a platform to build on."

Since the thought held merit, Doro wrote about what she had seen upon arrival. When she finished, she looked back at Ev. "I included Mrs. Frotis' views on using the ladder."

"Good. Those are significant points."

A tap on the door preceded Wade Lammers' entrance into the compact office. As usual, one lock of his straight black hair fell over his broad forehead. He brushed it back, but it fell down again. "I need a haircut," he murmured.

"Or some brilliantine," Doro suggested with a smile.

He made a face. "That'll be a last resort."

"Same here. That goo is awful." Ev rose and shook the other man's hand. "Sit down, Wade. Doro noted some of the basic facts, along with a little pertinent information about Mrs. Frotis' habits."

Before taking a chair, the constable exchanged greetings with Doro and addressed the case. "You discovered her body."

After nodding, Doro provided details. She concluded with her observations about the chairwoman's rules. "It's unlikely she'd get on a ladder with high heels on and without someone holding it."

"I agree," Ev said.

Wade released a long, low breath. "If she hadn't run off most of the committee, she wouldn't have needed to be there so early. I hate to speak ill of the dead, but Mrs. Frotis has ruffled more than a few feathers due to her highhandedness. I've heard the committee is down to bare bones after some harsh words at the last few meetings."

Annoyance at the dead woman rose inside Doro. "That's accurate, and Mrs. Green quit last night."

Wade's gaze widened. "Her brother and I went to school together, and Irma is one of the easiest going folks in town.

Always has been. What in the world got her upset enough to quit?"

As Doro thought back to the previous evening, she grimaced. "Mr. Green and his brothers brought the tree. Mrs. Green and the boys stayed to help decorate. Mrs. Frotis got after the kids for fooling around, although they weren't doing anything wrong. But that was the last straw. Irma has never complained about how Mrs. Frotis treated her, but treating the boys badly put a quick end to her tenure on the committee."

A somber expression blanketed Wade's face. "That would do it. The sun rises and sets on Irma's sons, and you better not speak ill of them unless they mess up real bad."

Doro shook her head. "They didn't do anything wrong, but you know how Mrs. Frotis always is. How she was."

"I sure do, as does everyone in town," Wade agreed. "I'm afraid she won't be missed all that much."

The observation, while accurate, saddened Doro, who had to concur. "That's true. She had a way of antagonizing people with her bossiness and snobbery. When I was little, I recall my mother saying Mrs. Frotis left the Ladies Aid Society because she wasn't elected president."

"My ma said the same about the woman not wanting to join the local women's knitting group during the Great War, if she couldn't run it," Wade put in.

Confusion turned Ev's eyes from silver to gray. "I remember my mother and others in the neighborhood knitting mittens, scarves, and socks for soldiers. Wasn't the Red Cross managing the effort?"

Doro nodded. "It was. My mother and grandmother knitted many items. I helped, although my knitting wasn't good. When a big lot was ready, someone took them to a central place for shipping." Doro looked at Wade. "I never saw Mrs. Frotis at any of the knitting nights. Do you know if she ever went?"

"According to Ma, the woman wanted to have a formal meeting every time the ladies got together. The rest of the group was focused on getting much-needed garments to the boys in the trenches." Wade slumped back in his chair. "Mrs. Frotis had Mrs. Otten and the maid knit garments and take them to the group. Not sure how many things the old harridan created herself." When the last statement was out, he put one hand over his mouth. "Shouldn't use such names."

"Maybe not but it's accurate." Before continuing, Ev leaned back in his chair and folded his arms across his lean waist. "We're all in agreement that her death wasn't accidental."

His words, both question and statement, signaled Doro's continuing involvement. Surely, Wade wouldn't disagree. Would he? Heart racing, she waited for his response.

"I am," the constable said, "and Doro seems to think so, too."

Since both men were still including her, Doro nodded. "Definitely. But who might've been in or around the auditorium so early?"

"Mrs. Parson lives next door," Doro said.

Ev glanced at Wade. "You've heard some of her malicious gossip about Mrs. Frotis?"

The constable nodded. "Not directly, but several folks have mentioned it. Mrs. Parson hasn't made a direct threat, so I'm not ready to question her."

"Have you heard what she said at the committee's Monday meeting?" Doro asked.

"No. Why?" Wade replied.

Doro shared the exchange about the dogs and the mums. "Veronica was madder than I've ever seen her."

Wade reached into his pocket and extracted a notepad and pencil. "She actually used the words "You'll live to regret it, but you won't live long?""

"She did. The others can confirm her tirade," Doro said.

Wade's dark gaze focused on her. "I believe you. I just want to get it right." He scribbled on the paper before continuing. "It's not enough to pinpoint her as a suspect, but I want to keep her in mind. Any other threats from committeewomen?"

Doro shook her head. "No, but Eloise Vining has been following Veronica's lead. The two of them quit yesterday because they were going to Toledo for dinner and wouldn't hurry back to help decorate."

After jotting more down, Wade leaned back in the chair.

Curiosity got the better of Doro. "Are you putting both Veronica and Eloise on your suspect list?"

"I have them as people who need to be interviewed. Before we identify suspects, we need more details." Wade glanced at Ev. "What's your perspective?"

Ev folded his hands on his desk and twirled his thumbs. "Whoever killed her had to know she was going to the auditorium, or saw her on her way and followed her. Someone with a grudge against the woman. You've known Mrs. Frotis a lot longer than I have. It's obvious the woman antagonized many folks, but how many would be angry enough to kill her?"

Wade sat back in his chair. "I don't know. Few probably." He glanced at Doro. "I can't believe Irma Green would confront the woman this morning. It's not in her nature."

"I agree, and she was probably at home doing chores and getting her boys ready for school," Doro added.

The constable nodded. "Not many are left on the committee, I know, but did she throw anyone off recently?"

"Drove them away would be more accurate," Doro replied. "Like I said, Veronica Parson and Eloise Vining quit yesterday."

"Why did they have to go into the city for dinner?" Ev asked. "The party is only days away. Couldn't they have stayed on until then? Even with the quarrel between Mrs. Frotis and Mrs. Parson, it makes no sense to quit suddenly."

Doro shrugged. "Veronica claimed to be meeting friends. As you say, it's odd, especially when there's so much left to do. It seems like Veronica and Eloise planned to quit. They were quite pleased with themselves as they rushed out."

Wade drummed his fingers on the chair arms. "Eloise has always been a quiet little mouse. I know she's been going around with Veronica Parson, who's spreading nasty tittle-tattle. But it's hard to see Eloise as a killer or accessory to murder."

Ev nodded. "I don't know her well, but might she have gone to help, gotten upset when the chairwoman criticized her—which is apt to have happened—and let go of the ladder? I caught part of Monday morning's meeting, and Miss Vining was upset with being ordered around, although not to any great extent. Did she say anything about Mrs. Frotis living to regret treating the Parson dogs, Duke and Duchess, badly?"

"A little, and she mentioned Tee," Doro replied before reviewing Eloise's remarks from their Friday morning conversation.

Ev frowned. "We don't know what happened to the mother and other pups, which is disturbing. I agree that a vagabond coming to town and being paid to harm them isn't likely."

"So do I," Wade said. "We occasionally get a stranger passing through, but seldom and not recently. It sounds like an excuse to me."

"It does," Ev said.

Doro turned to Wade. "You know Eloise from when you were growing up, right?"

The constable nodded. "She's a few years older, but I knew her. Eloise was even quieter than Irma, and she never went around with other girls. As far as I know, she never had a sweetheart, either. Her folks were strict, and her mother was poorly for years before her health declined badly, so Eloise took care of her. Not much fun for a youngster."

"Mrs. Parson befriending her probably makes Miss Vining feel good," Ev suggested.

"I'm sure it does," Wade replied.

"I agree," Doro added, and the certainty increased her uneasiness. Monday's heated exchange between Veronica Parson and Hortense Frotis had revealed a dark side to the younger woman. Would she have used Eloise in a plot to eliminate the matron? A shiver ran through Doro.

"Are you all right?" Ev asked.

"I am." Doro tried to smile as part of her reassurance. "But Veronica was ferocious when Mrs. Frotis threatened her dogs on Monday." She glanced at Wade. "I told Ev when he got to the auditorium this morning. Maybe I should've told both of you right away, but I didn't think Veronica was serious."

Wade shook his head. "I don't think she was, either. She can be quite dramatic. Don't you agree, Ev?"

When color swept into Ev's lean cheeks, he glanced down at his desk. "I guess so."

Although Wade didn't laugh, his lips twitched. Doro wondered about the interaction between the two men. After seeing Veronica fawn over Ev, her curiosity was piqued. Not that she planned to ask. Instead, she returned the conversation to the case. "I've seen her be theatrical."

"Where is she from originally?" Ev asked.

"Toledo," Wade replied. "Urban Parson met her there. Neither ever gave a lot of details about their initial acquaintance, but she's supposedly from a wealthy family. None of her relatives have visited here, though."

The comment made Doro review her association with the widow. "She never talks about family. Has she to you, Ev?"

Red swept back into the security officer's face. "No. Why would she? I hardly know her."

Doro withheld a direct response and explained more possibilities. "Others have grudges against Mrs. Frotis. Mr. Adler would fall into that category, and he's furious."

"I understand his anger," Wade observed.

"As do I," Ev added. "Motive is there and, maybe opportunity. When Tee and I are out especially early, I've seen him in his wagon making deliveries."

"He takes baked goods to the diner, the school, and a handful of other customers. I see him, too, and it's always between six o'clock and seven-thirty." Wade drummed his fingers on the chair arms. "He's got as much or more motive than Mrs. Parson. Her dogs have been threatened, but the Adlers' bakery has already been harmed by losing the party business."

"I suppose that makes him a strong suspect," Doro murmured with reluctance.

"You don't agree with Wade?" Ev asked.

"It's not that. I feel bad about Mrs. Frotis changing bakeries, and I hate to think that caused Mr. Adler to harm her," Doro replied.

"Maybe that wasn't his initial plan. Or anyone else's. It could be that the aggrieved party offered to help, held the ladder, and shook it to frighten her. Mrs. Frotis could've panicked, which caused her to fall," Ev said.

Doro considered the idea and expanded on it. "What if the killer only wanted to confront Mrs. Frotis? Maybe an argument led to loss of control. The person might've even offered to help to influence her. Then, if she got officious and abrasive, as she often did, the guilty party lost his or her temper."

Wade slowly nodded. "That's a good point. But we need to figure out who knew she went to the auditorium alone. We have a few possibilities, but is there anyone else?"

For a slice of time, Doro rolled her pencil between her palms. "None of the committeewomen who quit knew we planned to work early this morning."

"You and I knew," Ev said. "And the Frotis housekeeper had to know, too."

"She did," Wade said. "Mrs. Otten answered when I called before coming over here. I didn't want her and Ralphie to find out about the death from town gossip. I was hoping to get in touch with Retty, but Mrs. Otten doesn't know how to contact her in Toledo."

The comment piqued Doro's curiosity. "Did you know Retty Hood when she lived in Michaw?"

"In passing. She's a decade older than I am, but Retty was a pretty girl. All us boys thought well of her," Wade said.

"Floyd Quartine knew about her from Doc Frotis, since they were friends. At some point, she got married—although she's a widow now—because she's Mrs. Hood," Doro explained. "Although the two sisters weren't close, I'm sure the death will come as a shock. Retty mentioned coming home to reconcile. Now, that won't happen."

"Sad," Wade said.

Ev leaned forward. "Do either of you have any idea about why they were initially estranged?"

"I heard the details later from my ma," Wade replied. "When Retty left town, Mrs. Frotis didn't like it. She said proper young ladies stay home until they wed."

"Some people still believe that," Doro murmured, thinking of her own experiences.

"They do," Wade agreed, "and Mrs. Frotis took great stock in propriety. I'm surprised Retty never visited after her marriage, though."

"Floyd Quartine was close friends with Dr. Frotis, who stayed in touch with Retty. Evidently, she and her husband went West to hit it rich. When that didn't work, the two of them went on the vaudeville circuit."

Wade's jaw dropped. "That had to upset Mrs. Frotis, but I never heard a word about it."

"Doc Frotis asked Floyd not to repeat the information," Doro said.

"Understandable," Wade put in.

Ev looked at his watch. "We should probably go back to the auditorium."

"I agree," Wade said. "I telephoned Doc Silven, who will meet us there as soon as he gets back from his house calls. His wife told me about an hour, most likely, but that was forty minutes ago."

After rising to his feet, Ev slipped on his jacket. "Since you don't have to start work until noon, you're coming along, aren't you?" He addressed the question to Doro.

"Sure," she replied as she let Wade help her don her coat. Although Doro was sorry about the matron's murder, she was eager to help crack the case. Very eager.

Chapter Five

When the trio went back to the auditorium, they found Dr. Silven, a trim man in his mid-thirties, approaching the building from the parking area. He tapped the bill of his hat and greeted the group.

"Good to see you, Doc," Wade said, "although I'm sorry about the circumstances."

A long exhalation left the physician. "I am, too. Dr. Frotis welcomed my wife and me to town when he retired. A fine man."

"He was," Wade agreed.

Doro noted the doctor's failure to praise Mrs. Frotis, which seemed odd. She, not her late husband, was the victim. Had the woman not been gracious to them? For a moment, she reviewed the interactions between the physician's wife and the murdered matron. Stilted was the best word to describe their exchanges. While Mrs. Silven was always pleasant, she showed no signs of actually liking the older woman. But who did?

After Ev unlocked the door, Doro stepped inside, and the men followed. Dr. Silven examined the body, while Ev and Wade stood beside him. Doro stopped farther away.

The physician grimaced. "She had to be a few feet up to fall hard enough to break her neck, although the angle of the tumble is important, too."

A shudder went through Doro, who had tried to repress seeing Mrs. Frotis' fallen form. She only hoped the woman hadn't suffered. Ev's question and Silven's response eased her mind.

"Do you think she lived long afterward?" Ev asked.

"She might've lived for a short time, but unconsciousness probably occurred in under a minute," Silven replied with a shrug. "When I was in medical school, I had a case where the patient survived a broken neck, but it wasn't as severe as this one. Falling from far up is the main reason for fatalities." After getting to his feet, the doctor looked at Wade. "When my wife told me about your call, she also said Mrs. Frotis always insisted the committeewomen not get on ladders without someone holding them. It makes me wonder why she did this morning."

"Doro said the same thing," Wade replied.

When Dr. Silven turned his attention to her, Doro stepped forward. "Your wife is right, which is why the fall is so strange."

The doctor nodded. "And why two lawmen are on the scene."

"You're right, Doc. The situation is disturbing," Wade said, "but we'd like to investigate more before we decide the death wasn't an accident."

"We would," Ev agreed.

Silven put up both hands. "I won't say anything to anyone, except my wife, who's already suspicious. You can count on her not to gossip."

"Thanks," Wade replied, shifting from one foot to the other. "I'm not sure where to have the body taken. With no family in the area, she won't be laid out at her home here. Unless Retty wants to do that."

"Magenta said Mrs. Frotis' sister was in town yesterday but planned to visit friends in Toledo," Dr. Silven said. "She'll need to be contacted."

"I've spoken with Mrs. Otten, but she doesn't know how to do that. We may have to wait until tomorrow when Retty returns," Wade said. "In the meantime, I'll get the body to my office, since we have proper facilities."

After the last details were discussed, and Dr. Silven left, Ev addressed Wade. "I'll help you get her out of here."

"Thanks," the constable replied. "I'll bring my vehicle to the back door."

"Good. Fewer prying eyes in that direction," Ev said. "We can discuss the situation more after we get her moved. If you don't mind, Doro and I will go over the committee members in more detail. Then, you and I can review the notes and other information later today."

After expressing his agreement, Wade bid farewell to Doro and went out. When he was gone, Ev turned to Doro. "Maybe you and I can talk in my office around ten o'clock?"

"That's fine. I don't need to get to the library until noon." Her gaze strayed to the tree. "We'll need to decide what to do about the party."

"No decision has to be made yet," Ev replied. "We'll know more by later today. Then, you can meet with the remaining committee members."

A sigh left her. "There's only Mrs. Silven and me. We can't do everything in time, especially not when her children are sick."

"I'll help, and I'm sure others will, too." Ev paused for a moment. "Wade will undoubtedly tell the mayor, who will have to be involved along with the town council. Try not to worry about all that right now. You had a shock at finding the body. Why not go back to your apartment for a cup of tea? If it's easier, we could talk in the reception area later."

Doro shook her head. "No. We'd be interrupted. I'll come to your office."

"Are you all right to walk back by yourself?"

The concern in his voice and expression touched Doro. But she did not want to appear weak or needy. "I'm fine. Remember, this isn't the first body I've come across." With effort, she managed a note of levity.

"No, it isn't," he agreed, "but let's hope it's the last."

Doro gave a sharp nod. "Yes, let's." Although she loved whodunits and teaching a course on the mystery novel, Doro hated to consider anyone else dying at the hands of a killer. Fictional murders were far afield from a real life homicide.

⁂

After leaving Ev, Doro returned to Wheaton Hall. Some of the residents were in the reception room having breakfast, so she crept up the stairs. Chatting with others was the last thing she wanted to do. On the way to her apartment, Doro ran into Aggie.

"Are you finished decorating already?" Aggie asked.

"No," Doro replied before glancing around to ensure they were not overheard.

"What's wrong? You look upset. Did that awful woman get after you?" Concern etched her friend's freckled face.

"Do you have to leave right now, or could we talk for a bit?"

Aggie's frown intensified. "I don't have to be in my office for forty-five minutes, so let's go to my place."

Doro followed her friend to the second-floor suite. Immediately, tension drained from her. Aggie had made the space a haven by putting two comfortable armchairs in front of the small fireplace and placing a little table between them. Added touches, like needlepoint pillows and soft afghans, created a sense of home. Of course, the apartment was home to Aggie, and she had made the most of it. With both of her parents dead and her brother in France, Aggie had been alone for years, so having her own place, and making it hospitable, was important—as important as getting her education had been. Her friend had worked hard to become an English professor, and to make a place for herself at Michaw College.

"Do you want a cup of tea?" Aggie asked.

"No, thank you." Doro pulled off her mittens and clasped her frozen hands in her lap. The chill encompassing her was not from the weather. It was a soul-deep coldness.

"You haven't said what's wrong, and something must be or you wouldn't look so stricken."

A deep breath helped Doro settle her nerves. "Mrs. Frotis is dead."

Aggie's jaw dropped. "What happened?"

After providing a summary, Doro finished by saying, "I'm meeting Ev to discuss details about the committeewomen and others who had run-ins with Mrs. Frotis."

"That will be a long list." Aggie folded her hands in her lap. "Does he know about Mrs. Parson and Miss Vining saying nasty things?"

"I shared all that. Wade met with us, and he'd heard much the same."

"Then, they're suspects?"

"Not officially, but there are others who must be interviewed. Like Mr. Adler. There may be more people who deserve scrutiny. Irma Green quit the committee, but she isn't a likely killer."

"Not to mention she would've been home doing chores and getting breakfast for her family."

"Absolutely." Doro was glad her friend felt the same as she did. "There's a lot more digging to do."

Aggie rubbed her palms together. "Because so many people disliked Mrs. Frotis."

"I'm afraid so, but we can winnow the number down by determining who might've been out this morning. Not everyone would see her go to the auditorium, or know she'd be there." Doro's mind whirled with possibilities. Perhaps, her friend had some insight. "Does anyone come to mind as a likely killer? Someone who might've been out and about early."

A half-shrug lifted one of Aggie's shoulders. "I didn't know her nearly as well as you did, but I agree about Veronica Parson."

She chewed on her lower lip. "Since I'm from Toledo and she is, too, I asked what neighborhood she lived in. She cut me off, sharp as a knife."

The comment surprised Doro. "You never mentioned that before."

"It was in passing and didn't seem important."

"Maybe, maybe not. When I first joined the Christmas committee, I remember another new member asking Veronica how she and Urban Parson met."

"How did she respond?" Aggie asked.

"Rather oddly. Something about in a restaurant where she worked, but no name and no other details. But she also claims her family is wealthy, so why was she a waitress?" Doro drummed her fingers on the chair arms. "Veronica mentioned them courting for a year or two. They married after his folks were both gone."

"I saw old Mr. and Mrs. Parson in town sometimes, but I never got to know them. Did Urban bring Veronica to Michaw often when they were stepping out?"

Doro shook her head. "As far as I know, he never brought her home until after their wedding."

Aggie's expression grew speculative. "His folks seemed snobbish. Maybe they wouldn't have approved of the relationship."

"They were pretentious. Old Mrs. Parson inherited a lot of money from her parents. She considered herself to be the cream of Michaw society." A chuckle escaped Doro. "Not that Michaw has society."

"She sounds like Mrs. Frotis," Aggie observed.

For a moment, Doro considered the idea. "In some ways, she was. Anyhow, she might've thought Urban was too good for Veronica. I still wonder why she was a waitress if her family was wealthy."

"I agree with you about her claiming to come from a rich family but working. It doesn't make sense." Aggie's hazel eyes glittered. "You're in the thick of it again."

A rueful smile tugged on Doro's lips. "So far, Ev and Wade have been open to me helping, but I'm not sure how much or how long. For one, I need to report to the library at noon."

"And I have office hours soon. Maybe we can meet later. I'd love to help."

"I'd like to have your help, since we make a great team. After all, we've worked on two mysteries together already."

"The last one, you mostly worked with Ev," Aggie pointed out with a grin. "Which wasn't a bad thing."

Her friend often promoted the handsome security officer as Doro's potential beau, which seemed unlikely. Although she and Ev had overcome their initial antipathy, they had not moved past a friendly acquaintance. Nor did Doro want more. "You helped a great deal during the Corlon case," Doro replied. "And, with the stolen examination, it was mostly you and me working on finding out what happened, which was a puzzle."

"It was," her friend agreed. "I was afraid we wouldn't unravel it. If we hadn't, I wouldn't be here now because I would've lost my scholarship, and I couldn't have afforded the tuition. Even though it wasn't a murder mystery, it saved my life. Or at least the dream of my lifetime, which was to be a teacher. In fact, knowing you made me dream bigger. Not many young women become professors."

Aggie's heartfelt sentiment reminded Doro of the details. When the two girls met, Doro had been a recent high school graduate planning to attend Michaw College the following fall. After arriving to meet her father, Doro overheard a distraught Aggie being berated by another faculty member. As the man's student assistant, Aggie typed and mimeographed tests. Unfortunately, his final exam was missing from his office, and he had loudly blamed Aggie and threatened to cancel her scholarship. Wanting to comfort Aggie, Doro had suggested going to the ground floor café, where they discussed the problem. The pair, along with another student and Dr. Banyon, had cracked the complicated case. That had been nearly a decade earlier, but a strong bond had formed. Strong enough for Aggie and Doro to become best friends. "It was important for another reason. It brought us together."

Her friend beamed. "That was most important of all."

༈

After promising to report back to Aggie later in the day, Doro headed to Ev's office. She was crossing College Commons when she caught sight of Eloise Vining on the main sidewalk in front of the campus. Since the woman lived west of town, she rarely meandered around the campus. If Eloise had errands, she'd be two blocks north in the business district. But, if she was heading away from Veronica Parson's home, Eloise would be on the right track.

Suspicion and curiosity combined to change Doro's path. She was about twenty yards from the other woman when Doro noted Eloise walking faster. Undeterred, Doro sped up. When she was close enough to call out without hollering, she said, "Eloise, please wait for a moment."

The older woman slowed her steps before stopping to face Doro. "How can I help you?"

Doro bit her tongue to keep from giving a straight reply. Admitting she wanted to know why Eloise was in this part of town was too abrupt. A more circuitous response might glean valuable information. Since she hesitated to reveal Mrs. Frotis' death immediately, Doro spoke with care. "Have you been out and about this morning? I know you're an early riser."

Eloise's eyes narrowed to slits. "I am. Always have been."

The reply added nothing to Doro's knowledge, so she tried again. "Were you visiting?"

A frown knit Eloise's eyebrows. "Calling on folks before noon isn't typical."

Once again, the answer lacked information. "True. Are you taking a morning walk? Some people like that ritual. Walking around town while it's still quiet."

"I haven't been walking around town. I've been running errands." Eloise pursed her lips. "And you must be snooping, as usual."

The last comment, while made in a composed tone, smacked of criticism. Feigning ignorance seemed wise. "Snooping about what?"

Briefly, Eloise shook her head, as if to dismiss the question as foolish. "Everyone knows about you teaching that class on mysteries, so any time something odd happens, you get involved."

Again, Doro pretended to be unaware. "Has something odd happened?"

Eloise rolled her eyes. "Playing dumb doesn't suit you. When I walked past the constable's office earlier, I saw Wade Lammers and that campus security officer carrying a body into the back door. They'd backed Wade's automobile almost up against the building. If there'd been a natural death, they wouldn't do that, would they?"

Her pointed tone scraped Doro's nerves, but she schooled her features. How much did Eloise know? "Did you learn who it was?"

"The body was covered, of course."

Eloise's manner indicated Doro should know as much, which she did. Delving for details some other way was necessary. "So, you don't know what happened."

"No, but I suppose you do, and you're only asking me to find out if I have information that you don't." The other woman's lips flattened. "It's common knowledge that you see yourself as an amateur sleuth."

"I love to solve puzzles," Doro admitted.

"So do I," Eloise replied. "We didn't have money for college, but I read a lot—especially mysteries."

"Maybe we've read some of the same whodunits."

"I'm sure we have." Eloise pulled her faded wool scarf more closely around her scrawny neck.

Wade's characterization of Eloise as never having many friends influenced Doro's next comments. "We have a mystery book club on campus, and it's open to townsfolk. You'd be more than welcome."

Surprise flickered in Eloise's eyes. "You never invited me in the past. You're usually too busy for a brief chat. Friday was an exception."

Embarrassment assailed Doro. Countless times, she had cut off conversation with Eloise by citing her need to be in class, at work, or at a meeting. As a forty-plus year-old spinster, the other woman was apt to be lonely. Little wonder, she welcomed Veronica's friendly overtures. Doro resolved to be kindlier herself. "I'm sorry. I rush around too often, but I'd love to discuss mysteries with you."

Eloise did not look convinced. "I don't need you to humor me, but you ought to have a life away from school. That's all you've ever done. Go to school and work at a school. Veronica says you're naïve and foolish, due to your life in the ivy-covered tower. I agree with her. You think you're up-to-date, but you're unsophisticated and one-dimensional."

Even though the other woman was hardly a worldly trend-setter, the criticism stung. But the censure had probably not originated with Eloise. The observations were undoubtedly direct quotes from Veronica Parson, who was more experienced. Although the urge to defend herself was strong, Doro resisted. Despite what Veronica said, Doro was a modern young woman, a career woman. Eloise's voice broke into her thoughts.

"What about the dead body? Do you know who it is?" Eloise asked. "I could guess."

After a moment, Doro replied. "Mrs. Frotis died early this morning."

"As mean as she was, I thought she might live forever," Eloise replied in a flat tone that belied the slight upturn of her lips.

"No one lives forever."

"No, they don't." The words hung heavily before Eloise continued. "Why take her to the constable's office? That's only happened once in my memory, and it was when the professor was killed. Usually, folks are held at the doctor's home until a mortician comes. That's what happened with both my father and my mother." A speculative gleam entered her eyes. "She didn't drop over dead, did she?"

"You already guessed as much when you saw Wade and Ev with her body," Doro stated. Or maybe Eloise had known before then.

"I figured it was an accident."

Doro wasn't sure she believed Eloise, so she latched on to the possibility—although she, Doc, Wade, and Ev all agreed murder was more likely. "It might be." Doro followed by providing the bare bones of what had occurred.

A frown darkened Eloise's face. "Mrs. Frotis would never have climbed a ladder without someone to hold it. You know how she was."

The observation was correct, but was it significant? If Eloise was involved, would she make such an admission? Or could it be a comment intended to lead Doro astray? Questions abounded, while what she needed was answers. "I agree, but people sometimes act out of character, especially when there's an emergency."

"What emergency?"

"We were shorthanded and working with a deadline."

Color rose in Eloise's thin cheeks. "I hope you're not blaming me or Veronica. Both of us put up with a lot from that woman, especially me."

Since she didn't want to alienate Eloise, Doro rushed to offer reassurance. "Of course not. I was only making an observation. Mrs. Frotis planned to arrive later, but she may have fretted over getting everything done on time. That could've led to her getting on the ladder with no one else around." Doro mentally crossed her fingers that the speculative comment would evoke a real tidbit, instead of more banality.

"Knowing Hortense Frotis, that's quite likely. She thought she was better, smarter, and abler than anyone else. I always figured her arrogance would be her downfall, and it was." A snort escaped Eloise. "Downfall. Fall down. I made a pun."

Being annoyed with Mrs. Frotis was one thing, but laughing over her death...that was beyond the pale. When Doro opened her mouth to say as much, Eloise interrupted.

"I must be on my way." With that, she turned on her heel and strode off.

For long moments, Doro stared after the woman. The exchange left her confused and uncertain. Perhaps talking with Ev would put it all into perspective. A glance at her watch said she needed to hurry to be on time. As she walked along, Doro could not help but recall Veronica's flirtation with Ev. He had not seemed attentive, but did he also see Doro as an immature, inexperienced girl? Not that it mattered. Because it didn't. Not in the least.

Chapter Six

The door to Ev's office was ajar when Doro arrived. After she tapped, he looked up with a smile. "Come in and sit down."

After taking the chair across from him, she shrugged out of her cloak. "Everything—uh—settled?"

He nodded. "Yep. Wade talked to the Frotis housekeeper again. Mrs. Otten dug out the letter Retty Hood sent last week. It had her home address, so the local operator has a call in. It hasn't gone through yet, but Wade will pass word along when he hears something. Maybe her staff knows where the woman is, so she can be notified."

"That would help. I've thought about the interaction yesterday. Not all sisters are close, but they hadn't spoken for years and years. Then, there was the comment about mistakes Mrs. Hood made. I wonder about that. Leaving home, marrying young, being on the stage. I suppose those are the problems."

"True. Wade's mother will have more details about Mrs. Hood being here as a girl and why she left. Other than wanting to live in a city. In any case, we'll want to speak with her when she gets back, since she may have useful knowledge." Ev flipped open his notepad. "Speaking of knowledge, would you mind sharing more about the issues between Mrs. Frotis and the others? I already know about Mrs. Green, and about Mrs. Parson and Mrs. Frotis being at odds. And a little about Miss Vining. Are there other issues or people involved?"

"Nothing much more than we've discussed, but I wanted your viewpoint on an exchange I just had with Eloise Vining."

His brow furrowed. "You didn't call her, did you?"

The question sounded like something a lawman would ask. A suspicious lawman. Of course, not only was Ev a campus security officer, he had been a policeman and a federal agent. "I know better than that," Doro replied before providing the basic facts.

"Sorry," he began. "So, she was walking near the campus. Doesn't she live out the other way?"

"She does," Doro agreed, "but she was supposedly running errands."

"Why *supposedly?*"

"She was coming from a residential area, not uptown. Veronica Parson lives over that way."

"So did Mrs. Frotis."

Doro nodded. "I'm not sure that means anything, but Eloise's reaction to the death might."

Again, he scowled. "How did she know about that?"

His bossy tone annoyed Doro. "She saw you and Wade hauling a body into the constable's office. Evidently, you didn't look around to see if you were observed." The words were accusatory, but he had no reason to treat her like she would give details away to anyone and everyone.

A muscle jumped in his jaw as he stared back at her. "It was barely light, what with the heavy clouds and late sunrise."

She shrugged. "Eloise is no fool, so she knew there was a suspicious death."

"But not who died?"

Although both his voice and countenance were more amenable, subtle criticism seemed clear. "No, or so she said."

"Did you learn much?"

The terse query could be rhetorical, since she had already revealed Eloise's reaction to the death. "She wasn't bothered by the news. Not at all. In fact, she made a pun about Mrs. Frotis' arrogance leading to her downfall...or fall down."

Ev's gaze widened. "That's harsh."

"It is. But is she involved? I don't know. What do you think?"

After a sharp exhalation, Ev slumped back in his chair. "I don't know. You've said Miss Vining was upset with Mrs. Frotis. How much and how long could be significant. Simmering grudges often lead to retribution."

For several moments, Doro considered the valid observation. "A couple of years ago, Eloise wanted me to help her oust Mrs. Frotis as head of the committee based on her age. I couldn't agree with that, so I tried to avoid talking with her separately back then."

"Understandable. Was Miss Vining upset with you?"

Doro rolled her eyes. "When we talked on Friday, she was quite upset and stomped off."

With one hand, Ev stroked his jaw. "As in angry?"

"I'm afraid so," Doro replied. "But angry enough to commit murder? That seems impossible."

After writing more in his notepad, Ev looked up. "Does Miss Vining often come to campus? I can't recall seeing her here."

"No, she doesn't except for when the committee meets in the auditorium. Today, she was passing on the main sidewalk. I don't know that she was actually on campus."

Ev jotted notes on his pad. "If Miss Vining repressed resentment for a long time, she might've acted out toward Mrs. Frotis. But how would she know about this morning's decorating session, or that the woman was in the auditorium alone?"

"That puzzles me, too. Although Eloise rises around dawn, why would she be in town so early? Most shops aren't open until nine. And she's evidently been away from home since before she saw you and Wade."

"Wade may have some insight. For now, let's keep her on interview list, along with Mrs. Parson and Mr. Adler."

"Veronica seems friendly with you." As soon as the comment was out, Doro wanted to snatch it back. Then, Ev's reaction mesmerized her.

Scarlet suffused his lean cheeks. "I'm barely acquainted with the woman. She had a flat tire back a few weeks, and I changed it for her. Since then, I've crossed paths with her in town and passed the time of day." He cleared his throat. "She introduced herself with her first name, but it's not appropriate for me to address my elders that way unless there's a close connection."

A hearty laugh escaped Doro.

"What's so funny?" Ev asked, his brow wrinkling as he gazed at Doro.

His reaction reminded Doro of her initial impression of him—starched and straightlaced. The memory of him saying he had been the youngest agent in his office arose. As such, he had maintained a high level of decorum, but a more casual attitude was fine on campus and around town. Not that Doro thought he should get friendly with the young widow. "Don't refer to Veronica as your elder in front of her. She'd be incensed."

"She's a decade older than you and me," Ev pointed out.

"But she's only in her thirties. Plus, she strives to be modish and modern."

"I could tell," Ev said with a grimace, "and I don't want any better acquaintance with her."

Perhaps being standoffish with Veronica was a wise path for him, especially if she was interested in the handsome security officer. Her flirtation last Friday might've been one in a series of attempts to garner his interest. "Mr. Parson left her well-off," Doro put in, mostly because she didn't know what else to say.

"What happened to her husband?"

"He was killed in an automobile wreck a couple of years ago. Driving too fast on a wet road after a few drinks." Or maybe more than a few. When Ev's eyebrows rose a fraction, she expanded the explanation. "According to town gossip, both of them liked to frequent speakeasies in the city."

"Was Mrs. Parson injured in the accident?" he asked.

"No," Doro replied. "She wasn't with him on that excursion, since she was sick." At least that was the story Veronica and her household staff had told after the crash.

"And he left her alone?"

A half-shrug lifted one of Doro's shoulders. "He was in town on business and went out with cronies. Besides, they had a live-in couple and a maid. Veronica still does."

"What business was he in?"

The suspicion roughening Ev's voice made Doro wonder if he suspected the man of bootlegging. That would be natural, since Ev had been a Prohibition agent before becoming the campus security officer at Michaw College. Or maybe he had heard town gossip about the man. "Mr. Parson was an attorney, but his family owned several farms in the area. The land is rented out, so he mostly managed the properties. He sold a few holdings, which was what took him into the city that day." Or so he had said. Since his death, gossip had swirled around his activities, but no one knew for sure.

"Did he have frequent business deals in town?"

"Every month, from what I recall. I was in Ann Arbor for school part of that time." Urban Parson had often cited business deals as reasons for his frequent trips to Toledo.

"I see," Ev murmured. "With all that in mind, I have to wonder why his widow stays in Michaw. Seems like she'd be happier back in the city."

"She cuts a wide swath here," Doro pointed out, "and she enjoys being the center of attention. She's told people that her family is wealthy, but none of her relatives have ever visited here, and no one knows details."

Ev rolled his pencil between his palms. "That's a bit odd. Is there anything else?"

"Veronica gets a kick out of upending the status quo, but she and Mrs. Frotis argued more than once." As she spoke, Doro felt a stab of disgust. Why did two grown women act like squabbling children? Why couldn't they have calmly discussed a simple solution? Now, one was dead, and the other was a suspect. Doro felt sympathy for Mrs. Frotis but not for Veronica. The older woman was overbearing, but she voiced her criticism of people to their faces. Veronica said nasty things behind their backs. And to their faces at times.

"About the dogs?"

"Mostly, I think."

"That makes sense, but I doubt if Mrs. Frotis forgot it...or forgave Mrs. Parson and her dogs for repeated damage. And Mrs. Parson never forgave her for threatening Duke and Duchess, but what dog lover would?"

Doro, whose parents had their family dog in Colorado, could only agree. "I'm still concerned about what Eloise said the other day."

"About Mrs. Frotis getting someone to harm Tee's mother and littermates."

Doro nodded. "As Wade said, we don't get vagabonds often and, when we do, everyone knows. But I don't think Mrs. Frotis would do away with dogs."

"You're sure Ralphie wouldn't do it."

"I am," Doro replied.

Ev braced his elbows on his desk. "Tee's mother was in the backyard shed before and after her pups were born?"

"Evidently," Doro replied. "The house is at the south end of town, near the woods and not far from where you saw the mother dog in October."

Before looking back at Doro, Ev scrawled some notes. When he lifted his chin, Ev's gaze was dark with dismay. "When I got to campus this fall, the weather was foul—chilly and rainy."

Doro nodded as she recalled the conditions when she and Ev met. "We'd had colder than normal weather even before then, and days with fog and drizzle."

"A mother dog would seek shelter." Ev's voice and expression were thoughtful.

"You saw them in the woods," Doro pointed out.

"True, but a shed would be a better place to deliver pups and care for them until they were weaned. Dogs are smart, so she might've gone back to the Frotis place." A muscle twitched in Ev's jaw as he appeared to grind his teeth. "Did Mrs. Frotis use the phrase *get rid of the dog*?"

The question set Doro to considering how she had heard the assertion. "According to Eloise, Mrs. Frotis said Ralphie had to get rid of the cur—that's the word she used—before the pups came. As a handyman, he did a lot around the place. But he wouldn't harm any animal, and I'm not convinced Mrs. Frotis asked him to do so. She didn't want dogs digging up her flowers, which I understand."

"So do I, but what happened to the mother dog and the other puppies?"

"Ralphie goes out to a few of the nearest farms every week or so. He could've found homes for them there. I don't believe Mrs. Frotis planned to have them destroyed. She's snooty and bossy but not nasty. Ralphie could tell us exactly what she said to him."

"You and Wade have mentioned Ralphie, and I've seen him around town, but I haven't had a conversation with the man. When I offer a greeting, he gives a wave and hurries off."

"He's rather slow and very shy," Doro explained. "He's probably intimidated by a stranger, especially a lawman."

"That explains his behavior," Ev observed. "I don't want to upset him by asking about the dog and puppies. Maybe Wade could do it. They must be acquainted."

"Ralphie knows Wade in passing. But Wade is the constable. I'm afraid Ralphie would be unnerved by him wanting information, but I can ask about the dog. I could've done that when I ran into him yesterday." Doro explained how she had joined Retty to walk uptown and learned about the woman's kindnesses to the handyman.

"Nice of her to be good to him," Ev agreed.

"They seem fond of each other, like brother and sister," Doro observed. A wry smile touched her lips. "Retty spoke highly of her brother-in-law, too."

Ev ran one hand over his face. "But not of her sister."

Doro shook her head. "It's sad that they won't be able to reconcile."

"Maybe Mrs. Hood will decide to live here again. That'd work well for Ralphie."

"It would. In the meantime, I'll try to talk with him about the dogs."

"Please do. You'll know how to talk to him without causing upset. In the future, I'll keep his situation in mind when we meet again."

Relief spread through Doro. Not everyone was patient with those who were different. "Good. Ralphie is a nice man and, once he gets to know you, he'll be happy to have a new friend. He doesn't have many, due to his issues."

Ev offered a gentle smile. "I'll be glad to befriend him."

"Wonderful." Ev was a good man.

"Back to the case," he said. "I've got a handle on why Mr. Adler and Mrs. Parson could be suspects. But what about Miss Vining? What is her motive? Being picked on by Mrs. Frotis? That hardly seems like enough."

Doro considered his observation. "The criticism has gone on over a long period. For years, Mrs. Vining, Eloise's mother, served as the secretary. Eloise joined the committee when she turned twenty-one but only in a minor role. After her mother passed, a majority favored her taking over as the secretary. Mrs. Frotis wasn't happy, but she couldn't outvote everyone else."

"So, she repeatedly criticized Miss Vining, maybe to make her quit," Ev suggested.

Doro grinned. "Very astute. I'm sure that was her hope, but Eloise isn't easily deterred. At first, she didn't react, but this past year, she's spoken up on a few issues. One was Mrs. Frotis saying what a poor secretary she is. It's happened repeatedly, but the last few times, Eloise contradicted Mrs. Frotis." Doro summarized the exchange at the last meeting. "I was surprised at Eloise. Once again, Mrs. Silven interceded and got us on track. As I already told you, Veronica has been airing her grievances widely for the past couple of days, and Eloise has been right beside her."

"Then, Miss Vining has some motive to kill Mrs. Frotis, if only to help her new friend," Ev observed. "So does Mrs. Parson. I'd like to know where she was early this morning."

"So would I," Doro agreed.

He ran one hand over his face. "That brings up another idea. Mrs. Frotis would've passed near the business district on her way to the auditorium. Maybe she ran into someone and asked them to help."

Doro toyed with her lower lip. "It'd be more, someone she pressured to come along."

A corner of Ev's mouth quirked up. "All right. Who could've been pressed into service?"

Reluctance kept Doro from answering quickly. "She's co-erced Ralphie in the past. But he wouldn't hurt her. Or anyone."

For a long moment, Ev studied Doro's face. "We need to find out if he was with her. Maybe you could see how he reacts when you talk to him."

"That's a sound idea. I'll see if I can find him before I start work."

"Good," Ev replied. After making a notation on his pad, he continued. "Anyone else who might've helped this morning?"

"Not many people would voluntarily assist her. She was too critical and bossy. As for pressuring others, I'm not sure. I'll give it more thought."

"Good. What about others who might have a grudge against her?"

Once again, Doro searched her memory. "You know about the debacle with the Adlers. Mrs. Adler was upset, but Mr. Adler has been furious, from what I've heard. When I was in the bakery yesterday, he was out, so I didn't hear him directly, but I understand why he's distraught. Since so many items are needed, they bake some of the cookies ahead and freeze them."

"And now, they're stuck with dozens," Ev observed.

"They are. Many ladies do their own baking, especially at Christmas, so selling hundreds of cookies isn't likely. The Adlers make a decent living, but they aren't wealthy. Sustaining the loss may put them in the red for the month, maybe even the year."

"Which gives them a motive."

Anxiety formed a lump in the pit of Doro's stomach. "Yes, but why would she get on the ladder if Mr. Adler followed her?"

"Isn't it possible he might've offered to help and tried to convince her to change her mind?" Ev asked.

For several seconds, Doro mulled over the idea. "I suppose so."

"We already said he's often out making deliveries early."

"Since their shop is at the corner of Elm and Oak, Mrs. Frotis could pass by on her way to the auditorium," Doro replied with growing uneasiness.

"Would she stop for coffee and a sweet, or avoid them?"

An honest answer might shed more doubt on the Adlers, but the truth was necessary to solve the case. "From what I understand, she hasn't stayed away from the bakery, mostly because she doesn't think she's in the wrong. I still don't believe Mr. Adler would follow and attack Mrs. Frotis."

"But we have to pursue all possibilities," Ev observed in a soft tone.

"I know," she agreed with real reluctance.

"I've been in the bakery a few times, and they have several employees. Might any of them be angry with Mrs. Frotis?" he asked.

"None of them would've been in the front early," she replied. "Mrs. Adler handles the counter during the morning, and her husband makes deliveries after they finish baking."

"When Wade and I talk later, we'll determine how to proceed, but I'd like to interview the Adlers. Wade will, too, I'm sure."

Disappointment assailed Doro, who would have liked to be in on those interviews. During the Corlon case, she had helped Ev due to Wade having a family emergency. Now, it stood to reason that the lawmen would work together, perhaps without her assistance. At least she had the go-ahead to chat with Ralphie. Maybe she could parlay that into deeper participation. Time would tell. What really mattered was solving the case. "I'll see if I can find Ralphie before I start work. He's apt to be at the Frotis house or uptown. Maybe at the diner."

"If you can, give Wade's office a call this afternoon. We'll set a time to go over the information later today. After that, the mayor and council may have views about canceling the celebration on Saturday night."

His tone and expression were controlled, so Doro had no hint of Ev's perspective. "What do you think? Go ahead, cancel, or postpone?"

"It's a tough call, and I'm glad I don't have to make it," he replied. "I'd think canceling is out. Obviously, I haven't attended one of the Christmas parties myself, but I've heard lots about this one. People are excited. Townsfolk and students. Seems like folks would be real disappointed if it didn't happen."

"Everyone looks forward to the event," Doro agreed. "Canceling is unlikely, but postponing would mean students and others in the campus community would miss out. It's still more than two weeks until Christmas Day, but examinations end next Wednesday."

His gaze narrowed on her. "It sounds like you favor having the party, as scheduled."

A long breath escaped her. "I do, but that might be construed as disrespectful."

"What would Mrs. Frotis decide if someone else on the committee was the victim?"

A study of Ev's face convinced Doro that he knew the answer, but she confirmed it for him. "She'd insist the party go forward, as scheduled."

"Will anyone on the council object, if it does?"

Sadness filled Doro, sadness for Mrs. Frotis, who had no close friends in town, all due to her attitude and actions. "No. She's been critical of them and of the mayor, too. She's critical, period."

After a moment, she looked at her watch. "I better go, if I want to catch Ralphie before noon." She scooped up her bag and rose from the chair. Before she grabbed her coat, Ev came around the desk to help her don it.

"Thank you."

"You're welcome," he replied, in a slightly rougher tone than usual. "It's cold out, so you need to stay warm."

Although the remark was benign, Doro felt like a gawky schoolgirl with her first beau. But she was past girlhood and had never had a real beau. That realization had her remembering Veronica's cutting comments, conveyed by Eloise. Despite her education, Doro was not worldly. Not at all. If she had even a modicum of sophistication, she would not feel so ill at ease when a man helped with her wrap. Doro cleared her throat and stepped back. "I'll talk with you later."

"Sure thing."

Before he said more, Doro hurried out of the office and down the hall. Why Ev's gallantry nonplused her did not bear examination. Only solving Mrs. Frotis' death did.

Chapter Seven

On her way uptown, Doro crossed paths with her best friend. Aggie was as bundled up as Doro. A brown cloche allowed her wavy auburn bob to peek out, while a matching wool coat and thick gloves completed her outerwear. "Did you learn anything new from Ev?"

After summing up her talk with the security officer, Doro said, "Do you want to go along to the Frotis place? Ralphie likes you and might feel more comfortable." Aggie's kindness and patience worked wonders with a host of folks.

Several seconds of silence preceded a reply. "If you think it would help, I will. I don't have another class today."

Relief filled Doro. "I need to be at the library by noon. We planned to meet back at Wheaton Hall, but this came up since we spoke earlier. Could you go now?"

"Sure," Aggie agreed.

Within ten minutes, the pair was in front of the Frotis house, a Queen Anne Victorian with a porch on two sides. Doro stopped at the end of the sidewalk. "Ralphie lives in the little attic apartment above the garage, but we should check with Mrs. Otten first. Wade called already, so she knows about the death."

"I'm glad we don't have to tell her," Aggie observed.

"Me, too," Doro replied before heading to the front door.

The knock was answered by a tall, sturdy woman in her late sixties. "Morning." The housekeeper's voice had no inflection.

Mrs. Otten's appearance and demeanor seemed the same as usual. "Good day, ma'am. Aggie and I want to talk with Ralphie, and you, too, if you have time." She had not mentioned questioning the housekeeper to Ev or Wade, but why not ask a few questions while she and Aggie were here?

The housekeeper's dark gaze went from Doro to Aggie and back. "I know about the accident, but thank you for stopping."

When Mrs. Otten started to close the door, Doro stepped forward. "We wanted to ask you a few questions. Ralphie, too."

A scowl formed on the woman's angular face. "About what? She fell and broke her neck at the auditorium. I don't know nothing about it, and I don't know how to get ahold of Miss Retty. I gave her home address to Wade Lammers. As far as Ralphie, he may be in the back stacking wood, not that we need it. I'll be getting out of here as soon as I contact my brother and let him know I need a place to go. Now, I want to pack."

Dismay flickered through Doro. The housekeeper seemed nonchalant about Mrs. Frotis' death. Even an accident merited more concern, but a murder would hit most people like a sledgehammer. Surely, Wade had provided details, so why did the woman refer to the event as an accident? Doro cleared her throat. "How much did Constable Lammers tell you?"

Several seconds ticked away before Mrs. Otten responded. "He said he's investigating cuz maybe it's not no accident. But that's no never mind. She's dead, and I gotta get out—after nigh on to fifty years working here. No pensioning me off, although I asked about it plenty of times. Young doc's folks promised me some money before they passed, and he did, too. The missus kept saying she'd have to see. But she went to a new lawyer after he died. Told me every penny will go to charity, so I'm outta luck. So is Miss Retty."

Surprise hit Doro, who focused on the last revelation. "Does Retty know?"

The woman's hefty shoulders rose and fell. "Maybe, maybe not. The missus didn't say nothing about her and the will."

Beside Doro, Aggie shifted from one foot to the other, signaling that her friend felt uneasy, too. When she spoke again, Doro tucked thoughts of Retty away and tried for a sympathetic tone. "You worked for the Frotis family ever since I can remember."

A wistful expression blanketed the woman's face. "I came with them from the city, when I was a girl," Mrs. Otten said. "Long before you was born. They was good, generous folks. So was young doc."

Doro noted that Mrs. Frotis was not given the same praise. "I remember Doc's parents a little and him very well."

"I knew Doc, too," Aggie added. "He saw me through a bout of Spanish flu when I was a student. You tended to those of us who stayed here at the house. We were lucky to have wonderful care."

A slight smile played across the older woman's thin lips. "I was happy to help. Never got sick myself, which was a wonder." Her good humor dissolved. "The young Mrs. Frotis tweren't no use at all. She went off to some friend's lake house to keep from getting down with the bug all three times it came along. It was just young doc and me to handle the cases, and there was plenty, all three times."

"I was only here when the third wave hit," Aggie said. "It was great to have a place to stay until I got on my feet."

The housekeeper's expression softened. "For a bit, we was worried you wouldn't make it. So sick you were."

The statements surprised Doro, who looked at her friend. "You told me about having the Spanish flu, but you never said how bad it was. We met only months after cases surged in this area that third time."

Aggie shrugged. "You and I were busy trying to save my scholarship. Later, when we roomed together, we discussed other things."

What her friend said was true, so Doro smiled. "I'm glad you were in such excellent hands here."

"Doc and I sure tried," Mrs. Otten said. "Some days, we was run off our feet. He had a mild case himself, but kept going."

Since the woman now seemed more amenable to conversation, Doro pressed the advantage. "I know you need to pack but, if you could take a few moments to talk..." As she let her voice trail off, Doro glanced at Aggie, who gave a slight nod.

"We'd be so grateful if you would," the other young woman said.

A moment of silence passed before Mrs. Otten responded. "All right. Come into the kitchen. I've got muffins. Made them for tonight's supper, at the matron's command. She won't be here to eat any." The woman pivoted toward the back of the house and lumbered along the wide hallway and through the dining room.

After exchanging a glance, the two younger women followed along. When they reached the kitchen, Mrs. Otten gestured to the table. "Sit down. Already boiled water for tea."

Within a few minutes, the refreshments took a prominent place in the middle of the well-worn oak table. Mrs. Otten poured tea before taking a chair.

"Thank you," Doro said. "This is lovely."

Following a bite of muffin, Aggie grinned. "Your muffins are wonderful. I remember you baking them while I finished recuperating. I had so little appetite, which was odd for me. But your baking tempted me to eat again."

The housekeeper actually smiled. "That's what I wanted. You were the last one to leave us, and I was sorry to see you go. But glad you were well, of course."

Doro felt amazement at the exchange between Aggie and Mrs. Otten. Although her friend had mentioned staying at the Frotis home while recuperating from influenza, Aggie had never provided details. Should Doro have asked for more at some point? For the most part, she avoided discussing the epidemic. Some local people had died. Others had come close to death, her mother—who'd already been fighting consumption—included. With determination, Doro repressed the woeful memories. Those awful weeks were in the past. Time in a Colorado sanatorium had been the final cure, which was why Doro's parents now lived in the state.

Right now, Doro needed to focus on the present. And let her friend dig for information. To that end, she looked at Aggie and gave a slight nod. The other young woman smiled in return.

"I had mixed feelings about leaving, but it seemed advisable when Mrs. Frotis returned," Aggie said.

Mrs. Otten's expression hardened. "Doc and I tried to convince her to let you stay longer, but she were always selfish."

Aggie nodded. "It was her home."

A snort left the housekeeper. "And she ruled with an iron hand. Tried to control the neighborhood, too. And the town. Still was, right up until this morning."

The continuing lack of sorrow disturbed Doro. Eloise Vining was not the only one who wasn't mourning the matron's passing. How many more fell into the same category? And how many of them might have killed her?

"I've heard about her run-ins with Mrs. Parson." Aggie made the comment between sips of tea.

Doro was glad her friend had come along. As always, Aggie used her knack for putting people at ease.

"The two of them was a lot alike. It weren't right that Mrs. Parson let her dogs run, but the missus shouldn't have threatened them critters. Not that she would've followed through on actually harming them. Just stirring up the neighbor with threats."

The last comment led Doro back into the exchange. "Did Mrs. Frotis warn Mrs. Parson about her dogs more than once?"

The sound that left the housekeeper was more a cackle than a laugh. "Several times that I heard. Probably bullied her more. Not that Mrs. Parson didn't talk back. Always did. She's a spunky one."

Doro silently agreed. But was Veronica Parson worse than spunky? "Did they only argue about the dogs getting into the flower beds?"

Mrs. Otten shook her head. "Nope. They had words about Mrs. Parson's oak trees. The branches hang over the fence. When the wind is strong, the branches rattle against the missus' bedroom windows. She claimed the glass were going to break during a storm...never did, though. Doubt if it ever will, neither. Not that I'll know."

"So, Mrs. Frotis complained to Mrs. Parson about various issues," Aggie suggested.

"Sure did," the housekeeper agreed.

"Did Mrs. Parson seem agitated?" Doro asked.

After setting down her cup, Mrs. Otten focused on Doro. "Mrs. Parson were plenty het up, especially after the committee met this week. I s'pose you were there."

Doro nodded. "I've witnessed the two of them arguing. It wasn't pretty. Nor was Mrs. Parson quitting the committee, especially since Eloise Vining left with her."

"I can imagine," the older woman observed.

"Did Mrs. Parson have a particular complaint this week?" Doro asked. "I know what she said to the committee and part of what she spread in town. Did you hear more from her or her staff?" She particularly wondered if the couple and the maid who worked next door had shared information.

"Mrs. Parson always has a greeting for me and Ralphie. She aren't stuck up, but she don't share her business with us. Sometimes, I overheard her and the missus."

Those comments gave Doro hope of learning more. "Did they talk privately this week?"

With a sigh, Mrs. Otten leaned back in her chair. "Sunday, Mrs. Parson come over. I answered the door and had her to sit in the front parlor. When I told the missus, the woman were here, she scolded me something fierce and wanted me to send the lady packing. I said I weren't paid to lie and went back to the kitchen."

"I don't suppose you heard any of their conversation," Doro said.

Mrs. Otten's gray eyebrows rose. "Couldn't help but hear. With the two of them yelling at the top of their lungs, I'm guessing half the neighbors heard 'em. The missus told Mrs. Parson to git out and stay away. Mrs. Parson gave her what for about not being capable of heading the committee, said she were an old fuddy-duddy who needed to be replaced right off. The missus were mad as a wet hen. Fired Mrs. Parson from the committee and said for her to git."

Surprise rippled through Doro and, when she looked at her friend, she saw the same feeling on Aggie's face. Mrs. Frotis had not mentioned axing Veronica. Why? "How did Mrs. Parson respond?"

"First, she laughed," the housekeeper replied. "Then, she refused to leave the committee and vowed to get rid of the missus instead."

Dismay hit Doro hard. "Meaning remove Mrs. Frotis as the chairwoman."

One of Mrs. Otten's shoulders rose in a half-shrug. "Didn't say that. Said get rid of her. Then, Mrs. Parson swept out of the house like a queen bee. The missus were sputtering under her breath. Later, her sister called about visiting and got an earful. I overheard the missus talking. Couldn't make out much, but she were plenty upset."

"I can imagine," Doro murmured. Mrs. Frotis' attempt to fire Veronica had failed, but how could it not? Others had left the committee under duress, but the young widow was not one to give in.

The housekeeper narrowed her gaze. "I s'pose you can."

After offering a slight smile, Doro went on. "Did Mrs. Frotis speak with her sister often?"

"Nope. Almost never," Mrs. Otten replied. "The missus were furious when Miss Retty left home after high school. I were the housekeeper then, too, and the two of them argued plenty. Usually behind closed doors. When Miss Retty left, I were visiting my brother, so I don't have no idea of what got said then."

"Did Mrs. Hood stay in touch?" Aggie asked.

"She wrote to young doc every month or two until he passed, and she'd always put in a note for me and one for Ralphie. She wrote the one to him in real simple words, so he could read it himself. She were thoughtful." the housekeeper replied with a smile. "When Miss Retty got engaged, she sent a wedding invitation. The missus wanted no part of it, but young doc sent a gift of money."

"But he didn't attend the ceremony?" Doro inquired.

Mrs. Otten shook her head. "Nope. He tried to convince the missus to go, but she pitched a fit. Got so upset, she took to her bed. Poor man was afraid to leave and make her worse."

"That's a powerful reaction," Doro murmured.

"It sure is," Aggie agreed.

A harrumph left the housekeeper. "The missus wanted her way and usually got it."

"Interesting," Doro said. "Did Mrs. Hood write or call her sister after Doc died?"

"She telephoned about coming to the funeral. I talked to her before the missus got on the line. Miss Retty were grief-stricken, but she and her man didn't come. Maybe cuz her sister said not to. Can't say for sure." The housekeeper's expression became sad.

"That's a shame," Doro said. "Mrs. Hood called on Sunday about visiting?"

The housekeeper nodded. "She did. As soon as the missus got off the telephone, she told me to get Miss Retty's room ready."

"Her room? I thought she didn't visit much," Doro put in.

"She didn't visit at all," the housekeeper replied. "But she had a room when she lived here as a girl. We got plenty of space, and young doc insisted we keep it the way she left it, even though she hasn't been back in years and years. Mrs. Frotis let it be, maybe cuz it's what he wanted when he was alive. She were a hard woman, but she loved him and missed him something awful."

"Mrs. Hood must've gotten along well with her brother-in-law," Aggie observed.

Mrs. Otten nodded. "That she did. With him being an only child, he loved having more folks in the house. Doted on Miss Retty, despite her own sister putting up a fuss."

While the tidbit was not apt to be important to the case, Doro tucked it into the back of her mind. "She didn't like her husband being good to her younger sister?"

"Nope. Said he spoiled the girl, but she were only ten when they lost their folks. That's hard for a child." Mrs. Otten took another long swallow of coffee. "Miss Retty worshipped him like he were a beloved big brother, and he treated her like he would've a special little sister."

A wide smile lit Aggie's face. "That's how it is between my brother and me."

"Same with mine," Mrs. Otten put in. "But his wife is a bit like Mrs. Frotis. Not certain she'll welcome me into their home." Dismay darkened the housekeeper's gaze.

"I'm sure she will," Aggie said.

"I hope so," the housekeeper responded.

As anxiety played across the woman's face, Doro wondered about her own future. A woman alone had to take care of herself. Retty Hood was also alone. "Did you speak with Mrs. Hood when she called last weekend?"

"I answered but didn't talk much. Got the missus and went back to work," the older woman said.

"You didn't hear any of their conversation?" Doro posed the question.

"Nope. The missus closed the door to the telephone nook," Mrs. Otten said. "Not that I'd eavesdrop."

Doro suppressed a grin. Mrs. Otten was an inveterate gossip and much of her knowledge came from listening to others. Doro went on. "Do you know about anyone else who held a grudge against Mrs. Frotis?"

Mrs. Otten took a bite of muffin and a swallow of tea before replying. "Wade Lammers didn't give no details about the supposed accident. Truth to tell, he didn't even use the word *accident*. Only said she took a tumble from the ladder while doing some decorating. The missus never got up on no ladder by herself. Wouldn't let Ralphie or me do it, either."

The answer did not address the question, but Doro responded to it. "She was the same with all of us on the committee."

"It weren't no accident, right?" The housekeeper made her words more statement than query.

Doro responded honestly but carefully. "Probably not." She cleared her throat. "What about others who had run-ins with her? Can you think of anyone who was furious enough to confront her this morning?"

After eating another piece of muffin, the housekeeper replied. "I run into Miss Vining at the dry goods shop yesterday morning. She were plenty upset, too. Tired of the missus finding fault with her notetaking and being bossed around. Couldn't say I blamed her, but she's always been such a meek little thing. I've seen her with Mrs. Parson a few times, so mebbe that's the reason for the change in Miss Vining."

"Maybe so," Doro murmured. "What else did Eloise say to you?"

"Just that the missus ought to go."

"Those were her words?" Aggie asked with a grim expression.

"Yep," the housekeeper replied. "We got interrupted, so that's all I know."

Once again, Doro stored the revelation in her mind. The phrase *ought to go* was not as troubling as *live to regret it, but not for long.* People often made bold statements without meaning to act on them. "Anyone else at serious odds with Mrs. Frotis?"

Something flickered in the housekeeper's gaze before she focused on another muffin. After consuming half of the treat, she spoke. "Ralphie has been upset with her ever since she wanted him to move the momma dog a few months back. He didn't think she oughta be disturbed before the pups came."

"What did he do?" Doro asked.

"Kept the momma in the garage, and the pups when they came. Once they was weaned, Ralphie found homes for them. He got a farmer to take two. The momma is with another farmer." Mrs. Otten folded her hands in her lap. "Miss Vining took the other one. She's been careful about not letting people know, for fear of getting Ralphie fired. That's another thing she was het up about yesterday morning. Mrs. Frotis being a dog hater. But hate's too strong."

The detail made another point of commiseration between Veronica Parson and Eloise Vining. "I've never seen Eloise with a dog, so she's done a good job of hiding the pup," Doro observed. "I haven't been out by her house since last spring, though."

"Few goes down that road," Mrs. Otten said.

Aggie set her cup aside. "She lives on a little lane off the road going out of town, right?"

"She does," Doro replied. "All four cottages are set in a copse of trees. Two are occupied by elderly couples and one is vacant, since the owner died last year. It's a short walk to the heart of town, but a world away when you're out there. When I was little, my mother visited Mrs. Vining from time-to-time. I loved going along. Their backyard was a magical place with a beautiful garden, apple trees, and a narrow creek at the back of the lot." Wonderful memories warmed her heart.

"Then, hiding the pup wouldn't be difficult," Aggie commented.

"Not at all." Doro set her cup and saucer aside before continuing. "There used to be a fenced area where Mrs. Vining had a garden. Eloise was never interested, but I doubt if she took the wood slats down."

"I don't think she did, since she told Ralphie about having a safe place for the pup," Mrs. Otten put in.

"And a hidden spot, if there are a lot of trees," Aggie said.

"Yep," the housekeeper said. "That eased Ralphie's mind. Of course, he's vexed now. I can probably go to my brother's place, but Ralphie ain't got nobody."

Sympathy filled Doro because Mrs. Otten was right. Ralphie had worked for the Frotis family since he had been orphaned as a young boy. Where would he go? What would he do? While finding Mrs. Frotis' killer was at the top of her agenda, Doro vowed to help Ralphie. "I'll check with President Adams to see if there's a job on campus. Housing might be offered, too."

"That'd be fine." The housekeeper's expression softened. "I fret for him."

"I'll do what I can," Doro said. "If there's no work on campus, someone in town will have a place, I'm sure. But we should get back to the case. Anyone else come to mind as a person at odds with Mrs. Frotis?"

"No one as angry as Mrs. Parson," Mrs. Otten replied. "At least not lately."

"What about an old grudge?" Aggie asked.

"Most folks never got real mad at her," the housekeeper said. "A lot due to young doc's doings. He smoothed things over good with others and with her."

Aggie nodded. "He had a soothing way about him."

"He did," Doro agreed before pushing back her chair and standing up. "Were there some major quarrels in the past? Something that stands out?"

Mrs. Otten braced her elbow on the table and rested her chin in her hand. "There was trouble with the Adlers last year. The missus were furious about their delivery boy dumping the baked goods and taking off, even though the couple come and fixed the problem. Then, she riled them up this year by hiring out-of-town bakers. It were mean of her not to tell them right off."

Anxiety curled in the pit of Doro's stomach as she considered the housekeeper's words. "When did she decide to change bakeries?" The chairwoman had informed the committee on Friday, but she had to know sooner.

"Before Thanksgiving."

Doro and Aggie exchanged a long glance. "Did she forget to tell the Adlers?" Doro felt sure that was not the case, but she wanted confirmation.

A rueful smile pulled up the corners of the housekeeper's mouth. "Nope. Always planned to wait. She weren't only bossy. She could be spiteful." After a long swallow of coffee, Mrs. Otten set her cup aside. "Can't think of nobody else that might've been laying in wait for her. Just plenty of folks fed up with her nonsense. Course one of them could've gotten up a head of steam and blown. She could rile a body up."

The image seemed all too likely. "She certainly could," Doro said.

"I hope Wade Lammers can get in touch with Miss Retty soon. Her sister's death will be a terrible shock to her." A somber expression blanketed the housekeeper's face. "I were hoping the two of them would overcome their differences. The missus is stiff and starched, so it'd be a tough climb for Miss Retty, but I believe she planned to try. No chance of that now."

An answering sorrow assailed Doro. "That's a shame."

"It is," Aggie agreed. "I can't imagine being estranged from my brother. It's hard enough that he stayed in France, but we're still on good terms."

Mrs. Otten smiled. "You went on about him when you was with us. Sounded like a fine man."

"He is," Aggie replied with enthusiasm.

With no sisters or brothers, Doro did not fully fathom the connection between and among siblings, but she could not imagine being estranged from a beloved family member for years and years, especially when that person lived close-by. "You mentioned a will."

The housekeeper nodded. "Young doc insisted on having one, but she had a new will written right after he died. He'd insisted on making Miss Retty the main heir, with money for Ralphie and me. The missus changed that. Didn't want her sister to get a thing and didn't care a whit about us help. It's all going to some charity."

"That's sad," Aggie murmured, "although the charity can use the money, I'm sure."

After agreeing, Doro got to her feet and said, "We should let you get back to your packing. Thank you for the refreshments and your time."

After offering her own gratitude, Aggie also rose.

The housekeeper followed suit. "Good luck, girls. Ralphie might still be in the yard, so use the back door. If he's not out back, he'll be in the garage or the garden. Or in his rooms."

After excusing themselves, the friends took the suggestion. As they followed the brick path through the yard, Aggie gestured at the walkway. "Keeping grass and weeds out has to be a tough task."

"I'm sure it is, but whenever I've been here, the entire property is always pristine. Ralphie works hard to keep it that way."

"Maybe he can stay on after the house is sold," Aggie said. "It's been his home for such a long time. I'm sorry Retty Hood won't be inheriting it, but whoever buys it might consider keeping him on."

"Maybe so, but I'll still talk with President Adams. Settling an estate takes time, so there may not be a new owner for a while." Doro stopped when they got to the shed, where logs were piled high. "No sign of Ralphie here. Let's go to the garage. Maybe he's in his apartment."

The young women headed toward the white frame structure, where they found the main large door open and the smaller side door ajar. "I'm surprised Mrs. Frotis didn't insist on Ralphie closing the garage after she left. Snow drifted inside," Aggie commented.

For a moment, Doro looked around the dim interior. "It is odd. Mrs. Frotis is so fussy, and Ralphie usually jumps to do her bidding. He wants to please people."

Dismay darkened Aggie's hazel eyes. "Poor man."

The thought made Doro feel queasy. "I'm glad he found homes for the dogs, but I bet he would've liked to keep one. Not that Mrs. Frotis would've allowed it." Doro moved toward the wooden steps set against one wall. "I'll call up and see if he'll come down. I don't want to invade his privacy." After calling the man's name several times, Doro turned back to her friend. "Let's go upstairs and knock."

Aggie nodded before following Doro upstairs. When they reached the small landing, they found the door shut and locked, so Doro rapped on it. No response came. She tried again, to no avail. With a sigh, Doro faced her friend. "He must not be here. Let's head to the constable's office," Doro said before she and Aggie left the Frotis property. "I'll call the library from there and let them know I'll be a few minutes late."

Chapter Eight

When the pair arrived at the constable's station, they found Ev and Wade at the corner desk. Both men stood and greeted the young women before helping them remove their winter wear. "Thank you."

"It's good to see you again, Aggie," Wade said after taking her coat and hanging it on a wall hook.

Although Ev offered only a greeting, he narrowed his gaze on Doro. Since she did not owe him an explanation for Aggie's presence, Doro addressed Wade. "I ran into Aggie on my way to the Frotis house. I knew having her along would help, since she has a knack for putting people at ease."

"That she does," the constable agreed with a smile.

The blush rising in Aggie's face nearly blotted out her freckles. "I got to know Mrs. Otten when I recuperated from the flu at Doc's place."

Wade's lips flattened. "I was working on the railroad back then, but Ma shared how bad it was around here. I'm glad you got the best of care."

"I did," Aggie hurriedly agreed.

Ev cleared his throat. "So, the two of you talked with the housekeeper and Ralphie. Learn anything important?"

"We can go over everything." After answering Ev, Doro focused on Wade. "Could I use the telephone? I want to let my boss know I'm running late."

Wade quickly agreed. "Sure thing."

After Doro placed the call, she returned to the desk with a smile. "They don't need me to come in. Our student worker is feeling better, so she'll help this afternoon. Mr. Quartine said he can stay late." She did not continue by revealing his additional comments—that Doro's expertise was needed to solve the murder. The two lawmen would likely take the observation with good humor, but she didn't want to overstep her role, which was peripheral, at best. Ev already seemed uneasy about Aggie's involvement, so Doro did not want to test him.

"Great. The two of you were a big help during the Corlon case." Wade glanced at Aggie as he spoke.

The comment pleased Doro, but she waited for Ev to agree. Would he? Several moments passed before she got an answer.

"They sure did," Ev said.

Color swept into Aggie's face. "Mostly Doro helped."

"You were instrumental, too," Doro added.

"You most certainly were," Wade said with unbridled enthusiasm.

When Aggie's blush again blotted out her freckles, Doro hurried to ease the situation. To her eyes, Wade seemed smitten with her friend, but Aggie had refused to discuss the possibility. "We're both willing to assist again."

Ev's mouth quirked. "Nice to have enthusiastic volunteers."

His amusement indicated he didn't object to Aggie helping, but Doro wanted to press her point. "I'm the principal witness, since I found the body."

"You are," Ev agreed, "and you've been an armchair detective for a long time."

Dismay hit Doro. "I thought I'd moved up a notch to amateur sleuth."

A grin slowly turned up the corners of his mouth. "Maybe a couple of notches."

Her uneasiness ebbed, even though that still put her a long way down the investigative ladder from lawmen. "I see," Doro replied, although she was not sure how to take his response.

"You see a lot, which is great," Ev said. "Even though the cases are fictitious, your study of mystery novels has given you insight."

His explanation lifted Doro's spirits. Ev had told her as much at the end of the Corlon case. He had also admitted to a love of whodunits, but they hadn't discussed any books since then. Doro dismissed her disappointment and pulled out her notepad. They were both busy. "Reading is an adventure."

"It is," Aggie agreed. "I'm not a mystery expert like Doro, but I enjoy whodunits, too. My bookshelves are full of them and poetry books."

Wade leaned back in his chair. "I'm not much of a reader. When I was with the railroad, I worked long hours. Now, I've got more free time, especially with Ev helping, but the house and kids need my attention." As a widower with young children, the constable had a host of responsibilities.

His tone and expression indicated embarrassment, so Doro offered support. "Your children come first. When they're older, you'll have time to read." She glanced at Aggie. "Your poems are short, so Wade could read one or two in a few free minutes. You'd share some, wouldn't you?"

Wade shifted toward Aggie. "I'd love to read your work."

Aggie smiled. "I'm happy to lend books to you."

"Wonderful," Doro put in. A moment passed before Ev picked up the thread of conversation.

"You two can discuss that later," he said. "Right now, we ought to work on the case."

"Of course," Doro readily agreed. "Maybe we should start with what Aggie and I learned at the Frotis house."

"Good idea," Wade said.

"It is," Aggie chipped in.

Doro scanned her notes. "We didn't talk to Ralphie, since he wasn't there. Have either of you seen him?"

Both men shook their heads before Wade replied. "He sometimes goes into the hardware store across the street. Or to the bakery. He has a serious sweet tooth. But he hasn't been around today. At least, not when I've been in the office."

Ev added his own observations. "I don't see Ralphie much, and I didn't today, either. If he isn't at a Main Street business, where else would he be?"

Wade shook his head. "No idea."

"Me, either," Doro added before remarking on the open garage door. "He evidently didn't close it after Mrs. Frotis left."

"Maybe he planned to be away from the house," Ev said. "If so, he might've left it open, so she didn't have to get out of the automobile and do it herself when she got back."

"Could be," Wade observed.

"If he's not in town, maybe he went to visit some of the dogs," Aggie put in.

Both Ev and Wade looked perplexed, so Doro provided an explanation and ended with, "He could walk to the Vining cottage easily, but the farms aren't close to town."

"He goes out there at least once a week. I didn't know about the dogs, but the one of farmers' wives always feeds him. With the snow we've had, hiking to one wouldn't be easy," Wade added. "I'd like to hear what he has to say, so we need to find him. But did you learn anything from Mrs. Otten?"

"At first, she wasn't going to talk with us, but Aggie mentioned how much she appreciated the care she got while recuperating from the Spanish flu. That softened Mrs. Otten's attitude." Doro grinned at her friend.

Aggie put both hands up, as if warding off the compliment. "It was all true. Mrs. Otten and Doc Frotis were kind and caring. She was very good to all of us patients."

"What about Mrs. Frotis?" Ev asked. "Didn't she assist in the care?"

After explaining the woman's hasty departure, Aggie released a long, low breath. "As soon as she got back, Mrs. Frotis made a fuss about how I'd be more comfortable in my dormitory. Of course, I was much better by then, and I was the only one left staying at the house."

Wade drummed his fingers on the desk. "Mrs. Frotis rarely showed concern for others, although she always had cookies for kids visiting Doc. And milk or cocoa to go with them."

"The same was true when I was little," Doro said. "I'd forgotten."

"She was always snooty," Wade put in, "but she was nicer when her husband was alive. Happier."

"You're right," Doro agreed. "I suppose she got lonely and bitter, which made her more and more difficult."

"Which is why finding her killer is a challenge," Ev observed. "Too many people who didn't like her. Or worse. Detested her."

His frustrated tone encouraged Doro to provide additional details. "I didn't take notes while we talked with Mrs. Otten, but I can jot some down while we confer."

Ev sat up straighter. "Anything important?"

"You and Wade would be the best judges of that," Doro replied. Although she had her own opinion, she would wait to reveal it. "First off, Mrs. Otten wasn't distraught. More blase."

"She already knew about the death. Perhaps, she'd already gotten over some of her grief," Aggie suggested.

Her friend's viewpoint had to be affected by Mrs. Otten's solicitous nursing during the flu epidemic. Doro understood, but she still found the woman's lack of sympathy unnerving.

A grimace formed on Wade's face. "When I told her the news, she had the same reaction. She was going to pass the word on to Ralphie, so I don't know about his initial response. We know

Mrs. Frotis didn't evoke loyalty or friendship from folks, but to have her housekeeper not show a shred of grief...it's troubling."

"It is," Ev agreed. "I'm wondering about Ralphie."

"Mrs. Otten said he'd been stacking wood just before we arrived, but that was hours after Mrs. Frotis left."

Ev listened intently before commenting. "I'd sure like to know if he opened the garage door before she took off and left, or was he still there? Did he leave and come back? Or what?"

"Are you thinking Ralphie followed Mrs. Frotis?" Doro asked.

Ev shrugged. "It's possible. Or he could've gone with her. We just don't know. If he left, he came back. Otherwise, Mrs. Otten wouldn't have seen him."

The suggestion sent apprehension spiraling through Doro. Surely, Ralphie hadn't followed the woman and argued with her. "What do you two think about Mrs. Otten's reaction? Her primary interest was getting packed and hearing from her brother."

Ev rubbed the back of his neck, as if trying to dispel the tension. "While most folks get upset when someone they know dies, not all of them show sadness. Sometimes, it's due to shock. Other times, it's because they don't want to appear weak. Mrs. Otten could fall into one of those categories."

Doro watched his expression as he spoke. Ev had lost both of his parents, but something in his demeanor made her wonder if he'd experienced other deaths. In October, just before leaving his previous job, he had been shot during a raid on a speakeasy. The incident highlighted the dangers of being a Prohibition agent. Had any of his fellow agents died in the line of duty?

Was that why he looked morose? Had he witnessed a variety of crimes, including murder, in his work? Or in his life? Not wanting to evoke painful memories, Doro turned her attention back to the case. "Mrs. Otten is a curmudgeon and always has been, in my experience." She glanced at Aggie. "You saw her in a more hospitable role."

"I did," Aggie agreed. "She was very good to me and to the others. The patients were mostly students, but a few townsfolk stayed at the Frotis house when they were ill."

Wade nodded. "Doc kept some local patients when the flu hit here. I was working on the railroad, but Ma got it. Luckily, my aunt nursed her at home."

"It was bad everywhere, but the third wave was the worst one at the college," Doro observed. "Classes were canceled for two months."

"I was lucky to stay at the Frotis house during that time," Aggie observed. "Even after I gained strength enough to be out of bed a bit, Doc insisted I was welcome. Otherwise, I would've needed to rent a room some place. There was only one boarding house back then. Mrs. Otten was on edge today, but she mentioned needing to contact her brother about living with him and his wife. That isn't a simple situation."

Her friend's observations gave Doro pause. "You're right. She has to feel uneasy about the future." Not everyone had a loving family as support.

"Understandable, but being grumpy isn't unusual for her," Wade said.

Ev glanced around the group. "Did she mention others who were at odds with Mrs. Frotis?"

Doro shrugged before summarizing the rest of the conversation. "With what we know, Veronica seems like a strong suspect. Eloise might've helped her, but I can't see her acting alone."

The others agreed.

"What about women who left the committee in the last couple of years? Any hard feelings?" Wade inquired.

"Upset feelings, but those seemed to disappear quickly." Doro twirled her pencil. "One person was turned down last year."

"Anita Ressiger," Aggie filled in.

Doro nodded. "Yes. When Mrs. Frotis rejected her, it caused a stir. Anita's in-laws used to donate prizes for the raffle. His mother and sisters are talented quilters, and they made two every year. Jake and his dad always brought their team and sleigh for rides on the day of the party. All the children loved that."

"It sounds like they don't do any of those things anymore," Ev said.

"As the committee dwindled, we had to eliminate many activities. We used to have sleigh rides, a cakewalk, caroling, the raffle, ice skating, and sometimes, a skit with some of the schoolchildren," Doro said. "The Ressigers haven't taken part since Mrs. Frotis told Anita that the committee wasn't for the likes of her. Several women resigned then, and I almost did, too. I tried to lobby on Anita's behalf, but to no avail."

"When Anita found out Doro planned to quit, along with the others, Anita asked her to reconsider. She didn't want the event ruined," Aggie put in.

Doro appreciated her friend's explanation, but she still felt like staying on the committee was, in some ways, tacit support of the overbearing chairwoman. On the other hand, making the party fun for the community was important. It had been a conundrum...until now. With Mrs. Frotis deceased, someone else would take charge. Ambivalent emotions assailed Doro, but she returned her thoughts to the case.

"And the Ressigers don't come to the party?" Ev asked.

"Not since Anita was turned down," Wade replied. "I see them in town, and others in the family, too. Jake was the most upset over Anita not getting on the committee."

Ev looked around the group. "Is he still mad?"

Wade rubbed his jaw. "Maybe it's the time of year, but he was pretty het up when I ran into him earlier this week. He and Anita have two kids, not in school yet, and Jake's two sisters have a total of five. The older ones all come to Michaw for school. From what my brood says, the party is a sore subject among the young Ressigers."

Sadness filled Doro. "I'm sure the children don't understand why they didn't get to be at the celebration last year. They've probably been told they won't be going this year, either."

"How old are the kids?" Ev asked.

"Jake's nieces and nephews range from six to ten. The older ones remember the party," Doro replied. "Not going has to be disappointing and upsetting for a child."

With a sigh, Ev leaned back in his chair. "All because of Mrs. Frotis."

"Yes." Doro made the admission.

"You mentioned Jake Ressiger still being angry," Ev said to Wade. "Just talk or would he take action?"

Anxiety pressed hard on Doro as she waited for the constable to respond. Her acquaintance with Ressiger was only superficial, but his demeanor seemed off-putting, at best. Big and sturdy, he exuded strength and power. Although he was a man of few words, he always spoke in a gruff tone. Perhaps, he was softer underneath his rough outer shell. She did not know, and that was disturbing.

"He's got a quick temper with other fellows, but he's never provoked a physical fight, and he's respectful with womenfolk," Wade replied. "Not that I haven't heard him cuss out Mrs. Frotis since last year's set-to, although never to her face."

"Does he make a habit of cussing folks out?" Ev asked.

"He doesn't mince words," Doro put in. "More than once, I've heard him say a high school diploma is a waste in front of those of us who have college degrees." She hesitated before continuing. "But he'd likely be doing chores at that early hour. I was thinking about asking Anita to serve on the committee now. I could drive out there and chat. She might mention him being in town, although that seems unlikely."

"That's a good idea," Aggie agreed. "I imagine Anita would be happy just to be asked. That's if the celebration is going ahead." She looked at Wade. "What did the mayor and councilmen think?"

A half-shrug lifted one of his muscular shoulders. "They need to give it more consideration."

The news had Doro sitting up straight. "There are only two days left. If it's going forward, there's a lot of work to do."

"They'll have a decision this afternoon," Wade told her. "I'll pitch in and help myself, if they approve it."

"I will, too," Ev added.

Doro looked from Wade to Ev. "I appreciate that, but your primary concern will be finding the killer."

Ev folded his arms across his lean waist. "True, so let's finish going over what we've learned so far. Before we do, I don't think you two need to drive to the Ressiger place. You're right about him doing chores early. Let's wait and see what else we uncover."

"Yep," Wade agreed. "Unless none of the others pan out, I'd eliminate Jake. He's hot-headed, but not violent. Besides, how would he know Mrs. Frotis would be out so early?"

Ev looked at Doro. "Call the wife, if you like, but you've already plenty to do without adding a trip."

"I'm not sure I could take the time to run out to the Ressiger farm," Aggie added. "I have a tall stack of papers waiting for me, but calling Anita is a wonderful thought."

"All right, I'll call her later." Doro shuffled through her notes. "Mrs. Otten's behavior may mean nothing, as far as important details, but Veronica Parson and Mrs. Frotis arguing multiple times is important."

"More than we already knew about?" Ev asked.

"Yes," Doro replied before revealing the additional information.

"Mrs. Parson could've seen Mrs. Frotis leaving this morning," Wade said.

"We'll have to speak with her staff to find out," Doro said. "She isn't apt to tell the truth, although we can ask."

"Not sure if they'll be open with any of us," Wade said. "The housekeeper and handyman came with her from the city."

"A married couple?" Ev asked.

"Yes. Mr. and Mrs. Fulton. She has another maid, too. I believe she was hired more recently." Doro tapped her pencil on the notepad in her lap as she looked at Wade. "You know more about when Urban Parson married Veronica and brought her to Michaw. They wed when I was in graduate school. I spent the academic year in Ann Arbor and the summer in Colorado back then."

Wade's brow furrowed, as if he was dredging up memories. "Even though I was working on the railroad, their nuptials were an enormous source of gossip whenever I got home. Urban's folks had several long-time employees. He pensioned them off, and the Fultons showed up in no time. According to Ma and my aunt, the couple was never friendly with townsfolk. Even now, I rarely see them uptown."

"Neither do I," Doro added. "From what I hear, he goes into Toledo to buy most supplies."

"It's what I hear, too." Wade shook his head. "They pick up a few things here, but he goes to the city every week."

"We definitely need to talk with the two of them and the maid," Ev said. "I'm also interested in the run-ins between Miss Vining and Mrs. Frotis. I told Wade about your conversation with Miss Vining this morning, Doro."

"And I told Aggie, so she knows, as well." Doro made another note.

"Eloise has always seemed quiet and shy," Aggie said. "I was surprised at her awful pun."

Wade nodded. "So am I. It seems completely out of character."

"It does," Doro said, "but she's been spending a lot of time with Veronica. If Eloise has harbored anger toward Mrs. Frotis, she may have gotten to her limit after being egged on."

"But how would she know the woman was at the auditorium at seven o'clock? You already said Mrs. Frotis doesn't usually get up so early," Ev observed.

Doro nodded. "She was completely off-schedule today. Mrs. Otten verified her employer is a late sleeper."

"Are we eliminating her and Ralphie?" Ev asked.

"I don't see either as a suspect," Wade replied. "Neither has access to a vehicle, which means walking to campus. Ralphie tramps around town often, but Mrs. Otten's arthritis keeps her close to the Frotis house, especially in cold weather."

"She isn't on my list," Doro said.

"What about you, Aggie?" Wade asked.

"I agree with the rest of you. Mrs. Otten isn't the killer, and I doubt Ralphie is, either."

Wade shifted in his chair. "Probably not, but I can't reject him. Not when we don't know where he is."

"I agree with Wade," Ev said. "We can move Ralphie to the bottom, but not off the list."

"All right," Doro agreed. "Have we covered all possible suspects?"

A long moment of silence filled the room.

Chapter Nine

"The list of folks who disliked Mrs. Frotis is long. Those with a solid motive is shorter," Wade chipped in.

"And those with opportunity is even briefer," Ev observed.

Doro studied her list again. "We have several with motive and potential opportunity."

"Veronica Parson, Eloise Vining, Mr. Adler, and Ralphie," Aggie added. "We're leaning toward eliminating Ralphie, but he was around and knew Mrs. Frotis went to the auditorium."

The others nodded.

"Veronica Parson is a definite suspect to me. Eloise Vining would be further down my list, but ahead of Ralphie," Wade said.

"I agree. Especially since Doro encountered her this morning, and Eloise had no real reason for being near the campus," Aggie said. "We know Eloise was with Mrs. Parson when nasty gossip was being spread."

"And Eloise has one of the puppies," Doro reminded the group about Mrs. Otten's revelation. She glanced at Ev, who looked pensive. "Maybe you could interview Mrs. Parson, Ev."

His expression went from thoughtful to alarmed. "Why me? You were on the committee with her. You and Aggie should talk to the woman." Ev looked at the constable. "Or you could, Wade. You've known her for a while. I'm sure she'd feel comfortable with you."

A chuckle escaped Wade. "I think you're the perfect person, Ev. I've seen the two of you chatting a few times. Mrs. Parson seems much friendlier to you than she ever has to me."

Out of the corner of her eye, Doro saw Aggie narrow a speculative gaze on Ev. At the same time, the security officer spoke again.

"Only because she waylays me whenever we cross paths. She's interested in my time as a Prohibition agent, too." Ev scowled.

Wade's laughter grew louder. "I'm sure she's interested."

Dark color suffused Ev's face. "I'm not interviewing her by myself," he muttered. "Doro can go along and take notes. That's seemlier anyhow."

"It certainly is," Aggie agreed, with a lilt of amusement in her voice.

For Doro, the highlight of the exchange was Ev suggesting she accompany him, which meant more sleuthing. And, more time with Ev, although that was secondary. She did not seriously consider the amusement shown by Aggie and Wade. Let them chuckle. "I'd be happy to go along. I suppose Eloise Vining should be interviewed, too."

"You're right," Wade agreed. "I also want to find out if anyone else argued with Mrs. Frotis recently. I can ask around town. Although, once word about her death gets out, we may not have to pose many questions. Folks will gossip plenty."

Ev nodded. "Probably so. We'll learn more by listening. Someone might have information that we don't. Not that we have much. Certainly not enough to narrow our list."

Doro reflected on the conversation with the housekeeper. "But maybe enough to widen it. Mrs. Otten said Mrs. Hood was close with Doc. He was like a big brother to her, even though his wife thought he was spoiling her sister."

"What has that got to do with the murder?" Wade asked.

"I'm not sure it does," Doro replied, "but Mrs. Otten gave us some interesting information about the will." After sharing it, she posed a query. "What do you think?"

"Is Retty aware of the new will's contents?" Wade asked.

"Mrs. Otten didn't know," Doro replied, "but maybe so."

"*Maybe* doesn't make her a suspect," Wade insisted. "Retty isn't even in town."

"That's true," Ev agreed, "but why did she come back after such a long time? Could it have been for money?"

Wade shook his head. "Retty's in-laws were wealthy, according to town gossip."

"And according to Floyd Quartine," Doro agreed, "but money can get used up." She thought back to the woman's faded and dated outfit. If Retty Hood was well-to-do, would she wear old clothes? Doro presented the information to the group.

"Plenty of affluent folks don't keep buying clothes," Wade said. "Look at the bank president. He's got three suits, all more than a decade old."

Since Doro could not argue with that point, she made a benign comment. "You know Retty better than the rest of us."

"I do," Wade said in a firm tone. "And Retty wouldn't kill her sister, not even if the will was changed. But I'm surprised their lawyer did it. He's been working for the family as far back as I can recall."

Ev turned to Wade. "Did the Frotises use a local lawyer?"

"They went to a man in Sylvania," the constable replied.

Realization hit Doro. "When Mrs. Frotis told us about changing bakeries, she said the one in the city was near her new attorney."

A harsh breath left Wade. "She probably got him to leave Retty out. I think the fellow in Sylvania would've tried to talk her out of it. Maybe he did try, and that's why she went to someone else."

"Possible," Ev agreed, "but it makes me wonder if Mrs. Hood came to visit wondering about the inheritance."

Although he had not labeled Retty as a suspect, Ev seemed open to the idea. Wade did not. Doro mulled over the possibilities. "Why did Retty and her husband go into vaudeville, if his parents had money?"

"Retty was always unconventional," Wade replied. "Maybe her husband was, too."

Ev cleared his throat. "If Mr. Hood was no good with money, he might've gone through his inheritance. Do you know if his parents have been dead for a while?"

Doro chewed on her lower lip. "A few years, I think."

"That's plenty of time to spend their money," Ev pointed out.

Wade ran one hand over his face. "I don't believe Retty had anything to do with her sister's death."

For a moment, Ev studied the other man. "Probably not, but we need to know more about her and the others."

A tense silence followed his remark. Doro looked from Ev to Wade, whose expression was shuttered. Finally, she tried breaking the strain with a general comment. "Money often makes people do odd things."

Wade did not appear to be convinced. "The old Retty would never have done such a thing, and I can't believe she would now. Besides, she's in Toledo."

Doro didn't point out that Wade hadn't seen the woman for over thirty years or that they could not be sure of the woman's whereabouts. Not when they only had her word. "We won't accuse her of anything."

"Understood," the constable said. "And I'll be sensitive about her loss when I speak with her, but maybe she'll say something useful. Something to clear her completely, which is what I expect. Mostly, I'm hoping to locate her soon, so final arrangements can be made."

Final arrangements was such a chilling phrase. As Doro glanced around the group, she noted the others also felt stricken.

"Mrs. Otten said Mrs. Frotis spoke with her sister a few days ago," Aggie commented. "Just before she came here."

"Did they talk often?" Wade asked.

"Not at all from what Mrs. Otten shared," Aggie replied.

Ev shifted to sit on the edge of his chair. "Was the last conversation about the sister coming to visit?"

"Mrs. Otten thinks so, because Mrs. Frotis asked her to prepare Retty's old room right afterward," Doro replied.

A frown fell over Ev's face. "So, Mrs. Hood called wanting to visit after a long period of no communication."

"Remember, she stayed in touch with her brother-in-law right up until his death," Doro put in. "Only by mail, though. Somehow, she heard about him passing and called Mrs. Frotis. Retty wanted to come to the funeral, but her sister said she wasn't welcome."

Ev's eyebrows rose. "That was four years ago?"

Wade nodded. "Yep. Doc had a heart attack. Took him quick."

"Even though he had already retired, it was a terrible loss to the community," Doro put in. "The Frotis family had a history here. Sadly, the line ended with young doc."

"I assume there was a funeral," Ev said.

The others nodded before Wade spoke. "The whole town turned out to lay him to rest. Mrs. Frotis hardly spoke to anyone and left with her help right after the burial."

"No wake afterward?" Ev asked.

"None involving her. The minister invited folks to the church hall. Some of the church ladies provided food," Wade explained.

"Pretty odd, in my experience," Ev murmured. "Usually the family hosts a lunch."

"It was odd to everyone here, too, but people wanted to honor and remember Doc," Wade said. "It's a darn shame that Retty and her husband didn't come. They would've been welcome at the church."

Doro turned toward him. "We didn't ask Mrs. Otten about Mr. Hood. I assumed he never came to Michaw."

"I did, too," Aggie commented.

"He never did, to my knowledge," Wade said. "I'm sure someone would've mentioned the two of them coming. Plenty of folks knew and liked Retty." Wade did not need to say he was one of them.

"Did she stay in touch with anyone other than her broth-er-in-law?" Ev asked.

"Not that I know about," Wade told him.

"Me, either," Doro added, "but she left town before I was born."

"It's still curious that they were at odds going way back," Ev said. "There must be something in their past. Maybe related to their parents dying?"

As his eyes went wide, Wade leaned forward and braced his elbows on his knees. "I should've thought of this earlier, since I'm guessing none of you ever heard the story about her broth-er's death."

"Mrs. Frotis had a brother? I never heard her, or anyone else, mention him," Doro murmured in surprise.

"I only heard about him once, many years ago, and I haven't thought about it since then." Wade scratched his head.

"Do you remember the details?" Doro asked.

He slowly nodded.

"When they were kids, Mrs.Frotis' kitten got on the roof of the family's shed. Their folks weren't home, and she was scared the little thing would fall off, so she begged her brother to rescue it. He didn't want to, but according to what I heard from Dr. Frotis, he finally agreed. The ground was wet and muddy from heavy rain. The brother was older and had to realize getting on the ladder wasn't safe. Mrs. Frotis cried and cried, which had to be hard for a big brother. Anyhow, when he went up to get the cat, the ladder slid sideways. He fell off and broke his neck."

Shock and horror hit Doro. "How awful," she gasped.

Aggie's hand flew to her mouth. "Truly horrible."

"Yep," Wade said. "Doc only told me because I'd gone over to clean out eaves for them. That was way back when I was still in school. I had the ladder against the house and was climbing up when she came out caterwauling about how I needed to get right down. The woman was hysterical until her husband ushered her into the house. Then, he returned and told me the story. He asked me not to repeat it, because she didn't want folks gossiping about her, and he didn't want her to be upset."

As she listened, Doro felt her distress grow. "What a ghastly memory for her." She paused briefly. "She was a private, reserved person, so I understand her not wanting gossip spread—even though most people would've been sympathetic."

"It's little wonder she was adamant about being cautious on a ladder." Ev drove his fingers through his dark hair. "And it's powerful support for what you've shared, Doro."

"Very strong." Wade clasped his hands together before continuing. "I'd nearly forgotten about the story."

"You have a lot on your mind now, and you were young then," Aggie said. "It's understandable that you forgot."

Doro nodded. "Knowing about her brother's death, I understand some of her rules."

"Others would, too, although there's no excuse for the woman always wanting her way," Wade put in.

Briefly, Doro mulled over the statement. "No, but people sometimes do that based on a past tragedy. Maybe she felt partly responsible for her brother dying, because she insisted he save her kitten. After that, she might've tried to manage everything, even others."

"I wonder if Mrs. Hood saw him fall," Aggie put in.

Both Doro and Wade shook their heads and indicated they had no idea.

"Retty would've been very small," the constable added.

"Then, she might not have been old enough to have been left with them while their parents were away," Ev said, "but she has to know what happened."

"Does that make any difference?" Doro asked. "Whether Retty saw it?"

"I doubt it," Ev replied. "What's really significant is Mrs. Frotis' rules about ladders, and the reason behind them. It supports the idea that she wasn't alone when she got on it."

"Yep, it's solid support," Wade agreed. "Now we need to move forward. What about talking to Mrs. Parson, Miss Vining, and Mr. Adler?"

"We also need to find Ralphie," Ev said. "Doro and I can talk to the others, while you wait to hear from Retty Hood."

"I'd like to go along," Wade said, "but our young clerk can get messages mixed up. I don't want her doing that in this case. Besides, I knew Retty, so maybe that'll help soften the blow."

"I'm afraid I won't be able to pitch in until after my three o'clock department meeting," Aggie said. "I'll come back here when it's over."

"Good," Wade said. A broad smile chased the frown from his face.

"Should we meet here around four o'clock?" Ev said to the other man. "We'll have more to review, then."

A smile lifted the corners of Wade's wide mouth. "I'm glad you have permanent deputy status."

"Happy to help when needed," Ev replied.

After getting off to a shaky start back in October, the two lawmen worked well together. Since then, they had established a solid friendship. Doro sometimes saw them sharing the noon meal in the diner. The gregarious constable, a lifelong Michawan, had warmly introduced the new campus security officer to townsfolk. Wade's support had led to Ev, who was more reserved, being welcomed into the tightly knit community.

"You're needed now," Wade observed before looking at the two young women. "You two are, as well. I want to untangle this case as soon as possible. If we get leads today, the mayor and councilmen are more likely to let the party go ahead."

"Then, we'll do whatever we can to help," Doro vowed.

"We will," Aggie agreed, "but I have to get back to campus soon. My office hours start in twenty minutes, and my students are bringing their final compositions in. Then, there's the meeting."

Ev glanced at his watch before turning to Doro. "Why don't we talk with Mrs. Parson now? I'd like to catch her before she gets word from someone else. Although, if Eloise Vining knows, she probably does, too."

"Whether or not Mrs. Parson knows could tell us a little. Like if she and Miss Vining got together this morning," Wade agreed before turning to Ev. "I hate to put the burden of interviews on you two, but I'm stuck here waiting for calls. That's the downside of being a constable. With luck, I'll hear from Retty and the mayor by mid-afternoon. You may run into Ralphie, and I'd like to hear what the Adlers have to say, since he's let everyone in town know how he feels about the bakery being stuck with a lot of baked goods. He's a good man but known for having a hot temper."

Doro blinked in surprise. "Really? He seems stern, but not mean."

"Not mean, but volatile. A couple of my schoolmates worked for him years ago," Wade replied. "He got after them for even the slightest mistake. They didn't last long. Most of their help doesn't. He's passable to customers. Not as nice to his workers."

The revelation gave Doro food for thought. "Even though I've gone into the bakery hundreds of times since I was a little girl, I haven't seen Mr. Adler often. Mrs. Adler is usually at the counter, unless the two of them have left for the day. Then, a clerk is."

"It's been that way as far back as I know," Wade agreed. "She's pleasant, so it makes sense for her to be the face of the business."

With a contemplative look on his face, Ev nodded. "I've been in the shop a few times in the past couple of months. Mrs. Adler has been kind and welcoming on every occasion. I've seen her husband twice. He barely spoke."

A rueful grin tugged at one corner of Wade's mouth. "That's him at his best."

Ev's expression grew resolute. "Maybe you and I should talk to him."

Wade's humor dissipated. "Later today, I can get away from the office."

"Does he have a gun?" Ev asked.

One of Wade's shoulders rose and fell. "I've never seen him with one, but I wouldn't be surprised if he owns a weapon."

Annoyance trickled through Doro. "I can go to the bakery with you, Ev. We could do it after we talk to Veronica and Eloise. Or before, since the Adlers go home early."

"The Adlers stand to lose a lot of money due to Mrs. Frotis' last-minute decision to go elsewhere for refreshments," Aggie said as a reminder.

"True," Doro had to agree.

"Motive is there," Ev inserted. "Opportunity could be, too. After all, the man is up and around early. So, we've several solid suspects. Now, we need to gather more details and get down to one."

Chapter Ten

F ive minutes later, Doro was in the passenger seat of Ev's Willys-Knight roadster, and they were headed to the Parson home. As they rolled through the business district, she glanced out the side window. The sidewalks were filled with shoppers, and many people waved as the vehicle passed.

"Everyone in town knows you," Ev observed.

The remark made Doro smile. "I've lived here my whole life, except for when I was in graduate school. Even then, I was only gone when classes were in session."

"It must be nice."

His voice held an undercurrent of some indefinable emotion, which had her turning toward him. "You grew up in the city, but you must've known people in your own neighborhood well."

"We did, but we moved after my dad died. My mother went to work then, so she didn't get well-acquainted with the other ladies in the area, and I had a job after school. That meant no time to spend with the other boys. My sister made more friends."

"How old were you when your father passed?"

"Fourteen."

Although his tone held no hint of sorrow, his jaw tightened. Doro could only imagine how hard losing a parent at such a young age would have been. Ev didn't talk much about his past life, but he had mentioned both parents passing by the time he turned twenty. "That had to be difficult, especially when you moved away from your friends."

"It wasn't easy, but I adjusted."

"And you adjusted again when you moved from Detroit to Toledo, and from Toledo to Michaw."

His gaze briefly met hers before going back to the road. "I'm not sure I've completely acclimated to small town life."

The remark surprised Doro. "You just said it must be nice to know everyone."

"I was thinking about growing up here," he replied. "Although most townsfolk have been welcoming, thanks to Wade, a few are standoffish. Not that I blame them."

"I could guess who, because a handful of people are reticent with everyone. It's got nothing to do with you." And a handful were rumored to work for rumrunners. Those folks would not befriend a former Prohibition agent.

The corner of his mouth quirked. "Good to know."

Those words were barely out before he pulled to a stop in the Parsons' driveway. "Let's see what she has to say."

Before Ev moved to open his door, Doro laid one hand on his arm. "I assume you'll ask the questions, and I'll take notes."

He swiveled to face her. "We can start that way, but feel free to jump in. I don't know Mrs. Parson as well as you do, so you'll probably get insights after we talk with her a little."

"We're only acquainted in passing, mostly through the committee. I can't recall exchanging more than a few pleasantries outside that. She might resent me posing queries." Although Doro wanted to grill the woman, she would act in whatever manner helped to move the investigation forward.

For a moment, he pondered her response. "During my brief time at the meeting on Monday, I observed her being abrupt with Mrs. Frotis. Is she that way with you?"

She shook her head. "No, never." Hastily, she turned toward the car door. Before she got out, Ev was helping her by extending a hand. "Thank you," she murmured.

"You're welcome."

As she stepped away from him, Doro forced herself to focus solely on the case. "Let's hope she's home."

Ev laughed. "That would be useful."

When they reached the expansive front porch, Ev used the brass knocker to rap. The door opened so quickly, Doro wondered if the young maid who answered had seen them pull up.

"Good day," the girl said. "Can I help you?"

Ev introduced himself and Doro before ending with, "Is Mrs. Parson home?"

"Yes, sir. I can get her." The maid blushed prettily as she smiled at Ev.

"Please do," Ev replied.

After nodding, the girl rushed off, leaving Doro and Ev in the wide foyer. His silver gaze twinkled with amusement. "Do you know if Mrs. Parson usually has her staff make visitors wait by the door?"

Doro felt certain Veronica wouldn't want the handsome security officer cooling his heels. She wasn't as certain about what her own welcome would be. "That maid is new. The previous one was a local girl, who married last summer. She'd taken Anita's place. Veronica complained at our first committee meeting in October that she hadn't found a replacement. Evidently, she has now. But I've never seen this girl, so she must be from the city."

Before they continued their conversation, Veronica Parson swept into view from the back of the house. "I'm so sorry you weren't ushered in and offered comfortable seats. Colleen is new and desperately needs training. I've sent her for refreshments, so please come along." The woman stopped beside Ev and slipped her hand into the crook of his arm as she spoke.

Clad in a drop-waist lavender silk dress that skimmed her knees, Veronica exuded style and confidence. Doro unbuttoned her cloak and glanced down at her own attire. While her frock was also in the latest fashion, it was two inches longer and subdued in color. The navy wool was suitable for her job, while the widow's outfit was right for a party. Doro couldn't quell the thought that Veronica might have been expecting Ev to show up. If so, did that point to her guilt? Doro stared at the pair, and after a moment, she followed them into the adjacent parlor. When Ev shot a rueful glance over his shoulder, she forced a smile. Maybe Veronica's soft spot for him would lead to important revelations.

As the widow sat on the gold brocade loveseat facing the fireplace, she patted the space beside her. "Sit down, Ev." Almost as an afterthought, she addressed Doro. "Take a chair, dear." Her gaze went from Doro's head to her hands. "It is chilly this morning. I noticed on my trip into Sylvania. I'm afraid I suffered for fashion by dressing stylishly, as usual. You're more practical, since you're wearing your cute mittens. I've seen many of the coeds in similar attire."

The way the other woman said *dear* made Doro feel like she was twelve, not twenty-five. She wanted to point out that her hat, a light blue cloche with a navy silk flower, was not typical headwear for college girls. As for the mittens, Doro's fingers felt icy with them on. Fancy gloves, like the kind Veronica usually wore, would not offer much warmth. Nevertheless, she bit her lip to keep from voicing her arguments, shrugged out of her cloak, and sat down. Briefly, her gaze took in the elegant furnishings. Few homes in Michaw held such expensive items. Not even the Frotis home next door, which was one of the largest and finest in town, had such luxurious materials. Once again, Doro wondered if the rumors about Urban Parson were true. Had he been involved in bootlegging? Not personally, since he had rarely dirtied his hands with any physical tasks. Instead, he could have paid for others to run liquor down from Canada and distribute it to speakeasies in the city. Was that why Veronica wondered about Ev's time as a Prohibition agent? Was she carrying on her husband's trade? Abruptly, Ev's voice broke into Doro's reverie.

"We wanted to impart some bad news and ask a few questions," he said to their hostess.

Veronica's eyes narrowed on him. "Bad news? What sort of bad news would the two of you bring me?" she asked in a baffled tone.

Looking on, Doro thought the other woman seemed genuinely perplexed, but she continued to scrutinize Veronica.

Ev cleared his throat. "Mrs. Frotis died early this morning."

Silence echoed in the elegant room for several moments. "Such distressing news," Veronica murmured. Her words were at odds with her tone, which held no hint of distress. "But why come to tell me? We were neighbors, but not friends, and I left the Christmas committee. Someone else will have to oversee the last tasks for the party, although there shouldn't be much to do. The tree was to be decorated last night along with evergreen boughs and holly being hung. The tables can easily be set up tomorrow night or Saturday morning, even without Hortense bossing everyone around."

Although Mrs. Parson and Mrs. Frotis had often, almost always, been at odds, the former's passing sorrow stood out to Doro. So did Veronica not asking how Mrs. Frotis had died. Maybe she didn't need to ask. Maybe she knew. Doro continued to study the other woman's face, but she found no clues.

Before anyone could say more, the young maid brought in a tray with a teapot, cups, and a plate of cookies. Ev rose to help her set the burden on the low table near the fireplace. With one hand, Veronica shooed the girl away. "Go back to your other tasks. I'll let you know when you can carry the things away."

A quick nod was Colleen's answer before she hurried off.

"It's an onerous task to get decent help way out here." Veronica poured tea as she spoke. She handed the first cup to Ev, who passed it on to Doro with a wink. He followed up by putting two cookies on a plate and setting them on the small table by her chair.

After Doro murmured her thanks, she sipped the hot brew. Hours had passed since an early breakfast, and she was suddenly aware of gnawing hunger. She grabbed a cookie and took a bite before addressing one of Veronica's assumptions. "You must not have stopped in town before going to Sylvania this morning."

The other woman set her cup in the saucer with the clear clink of bone china meeting. "No, I didn't. Why?"

"Last night, Irma Green quit the committee before taking her boys and leaving. Without their help, we made little progress." Doro stopped before saying she and Mrs. Frotis had planned to work this morning.

Veronica pursed her lips. "I suppose Hortense drove her away with the usual bullying and bossiness."

Although Doro could not deny the assertion, she sidestepped responding to it. "Because the committee was down to three, and Magenta Silven is dealing with sick children, Mrs. Frotis and I planned to meet early this morning and get the bulk of the decorating done." She sipped her tea before continuing. "Unfortunately, Mrs. Frotis was dead when I arrived."

Veronica Parsons leaned back and folded her hands in her lap. "How sad for you to find another body."

Neither the woman's tone nor expression gave credence to the assertion, because she appeared far from sorry. Doro glanced at Ev, whose features resembled a hard mask. Because he looked ready to speak, she let him.

"It's unfortunate Miss Banyon found herself in such circumstances again. Luckily, she has a steady demeanor and isn't easily flummoxed. Not everyone would maintain calm like she did." As he addressed the widow, Ev met Doro's gaze.

Although he had been using her given name since October, Ev probably wanted to establish the proper formality with witnesses...and suspects. Doro followed suit. "It was lucky Officer Mallow stopped on his morning rounds, too."

Their hostess offered a weak smile. "Yes, it was, but I don't know why the two of you are here. Surely, you aren't visiting everyone in town to announce the death."

"No, we aren't," Ev readily agreed. "We're only speaking with people who might've seen something important early this morning. Since you were out, you could have a clue and not realize it."

"Clue? What are you talking about, Ev?" Veronica asked.

The woman sounded perplexed, but was she? Or was she acting? Doro was not sure. She wondered if Ev had a gut feeling. If so, his demeanor gave nothing away.

"Mrs. Frotis died in a fall from the ladder used to put decorations on the tree," he replied.

Veronica's eyes widened as she looked from Ev to Doro. "I thought you found her dead when you arrived."

"I did," Doro said.

"Who else was there with her?" their hostess asked. "Hortie wouldn't get on a ladder without someone holding it. She didn't let anyone else do that, either."

"Doro told me the same thing," Ev replied without revealing more.

"Then, who was there?" Veronica asked in a querulous voice.

"That's just it," Doro said, "we don't know."

For several moments, the crackling of the fire was the only sound. "You're here because you think she was pushed off the ladder, maybe by me," Veronica said in a strained whisper.

"We aren't accusing you of anything," Ev quickly put in. "As I mentioned, you might've seen something that didn't seem important, but could help us solve the case. Maybe on your way out of town."

As Veronica shifted restlessly on the loveseat, she stared into her cup but said nothing. The widow's behavior bothered Doro, who spoke without forethought. "I saw Eloise Vining in front of College Commons. She was coming from this direction. That was around nine 'o'clock or so. Maybe you were already back from Sylvania." Or maybe Veronica had never left Michaw.

The woman's reply was to stand up and gesture toward the French doors into the front hall. "You two need to leave. Before I say anything at all, I'm calling my husband's lawyer."

A glance at Ev revealed he was as taken aback as she was. "No one said you're a suspect, Mrs. Parson. We only want information," Ev said.

"As I said, I'm saying nothing more at present. Please leave now." Veronica's classic features resembled a frozen mask.

With little recourse, Doro and Ev followed the dictate. In silence, they left the house.

When they were again inside the vehicle, he turned to her. "I didn't expect to be ordered out."

"Neither did I," she replied. "Veronica's initial reaction had me leaning toward dropping her as a suspect. Maybe I shouldn't have mentioned seeing Eloise."

"It didn't hurt anything," Ev said. "She has no idea what Miss Vining told you, although Mrs. Parson may find out quickly."

A sigh escaped Doro. "Now, they might get their stories to mesh." Guilt plagued her. "All because I didn't stop and think."

Ev shook his head. "If they're guilty, neither of them would stand up under questioning at the constable's station. Especially if they're in collusion. Besides, we can ask around town. Maybe someone saw Mrs. Parson heading to Sylvania. If no one did, Wade can call the constable there. In any case, both women will be more, not less, nervous. Not a bad thing."

"So, you also think they're solid suspects?"

"I do, and I'm keeping both at the top of the list."

As shivers rippled through Doro, she wrapped her cloak more closely around her. The bitter cold put a chill in her bones, but so did considering neighbors as murder suspects.

"We need to get inside, since the temperature is dropping. My automobile offers little protection from the elements. We can go over our thoughts after we talk to the others. Preferably in a warm place."

"Good idea," she readily agreed. Unlike her Essex, Ev's Willys-Knight roadster lacked isinglass windows or even side curtains, so the winter wind had free rein, which meant Doro had to use one hand to keep her cloche on her head.

"I was going to leave the car here and walk next door, but I'm afraid Mrs. Parson will object."

A chuckle escaped Doro. "I agree."

Within a couple of minutes, Ev parked the car in the Frotis driveway and hurried around to open the passenger door for Doro. "Maybe we should knock, just to see if Mrs. Otten has seen Ralphie since you and Aggie were here."

After nodding, Doro ascended the porch steps and rang the bell. When several moments passed and no one answered, she turned to Ev. "Mrs. Otten may be in her suite, which is off the kitchen. Should we try the back door?"

He shook his head. "Let's see if Ralphie is in his apartment. You lead the way."

She took him around the side of the house and to the garage in the back. "He lives upstairs." Doro pointed to the rickety wooden steps. "Aggie and I called out before going up and knocking."

"Let's try that again," Ev said before shouting the man's name. When no response came, he led the way upstairs and rapped. When the door moved, Ev faced Doro again. "You didn't mention looking inside."

"Because we didn't. When I knocked, the door never moved. Aggie and I didn't think we should go in, so we called his name again. To no avail, so we left. After all, we aren't officers of the law. We're amateur sleuths," Doro said with a laugh.

Amusement twinkled in his silver gaze. "And good ones. You were right not to barge in. Since I have deputy status, I'm going to look."

After Ev opened the door wide, Doro followed him, since he had not drawn his gun, and she had glimpsed a slight bulge under his jacket. Forearmed could be a good thing in their present situation. When she glanced around the tiny space, she gasped.

Every drawer of the bureau was ajar, and the contents spilled out and on to the floor. The mattress was off the bed frame, and its stuffing laid in puffs on each side. The single easy chair had also been ravaged. Hunks of straw poked out of the cushions. Shock filled Doro as she took a more careful survey. "There's no sign of Ralphie, but who would wreck his home? And why?" She voiced her questions in a murmur.

"I don't know," Ev replied. "At least there's no sign of a struggle, so Ralphie was likely gone when this happened." He moved toward the bed before heading to the chair and bending down for a better survey. "Someone had to be searching for something. But what?"

"He wasn't paid well, so there couldn't be money or other valuables up here," Doro stated.

A long moment passed before Ev spoke again. "We can't be sure he wasn't stealing from someone. Maybe Mrs. Frotis."

Doro's hand flew to her mouth. "Ralphie has never taken anything in his life. Why start now?" The defensiveness in her tone was obvious, but she didn't care. Ev barely knew Ralphie, but Doro did. She refused to let the man-child fall under suspicion for theft, and certainly not for murder. He might be at the bottom of the lawmen's suspect list, but he was not on Doro's at all.

Ev rose to his feet. "I don't know. Maybe he was keeping items for someone else. Maybe the person came to get them back. Both are possible, but maybe not probable."

"Weeks go by without even a minor crime happening in Michaw. Now, we have two on the same day. Something is amiss." Anxiety gripped Doro's insides. Who was responsible?

"I won't argue that point, although the two may not be related." He gestured around the room. "You've known Ralphie all of your life. Would he hide evidence for someone?"

Incredulity filled Doro and rang in her voice. "You believe he might've been keeping solid evidence, not simply storing benign items?"

His jaw worked. "Teaching your mystery course affects your perspective."

The comment seemed odd. Was the undercurrent in his tone amusement, admiration, or annoyance? "I'm not sure what you mean."

"You've considered ideas used in whodunits." His response did little to clarify his point.

"But I've gone from armchair detective to amateur sleuth, right?" After the query was out, Doro silently chastised herself for sounding uncertain. She didn't need Ev's praise. But she and Aggie couldn't effectively pursue the case if they were at odds with Ev and Wade. The lawmen had jurisdiction. The two young women didn't.

Ev pressed a hand to his forehead. "I didn't mean the comment as criticism. You're quick to pick up valid points and read between the lines. And, yes, I'm entertaining the idea that someone convinced Ralphie to hide evidence. What type of evidence and why, I don't know. Then, there's the chance that he took money or valuables himself. And there's one additional idea."

As she studied Ev's solemn expression, an idea popped into her mind. "The killer vandalized the place to point a finger at Ralphie."

"Also, possible."

"Then, it's more important than ever to find him." Even as she spoke, Doro felt fear strike her heart. Could Ralphie be a victim, too? She realized her anxiety must be visible when Ev clasped her shoulder.

"He's probably fine."

Doro nodded. "Probably so." But *probably* was a long way from *certainly*.

"I want to be careful, in case we can get fingerprints." With his gloves on, Ev looked into the open drawers and cupboards, checked the windows, and studied the items strewn about the place.

While Ev worked, Doro studied the room again. The corner of a pillow, wedged between the bottom of the bed frame and the wall, grabbed her attention. She pulled it loose and noticed a heavy lump at the bottom. "Ev, look at this."

When he joined her, Ev frowned. "Something besides stuffing is in there."

"Let's see what," Doro murmured.

"Go ahead. We can't get prints off fabric."

Since there was a gap in one seam, Doro reached in and pulled out a handful of gold coins. Shock hit her.

Ev took several and studied them. "Some are old, but a few are recently minted. How would Ralphie get them? As pay?"

"I don't think so," Doro said. She glanced around again. "It wasn't easy to see the pillow, but it might've been planted to make him look guilty."

"Maybe," Ev said. "Let's take them to the office and tell Wade what we discovered. He's got a fingerprinting kit, so I can get some from here today. As for the coins, they might be evidence. They might have prints, too, so we won't touch them with our bare hands."

In October, Doro had watched in fascination as Ev took prints. Reading about the procedure in books was one thing. Seeing it done was mesmerizing, and she'd like to witness the process again. "Do you want to come back and do that before we talk to Eloise?"

Ev nodded. "We should."

Chapter Eleven

During a stop at the constable's office, Doro and Ev shared their findings. Wade studied the coins with interest. "Some could've been given to him. Or, as you say, they were planted to make him look guilty, because the Frotises had gold coins. Doc liked to collect them. In any case, I'll hold them as evidence. If you get fingerprints, those will be, too, even if we can't match them to other prints yet."

Before leaving again, Ev tested the coins. "Smudged and partial only."

Wade shrugged. "Let's hope you have better luck in his rooms."

In a matter of minutes, Doro and Ev returned to Ralphie's apartment. Ev took prints from several places before turning to Doro. "Do you want to try your hand at it?"

Surprise mingled with anticipation. "I'd love to, but I don't want to mess anything up."

A grin tugged at one corner of his mouth. "You won't. I've hit the areas where most prints would be already. Why not take some from that chair?" He pointed to an overturned rocker.

"All right." Doro took the tape and special powder from him. Like Ev had done, she brushed the dark dusty substance on the wooden chair arms before pulling out adhesive tape and carefully applying it. Mimicking Ev's actions, she pressed hard and thoroughly. Then, she methodically removed the tape and crossed to the table, where blank paper waited. Doro applied the tape and breathed a sigh of relief when a pristine print became visible. For a long moment, she studied her work. "I did it."

"Great job," Ev observed, "but I'm not surprised."

Pride warmed her insides. "Thank you," she murmured.

After putting everything back into the fingerprinting kit, Ev let Doro precede him down the stairway and into the yard. "Let's stop and see Mrs. Otten before we head back to the station."

Before Doro could respond, a girlish voice interrupted. "You looking for someone?"

Both Doro and Ev turned to see Colleen, Veronica Parson's maid, standing on the other side of the fence between the homes. Although the girl spoke in a hushed tone, she was only twelve feet away, so her voice carried to them. Without hesitation, Doro closed the distance. Ev followed.

After offering a smile, Doro explained their presence. "We were looking for Ralphie and Mrs. Otten." Not the complete truth, but she did not want to discuss the vandalism or fingerprints.

The girl glanced over her shoulder, as if making sure no one was watching her, before looking back at Doro. "I saw Ralphie real early when he got the automobile out for Mrs. Frotis."

"Did he go with her?" Doro asked.

Colleen's slender shoulders lifted and dropped. "I didn't see her leave, cuz I had work to do."

"What about Ralphie? Did you see him after that?" Ev posed the question.

"No, sir, but I were busy."

Disappointment filled Doro. Ralphie might have gone with his employer. "Have you seen Mrs. Otten today?"

"Yep. She left an hour ago."

"Did someone pick her up?" Ev asked.

The maid shook her head. "No, she were headed for town. Maybe doing errands or such."

"Maybe so," Doro agreed. Perhaps, the woman needed to pick up a few items before moving out. She and Ev could check. "Would you answer a few questions? That could be a big help, Colleen."

A nod was the reply.

"Is Mrs. Parson still home?" Ev asked.

"Yes, sir," Colleen replied, "but after she made a telephone call, she went back to her room for a nap. We're not to disturb her."

Relief filled Doro. Although Veronica must have contacted her lawyer, she wasn't apt to notice them chatting with her employee. "Good. What time did she leave for Sylvania this morning?"

Colleen frowned, as if in concentration. "About six-thirty, but I think she went to Toledo, not Sylvania, although she coulda passed through there. Anyhow, she were gone a while and came back without no packages, so she weren't shopping like she claimed."

Last evening, Veronica had gone to the city for dinner with friends. Why go again so early this morning? "She drove herself?" Doro inquired.

"Yes, miss. She loves to drive her roadster real fast." A shudder went through Colleen. "She picked me up at the station in Sylvania. I were scared to death on the ride here."

"What time did Mrs. Parson return?" Ev added his own query.

"About a half-hour before you two came," Colleen said.

"Does she often leave so early?" Doro asked.

Colleen vigorously shook her head. "No, miss. She likes to sleep in. Since I been here, today is the first time she got up before eight-thirty."

When Doro studied Ev's expression, she noted his interest. They had more to discuss, since people acting out of character was often a red flag.

"Have you noted anything else that was different?" Ev continued to use a warm, comforting tone. As the girl licked her lips, he smiled. "We'll only share the information with Constable Lammers."

Colleen's dark lashes fluttered. "Do you think Mrs. Parson done something wrong? I couldn't help but hear you telling her about Mrs. Frotis. The two of them was mean to each other, and the other help said that'd been going on a long time. If I'd known, I wouldn't have come out here, but she were nice when she hired me. Real nice, and I needed a job bad."

The comments troubled Doro. "Is Mrs. Parson nasty to you?"

A shrug moved the girl's slender shoulders. "Not like with Mrs. Frotis, but she finds fault a lot. I never been a maid before, and I told her so. She said I could learn. I don't learn so fast, though."

Her hang-dog expression wrung Doro's heart. Colleen could not have been more than seventeen. Was the girl alone in the world? Not wanting to dig deeply into the maid's personal life, Doro resisted. But she planned to get more details soon. "Did you hear many arguments between the two?"

"Three, since I got here," Colleen said. "And Mrs. Parson ranted afterward about how Mrs. Frotis ought to get what was coming to her."

Fresh dismay hit Doro, but Ev was the one to respond.

"Did Mrs. Parson make any specific threats?" he inquired.

"No, sir. Just said what I told you," Colleen replied. "Last evening, Miss Vining come so the two of them could go to the city. They raved about how bad Mrs. Frotis was, how they'd like to get even. They was on their way out, so it's all I heard. All that scares me. Talking bad about people aren't nice." The girl's hazel eyes went wide with fear.

"I think you're safe here," Ev reassured her. "Just don't tell anyone else what you overheard."

Colleen's expression did not relax as she wrapped her arms around her waist. When she spoke, her voice was barely audible. "I don't have nowhere else to go, so I guess I'll stay."

The last assertion clarified the girl's situation and convinced Doro to help her as soon as possible. "I wish I could offer a job, but I live in faculty housing. Officer Mallow does, too. But I'll ask around and see if someone else can hire you."

Hope blanketed the girl's face. "Thank you, miss. Thank you. Now, I best get inside."

"We appreciate your help," Ev added. "And don't worry. You'll be fine for the foreseeable future, and Miss Banyon is as good as her word. She'll help you, if she can."

"You're both kind," the girl said before wrapping her shawl around her shoulders and running back to the house.

Once she was inside, Doro turned to Ev. "More to consider."

"That's for sure," he agreed. "Let's move on. Before we speak with Miss Vining, we can drive down Main Street. Maybe we'll see Mrs. Otten there. Even though Colleen is probably right about the woman running errands, I'll feel better if we know for sure. I'd also like to leave the kit with Wade."

Doro nodded. "He might've heard from Mrs. Hood, which would be good."

"My thoughts exactly." After they were inside his vehicle, Ev continued. "Do you have ideas for Colleen? I thought there aren't a lot of wealthy people in Michaw."

"The Parsons and the Frotises are—were—the wealthiest. Some college administrators have housekeepers. Even if anyone needed one, Colleen doesn't have experience."

"She isn't even qualified to be a maid, from what she and Mrs. Parson said. I have to wonder why she got hired. Is it so hard to get help here?"

"Folks from the city sometimes balk at coming to a small town. Others aren't interested in being live-in help, which I can understand. It doesn't seem like much of a life when you never leave work."

Low laughter rumbled out of Ev. "You live on campus, so you don't leave work, either."

"But I leave the library. Besides, I'm not at someone's beck and call every hour of every day." She swiveled to study his firm profile. "Your rooms are in the garage at the President's house, and you're on call all the time."

After shooting her a rueful grin, he looked back at the road. "I'm happy to have a quiet place to live. It'll be easier to get meals when a room is free in the male faculty residence, but—for now—I'm fine with my current accommodations. As far as Colleen, she needs a roof over her head and a job."

"I know, and I'll work on it. As soon as we solve this case."

‹‹‹•›››

Back at the constable's office, Ev and Doro chatted with Wade, who revealed his only news: the mayor and town council were leaning toward the party going forward and would have a final decision by late afternoon.

"I wonder why they're waiting to decide," Doro said.

Wade's eyebrows rose a fraction. "Probably want to see if many folks think it'd be unseemly. If anyone other than Mrs. Frotis was the victim, I'd be willing to bet the party would be pushed back a week or more. I'll admit to having mixed feelings about the celebration going ahead, but students will leave for home next week."

"That's my biggest concern, too," Doro said, although she also wondered how everything would get done. For now, she pushed the problem away. Catching a killer came first. If the decorations and food were not perfect, few people would mind. Gathering as a community—town and college—to celebrate the season was most important.

"I'd sure like to solve the murder before then," Wade put in. "You two made more progress than I have, but I learned a little. Since no one answers at Retty's house, I asked our operator to connect me with the operator down there. Turns out the housekeeper was let go nearly two years ago."

The news made Doro glance at Ev, who looked as surprised as she was. "Is there any household help?" she asked.

Wade shook his head. "Nope. At one time, there were two maids, a handyman, and a cook. They went one-by-one after Mr. Hood's folks died. The housekeeper was the last to leave. The operator doesn't know where any of them went or I'd try to contact them."

"That gives credence to Mrs. Hood and her husband running through his inheritance," Ev observed.

"It certainly does," Doro agreed.

"But it doesn't mean Retty killed her sister," Wade said.

"Of course not," Ev put in. "But she's more of a suspect now. Don't you think so, Wade?"

"Maybe, but Mrs. Parson and Mr. Adler remain at the top of my list," the constable replied.

"They're definitely in the running," Ev said.

Since Doro held the same perspective, she nodded. But, like Ev, she wondered about Retty Hood.

A momentary silence filled the office before Ev addressed the constable again. "There's not much we can do in regard to Mrs. Hood until she returns. On another note, I hope those fingerprints," he gestured to the kit he had placed on Wade's desk, "are useful. Of course, we need some to use as matches. With several suspects and a few leads, that may take a while."

Fingerprints had been crucial during the Corlon case, but they had made clandestine forays into some suspects' offices and convinced others to voluntarily provide evidence. "Veronica isn't about to cooperate, and I doubt Eloise will, either," Doro observed.

"You're right," Wade said. "If it comes down to it, Adler isn't apt to, either."

"We're stymied until we have enough evidence to arrest someone," Ev muttered, frustration clear in his voice. "But the break-in may not relate to the murder. There's no way to know yet."

"Other evidence is out there," Wade said. "We only need to find it."

The exchange increased Doro's frustration. "I hope we narrow the field down soon."

Ev glanced at the desk, where he had laid the gold coins. "Not sure what to make of the coins left in the pillow."

"I'm puzzled, too," Wade said, "especially when you said the rest of the place was turned upside-down and inside-out. Why not tear open the pillow, along with the mattress?"

"It wasn't easy to see," Doro pointed out.

"True," Ev agreed. "But did Ralphie put the coins in it, or were they planted?"

Wade rubbed his forehead with the heel of one hand. "Another question to answer. I'm worried about Ralphie."

"We all are," Doro added. "Colleen, Veronica's maid, stopped us when we were at the Frotis house. She said Ralphie got the automobile out for Mrs. Frotis, but she didn't see the woman leave."

"So, she doesn't know if he went with her," Wade suggested.

"No, she doesn't," Doro replied, "but she mentioned overhearing some heated arguments between Veronica and Mrs. Frotis. More than words about the dogs, too." Doro added the details given by Colleen.

A long exhalation left Wade. "Such foolishness, but it gives Mrs. Parson more motive. By the way, Mrs. Otten really is running errands. I dashed out to speak with her, and she can't imagine why Ralphie's room was vandalized."

"At least she's safe," Ev observed.

Wade nodded. "I'm not sure she should stay in the house. I called my ma. She's got an extra room, so Mrs. Otten will be there until her brother comes for her."

"She can live with him and his wife?" Doro asked.

"Yep. It's settled, and she seemed happy about it," Wade replied. "He'll come for her when he's off work on Sunday."

"Good," Doro said. "Now, Ralphie needs a place. Of course, we have to find him first." And clear him of potential involvement in Mrs. Frotis' death.

Ev's jaw tightened. "Have you called the farmers who took the mother and pups?"

"I got through to one. He and his family will keep an eye out. No one answered at the other place, but I'll have my clerk keep trying when she gets here," Wade said.

Ralphie's absence disturbed Doro almost as much as Mrs. Frotis' death. The handyman was childlike in many ways and could easily be influenced. Or victimized. But neither explained the condition of his rooms. "Ev mentioned the chance that Ralphie's rooms were vandalized to frame him."

"I wouldn't rule it out," Wade said, "although I wonder who would be so devious."

"Someone desperate." Ev supplied the perspective. He leaned back and folded his arms across his chest. "To me, it's significant that Ralphie's place was wrecked after you and Aggie were there, Doro. Maybe the person knows you looked around. Mrs. Parson was back in time, and Miss Vining might've gone there, too. Actually, anyone could've gone through the woods and into the backyard."

"But not everyone would know Aggie and I were at the Frotis place earlier," Doro pointed out.

"True," Ev admitted. "We need more information. A lot more."

"Which we might get this afternoon." Doro wanted to be optimistic, but doubt plagued her.

"Why don't you two head out?" Wade suggested. "There's no point in all of us cooling our heels while waiting for telephone calls. The mayor suggested I stay here. He'd like Mrs. Frotis out of the back room as soon as possible, and so would I. Meanwhile, if I see Ralphie, I'll get him to come into the office. I don't believe he was injured, or you would've seen some sign of that."

"I agree." Ev rose to his feet. "We'll be back by four."

"Me, too," Doro agreed before looking around. "Where is Nola?" The clerk typically worked from nine until six, but she hadn't been in earlier or now.

A long exhalation puffed out of Wade. "She's running late...again. At least, she called this time. The girl is more interested in moving to the city than in her job. I hate to say it, but I'll be relieved when she does. Maybe I can find someone more reliable."

The observations caught Doro's interest. Although she did not mention Colleen, Doro smiled. "The right person could come along any time."

A chuckle left Ev as his gaze met Doro's. "Indeed, she could."

"I hope so," Wade murmured. "Right now, arrangements should be made for Mrs. Frotis' burial, but I don't want to overstep my authority."

"There's not much more we can do until Retty comes back," Doro observed.

"No, there isn't," Ev agreed in a resigned tone. "But we can interview suspects and witnesses. It's been a long day, and barely afternoon."

"It seems like two days already," Wade agreed. "The two of you should probably talk to the Adlers. It isn't what we planned, but I don't think he'll give you a lot of trouble." He glanced at Doro. "You may hear some harsh words, though."

"That's all right," she replied. If she got to go along, Doro could turn a deaf ear to vulgar language or loud ranting. No problem.

Ev got to his feet but did not move. When he looked at Doro, his expression revealed profound anxiety. "I could go alone."

While Doro considered how to convince Ev, Wade stepped in. "I really don't think it's necessary. Or even advisable. Doro is a second set of eyes and ears, so she may pick up things you don't."

While waiting for Ev's reply, Doro crossed her fingers—out of sight, of course—and held her breath. Ev had faith in her as an amateur sleuth, so why was he hesitating? Out of concern? She studied his expression, but the source of his reluctance was impossible to decipher.

After what seemed like an eternity, Ev shrugged. "I suppose it'll be fine."

"Great." Doro jumped to her feet. Before she could say more, the telephone rang.

Wade went to the counter to answer. After a few moments, he turned back to Doro and Ev. "That was Carlton Whiggs. There's a bad accident in front of his place. He's already called Doc Silven, so the both of us are headed over." He grabbed his jacket and hat. "Ev, will you call Nola and ask her to get over right away?"

"Sure thing," the security officer replied. "Doro and I will stay until she arrives, just in case Mrs. Hood calls."

"Thanks. Tell Nola that I'll be back as soon as I can, but she needs to stay until then," Wade said.

Ev nodded his response. After Wade left, Ev made the call and returned to his chair.

With reluctance, Doro sat back down, too. "What did Nola say?"

"She'll come over. It shouldn't be long, since she was ready to leave."

"Good. We have plenty to do," Doro observed. "You and I agree. Retty Hood has become a suspect, but Wade didn't act like she should be."

"No, but it sounded like he might've been sweet on her when he was a kid. That often happens with young boys and older girls, especially if the girl is nice. He probably still wants to think well of her."

The observation made Doro wonder if Ev had been as smitten with some older girl as a boy, but she did not want to intrude or get off track. Instead, she voiced a growing suspicion. "I'm wondering if she will come back. What do you think?"

He scratched his head. "If she needs money, she most likely will, whether she's guilty or not. Mrs. Otten didn't mention any valuables being taken, did she?"

"No. I'm dubious, I guess. But I'm equally dubious about Veronica and Mr. Adler."

"We'll learn more about her when we talk with others today."

"Maybe so," Doro replied. "Do you want to go to the bakery before we talk to Eloise?"

Ev glanced at his watch. "No, we have time to see her before the Adlers leave for the day."

"All right, we'll still be back here to meet, although Wade might not be."

"Aggie, you, and I could go over the evidence," Ev suggested. "Later, I could fill Wade in."

The suggestion appealed to Doro, since it kept her involved in the case. "Good ideas," she replied with a smile.

Fifteen minutes later, Nola arrived. When the girl chattered about various things—the party, Mrs. Frotis' death, and more—Doro cut her off. "Officer Mallow and I need to go. If Mrs. Hood calls, please tell her only that her sister died, and she needs to return to Michaw right away. Don't share any gossip you've heard. Wade will speak with her in person."

"All right," the clerk said without enthusiasm.

After helping Doro with her cloak, Ev donned his uniform jacket and cap. "Wade will be back as soon as possible. Like I told you on the telephone, you'll have to stay in the office until then."

Nola nodded. "I just hope he's not too late. I've got plans for tonight."

Doro bit her tongue to keep from chastising the girl, while Ev nodded and smiled. "I'm sure he'll be back long before evening."

After Ev ushered Doro into the passenger seat and got behind the wheel, he turned to her. "I haven't been down the road where Miss Vining lives, but I think I know how to get there. It's off the street in front of the campus, right?" Ev asked.

"It is. Trees block any view of the little neighborhood. The lane is dirt and rutted, even in good weather. With the snow we've had, it may be filled with holes."

"I'll be careful and not bounce you around too much." A note of humor was in his baritone.

"I thought you'd be most concerned about your beautiful vehicle."

"I'm not emotionally attached to it like you are to yours," he observed with a chuckle. "I refer to my automobile as it, not she...or he."

"Laugh at me, if you want, but mine is a beauty. You have to admit that," she said.

"I do, and I'm glad she's safely in a parking lot instead of traversing bad roads." The statement was made as Ev turned off the main road. Almost immediately, the car jolted as it hit a bump.

Doro put both hands against the dashboard to steady herself. "This stretch is bad."

Ev shot her a glance. "You all right?"

"Sure," she replied, despite her insides feeling like they had been mixed and melded by an egg beater. No wonder Eloise had been on foot this morning. Walking would be less jolting than driving.

"I can't slow down much more or we wouldn't move forward. The trouble is, the holes are covered by snow, so I can't see them well. The road isn't easy to see, either."

"Just go ahead. The Vining cottage is the last one on my side."

Although the distance could usually be covered in under five minutes, plowing through the drifts turned it into ten. Doro breathed a sigh of relief when Ev pulled to a stop.

"The snow seems deeper here than in town," he observed, "but I suppose the evergreen trees block the sun."

"They do, which makes the neighborhood cool in the summer. Luckily, no one living here has to get to work every day.

After a heavy snowfall, they're stuck for a few days." By the time Doro stepped out of the vehicle, Ev had come around to assist her. The walk was slippery. Luckily, there was only one step up to the cottage's porch. Although Doro wore ankle boots, she felt like her feet could fly out from under her. After reaching the door, Doro knocked. Almost immediately, Eloise answered.

A scowl darkened the woman's face. "What do you want?"

Ev smiled. "We'd like to speak with you for a few minutes, Miss Vining."

Eloise's eyes narrowed to slits. "Why?"

When a gust of wind blew her cloak open, Doro shivered and grasped it more tightly around her. With temperatures falling, being outside felt worse and worse. Doro grimly focused on the case. This evening, she could take a hot bath, don her flannel nightgown and wool robe, make hot tea, and settle in front of her own fireplace. At least she would if they made progress on the case. If not, Doro planned to keep investigating because Ev and Wade would. But what about last-minute preparations for Saturday? Who was in charge? When they got back to the station, Doro had to find out. But now, she answered Eloise. "We're talking to everyone who was out early this morning, in case they noticed someone or something unusual."

A snuffle left Eloise. "You and I already talked."

Frustrated and annoyed, Doro opened her mouth to voice a harsh retort, but Ev spoke first.

"I'd like to speak with you, Miss Vining. As you know, I'm a special deputy with the constable's office, so I have jurisdiction." He let his assertion sink in. "We don't need much of your time."

"All right." The woman stepped back and gestured toward a small parlor. "We might as well sit down while we talk."

Although the grudging tone offered no welcome, Doro followed Eloise into the other room with Ev at her side. The cramped space held a plethora of furniture: two large horsehair divans, each with a lamp table behind it; an antique wooden rocker; a small needlepoint footstool, along with a massive keyhole desk and chair. The divans flanked the grate, while the rocker faced it. Amid the grouping sat a square, short-legged table. The desk was pushed against the far wall. On the opposite side of the parlor, a window seat looked out on the front yard. Or it would if the yard could be seen. The closed drapes gave Doro a sense of claustrophobia. She did not recall such crowding when she had visited with her mother years ago. Evidently, Eloise had moved furniture into this room. But why? A Sunday parlor—a fancy room reserved for special days—was on the other side of the structure, and a dining room was off that. As Doro studied the space, she felt sure some of the pieces had come from those places. A second survey revealed a plate with remnants of a sandwich on the mantel. "I'm sorry if we interrupted your lunch."

Eloise flushed. "I eat in here, because I only keep one fire going. It's hard to haul enough wood for all of them."

The low flames hardly made up a roaring fire, nor did they offer much warmth. "You could hire a boy to chop and carry logs," Doro said.

A snort left Eloise. "You were raised with every advantage, and you have free food and housing now, unlike some of us who have to fend for ourselves."

The older woman's cutting tone and harsh countenance slashed like a knife. A few days ago, Doro would never have imagined Eloise could be so snide, but her urge to strike back was tempered by accepting the validity of the assertions. Doro was fortunate and always had been. And she was grateful when Ev entered the exchange because she was not sure how to respond.

"I'm sure some of the young men on campus would help," he said.

"I don't want charity," Eloise snapped.

One of Ev's shoulders rose and fell. "It'd be more of a goodwill gesture. President Adams wants to more closely connect the students and townsfolk. He's said the ties were always strong until he retired. Now that he's back temporarily, he plans to get school groups doing various tasks around town."

Doro latched on to the positivity. "The faculty and staff love the idea. You can call the President's office and ask Mrs. Jones, his secretary, about help, Eloise."

"We'll see," the older woman replied before shifting toward Ev. "Now, what do you want?"

Before he formed a response, a puppy ran into the room and right to Eloise. The ball of fur wiggled all over and yipped.

"That's enough, Lou May," Eloise might have tried for a stern tone, but she failed. After a moment, she bent to pick up the dog. When the little one was safely in the woman's lap, she laid down.

While Eloise's attention was on Lou May, Doro glanced at Ev, whose expression was speculative. After a few seconds, he addressed their hostess.

"Cute dog. How long have you had her?" he asked.

The softness did not completely leave the woman's features, but her tone was chillier than it had been with Lou May. "I'm sure you know by now."

The comment proved Eloise Vining was no fool.

"We heard about Ralphie finding homes for the mother and puppies earlier today," Ev replied.

With one hand, Eloise petted the puppy, who hummed in response. "Ralphie was worried about the mother and litter. When he told me, I promised to take one and keep it a secret. Lou May and I walk early and late, so we aren't seen. Not that my neighbors are nosey. If they see us, they don't say anything. They're old and keep to themselves, thank goodness. Since my backyard is fenced, I can let her run during the day. She's a good girl." Eloise made the last comment with a broad smile.

"I can see she is," Doro put in. "And she looks a lot like her sister, Tee."

Eloise lifted her chin a fraction. "She's the puppy who accompanies you on campus, isn't she, Officer Mallow?"

"Indeed, she is," he agreed before posing a question. "Why do you call her Lou May?"

A true grin lit Eloise's lined face. "She's named after my favorite author, Louisa May Alcott."

Both Ev and Doro laughed.

The older woman's amusement flattened. "What's so funny?"

"Tee is named for one of our favorite authors, Agatha Christie. Since my best friend is called Aggie, we chose Tee for short," Doro replied.

"Very nice." The rest of the woman's hardness returned. "Old Lady Frotis hated her, too. She said as much on Friday. Awful woman. She hated Veronica's dogs, as well. Wanted them dead."

Surprise jolted Doro. "Mrs. Frotis asked Ralphie to kill Duke and Duchess?"

"She told Ralphie to take care of them like he did the other dogs," Eloise replied. "Probably run them off. I don't know."

Ev shifted to sit on the edge of the divan. "Does Mrs. Parson know her dogs might've been moved?"

Eloise nodded. "He told us both at the same time. We were on our way to the last committee meeting, the one where we quit, and he stopped us as Veronica was backing the car out."

"Mrs. Parson must've been upset," Ev suggested.

A humorless guffaw left Eloise. "She was furious, and so was I. That old harridan was always mean. She said repeatedly I'm not a suitable replacement for my mother, but Mrs. Frotis treated her like a doormat. Always bossing her around, getting her to do the dirty work for every event. Then, when Mother was dying, the woman never visited or even bothered to send a basket. No flowers, no food, nothing." Eloise's nostrils flared with a sharp intake of breath. "My mother thought they were friends. But they never were. That old lady saw her, saw us, as servants."

The venom in Eloise's voice telegraphed the depth of her anger. Simmering resentment did no one any good, and it had obviously taken a toll in her case. Doro considered moving back to the dog situation, but letting Eloise rant was probably a better choice. "Your mother has been gone for several years."

"Nearly ten. I took her place on the Christmas committee that last year, because she was too weak to take part. Old lady Frotis had me running everywhere doing all the piddling, dirty jobs. I wanted to please my mother, so I did whatever was needed. I thought Mother would be able to attend the party, and she'd be pleased I worked to make it a success. But she died a week beforehand." Eloise's jaw quivered with her last words.

"I'm so sorry," Doro murmured with genuine sympathy. "I remember your mother. She was a kind, lovely lady."

Tears filled Eloise's eyes. With the back of one hand, she wiped them away. "She was, and she deserved to be treated much better—especially by her supposed friend. Mrs. Frotis didn't even come to the funeral."

While Doro agreed that Mrs. Frotis' treatment of Mrs. Vining, and others, was abominable, she still wondered if Eloise had killed, or helped to kill, the other woman. Her fervor disturbed Doro, who turned to Ev. Although his jaw was tight, his silver-gray gaze gave nothing away.

"That's a shame," Ev said. "Your mother sounds like she was a special lady."

Several sniffles preceded Eloise's reply. "She was special, and she was a lady—and better than Mrs. Frotis in every way, except for us not being well-to-do."

A smile pulled up one corner of Ev's mouth. "Most folks aren't well off. Most are doing their best to get by."

"Your family was like that?" Eloise inquired.

"Yes, ma'am. My dad died too young, and my mother had to work to keep a roof over our heads and food on the table. I helped, as I could," he said.

His openness with the other woman seemed out of character, since he had only revealed his past to Doro in dribs and drabs. A stab of jealousy pierced her heart, before Doro schooled her emotions. What was wrong with her? Ev was trying to get information. Sometimes, giving a little got a lot.

"My papa passed when I'd just started high school. We did all right for a while. Mother was a wonderful seamstress and sewed for a few ladies. She was always frail, and when she got ill, I couldn't keep up. Of course, I wasn't as skilled. It's been a Hodge-Podge, since she passed." Her gaze traveled around the room.

Doro looked more closely and realized that the area rug was threadbare, and the upholstered furniture was faded. Contrition filled her. Why hadn't she called on Eloise to chat? If she had, Doro would've realized the woman needed help. "You play the piano beautifully. Why not give lessons? Since Mrs. Harvey passed, there's been no one in town to teach music. I'm sure some people can afford lessons and would love to have their children learn."

Eloise focused on Doro. "I've thought about that."

"Let's discuss it more in a week or so," Doro said. If Eloise was not involved in the murder, and Doro hoped that was the case.

The other woman still looked harsh, but she nodded. "You're too busy to talk now, because you're hunting the killer and think I know who it is. Or maybe you believe it's me."

Silence hung heavily in the cramped room as Doro realized her sincere suggestion was being taken as a ploy. Insisting she wanted to help was apt to make matters worse, since Eloise clearly did not believe her. "We just want information. If you were up and out early, which you often are, you could've seen something crucial."

"But I didn't," Eloise replied.

The answer came fast. Much too fast. Doro shifted toward Ev for some guidance. After an almost imperceptible nod, he addressed Eloise.

"If you'd search your memory, I'd be grateful. Even a glimpse of someone could get us on the right path." He paused for a moment. "You have good reason to dislike Mrs. Frotis, but surely you don't want a killer on the loose."

The woman had no outward reaction, and her voice was steady when she replied. "Of course not, but I can't manufacture a clue for you."

"I wouldn't want you to do that," he assured her. After a moment, Ev stood up. "Thank you for your time."

His reaction surprised Doro enough to freeze her in place. It wasn't until he extended a hand that she rose. "Yes, thank you."

"Again, we appreciate your time," Ev said. "And I'll talk to President Adams about having some boys carry wood inside for you. Good day."

With little choice but to let Ev lead her back to the automobile, Doro walked along with disappointment nipping at her heels. "We didn't learn much," she said once they were back on the road. "And you gave up suddenly."

"As for giving up, she wasn't going to reveal more. Not now. But we confirmed the woman has a motive. Since she lives with only the dog and has a handful of elderly neighbors, she had an opportunity, too."

Doro nodded. "And the means is already in place."

"It is." A harsh breath rumbled out of him. "But my gut says, if she's involved, she didn't do it alone."

"I agree, and her most likely partner is Veronica."

"Yep. I wish we could've dug for more, but she was clamming up. I didn't want to push her hard and not be able to circle back around when she might be...let's say calmer."

His observations made sense. "Good points, and we could go back tomorrow. I wanted to ask about her trip to town with Veronica. Not that she'd reveal more than she did already. Probably not, but we can ask around town to find out who else might've seen her." Fatigue, frustration, and hunger were taking a toll on Doro. The last became obvious when her stomach growled. "Sorry," she murmured in embarrassment.

"I'm starving, too, so let's grab a bite at the diner."

"Sounds good."

Chapter Twelve

F red Carter, the diner's owner, called out a greeting when Doro and Ev stepped inside. "Can I bring you coffee while you decide what to eat?"

The pair accepted the offer as they sat in a booth near the back counter. After glancing at the menu, Ev laid it aside. "I'm having meatloaf. How about you?"

"That sounds good, especially with mashed potatoes and snap beans. A hot meal on a wintry day works wonders."

Ev's gaze narrowed on her. "The Vining cottage was cool, and so was my automobile. You must be chilled to the bone."

Since she had not removed her cloak, Doro could not make a valid argument. She was freezing. "I'll warm up in here." While the concern on Ev's handsome face appealed to her, Doro moved the conversation back to the case. "What did you think about Eloise? What she said and how she acted?" They had only scratched the surface after leaving the cottage.

The waitress bringing coffee and taking their order interrupted, but Ev responded after she went to the kitchen. "She has a deep pool of anger toward Mrs. Frotis, which was at odds with her compassion toward the pup and Ralphie. But you've known her for years. What were your feelings?"

Doro reviewed her impressions—past and present. "Eloise's vehemence surprised me, even though she's shown more spunk lately. I'm not sure why. Spending time with Veronica seems like the main reason."

"Mrs. Parson is more than spunky," Ev muttered.

His observation meshed with Doro's view of the widow. "She is, and she's appealed to Eloise's need for a friend." Once again, guilt plagued Doro. "I never stopped to think how Eloise has felt since her mother died a decade ago—alone and lonely."

"You were young when Mrs. Vining died. It wasn't on you to befriend the daughter," Ev pointed out.

"Eloise has worked hard for years, with little appreciation. No wonder she jumped to be Veronica's friend."

"More likely her sycophant. Mrs. Parson doesn't seem like the type to curry favor with anyone who can't do something for her."

"Do you believe that's why she's so charming to you?" As soon as the question was out, Doro flushed. "Sorry. That's not my business."

After a long drink of coffee, he set his cup down. "I'm sure she has some ulterior motive. What it is, I don't know and probably don't want to know. But her attempts to charm me, as you put it, won't work. I don't want to know the woman any better than I do right now." Ev cleared his throat. "What's bothering me is how angry both women were with Mrs. Frotis. Add means and opportunity to motive, and they're at the top of my list as partners in crime."

The waitress bringing their food briefly interrupted. After Doro and Ev thanked her, they both had a few bites.

"Excellent," he said with a smile.

"It is," Doro agreed after another spoonful of the fluffy potatoes. "Absolutely delicious, and the aroma is heavenly."

Ev let his fork rest on the side of his plate. He grabbed a roll from the basket the waitress had brought with their meals, buttered it, and popped a chunk in his mouth.

While they ate, she considered his perspective. "You couldn't have expected to investigate murders, when you took the job as our campus security officer."

His lips quirked. "You're right, but I'm happy to help. Even though Michaw is a peaceful place, Wade has his hands full handling petty crimes and caring for his children. A clerk isn't enough. He could use a regular deputy, not one with other responsibilities."

"You're juggling a lot yourself," Doro pointed out.

One of his shoulders lifted and fell. "President Adams understands me helping. Besides, Mrs. Frotis was killed on campus. He's as eager for the killer to be found as the mayor is." Ev glanced toward the kitchen. "The owner and the waitress didn't ask about the murder, so news of the murder hasn't spread everywhere...yet."

The last word told the story. News would be around town all too soon. Doro finished her coffee and laid her napkin on the table. "We should get over to the bakery before the Adlers head home."

Silence answered her observation. For a long moment, she studied the play of emotions across Ev's face and wished she knew how to interpret his expressions.

After finishing the last of his meal, Ev leaned back in the booth. "I don't know Adler well, but Wade's description of him disturbed me. In my experience, people can lash out at the drop of a hat. I'm carrying my gun and Adler may have one, too. I don't want you getting caught in the crossfire."

The idea seemed preposterous, but Doro had not been a city copper or a federal agent. Ev had, and his experience shaped his perspective. Although she wanted to interview the Adlers, she would not dismiss the security officer's concern. "Wade hasn't seen Mr. Adler with a gun, and he doesn't even hunt."

Again, time stretched out before Ev responded. "You know the man better than I do," he said without inflection.

Doro held her breath. At least he had not rejected her comment. Should she press harder? "He's reserved, which is probably why he mostly stays in the background, but he's always been civil to me."

A long breath rumbled out of Ev. "I'd rather chat with them at the bakery than at their house, so let's be on our way."

Doro wasted no time in donning her cloak and mittens. Ev was slower to slip on his uniform jacket and gloves before going to the counter where Mr. Carter was at work cleaning the surface. After Ev handed some money to the man, he and the owner chatted briefly. Doro could not make out their exact words, so she waited impatiently. As soon as they were on the sidewalk, she stopped. "Did Mr. Carter say anything interesting?"

"I asked if he'd seen Ralphie today, and he hadn't."

Disappointment hung like a heavy cloud. "Maybe someone else has," she murmured before moving on.

As they walked to the Adlers' shop, Doro pulled her cloak more closely around her. The icy wind had not eased. With fresh snow on the ground, the landscape was wintry. Too wintry to suit Doro, who longed for spring.

"You said Ralphie goes to the bakery, right?" Ev asked as they hurried down the sidewalk.

"He does. Mrs. Adler saves day-old baked goods for Ralphie and a few others, who stop by. It's one of the places he might've gone," Doro said.

"Then, we might accomplish two tasks with one stop."

"Let's hope so, but Ralphie hasn't been at the diner today, which is concerning. Although I suppose he doesn't go to both places on a daily basis," she murmured.

"Probably not," Ev said.

But Doro didn't think he sounded certain. Again, she wished the man-child would appear. What if he was in trouble? Or hurt?

As they made their way down Main Street, Doro looked around. Every shop was familiar. So were the townsfolk on the sidewalks. More than once, she lifted her hand to wave at people. "No one has stopped to ask about Mrs. Frotis. If someone does, what do you plan to say?"

A rueful smile touched his lips. "As little as possible."

Amusement filtered through Doro. "Thanks for the tip."

"Happy to share my expertise." Ev chuckled before his humor faded. "Seriously, if we get asked, let's say Wade is looking into it. That should work for everyone other than the suspects. All right?"

"Sure," she agreed.

When they reached the bakery, he held the door for Doro. Immediately, warm air and enticing scents engulfed her. Although Mr. Adler did most of the baking overnight, the couple made sure something wonderful was in the oven before leaving for the day. A clerk took the baked goods out and displayed them. "Sugar cookies." Doro inhaled deeply. "The Adlers make good ones, but my family has a wonderful recipe for soft cookies. Thick and cakey. They melt in your mouth."

As Ev followed her into the shop, he replied, "My mother made crisp sugar cookies, but your kind sounds great. I can't remember when I last had homemade cookies."

Doro opened her mouth to say she would make some for him, but snapped it shut. She had not baked in years, so why start now and for Ev? Not a good idea.

When the pair stepped toward the counter, a woman of late middle years and plump stature emerged from the back. "Doro, Officer Mallow. How nice to see both of you."

Mrs. Adler's manner indicated she knew nothing about the morning's crime, which was a relief. The speculative gleam in her dark eyes was not. In fact, it made Doro squirm. How many times in the past seven years had the woman asked Doro when she planned to wed? A countless number and, on each occasion, the baker had shared her own romantic history.

The Adlers had married when they were both seventeen and had produced five children by their seventh anniversary. By that standard, Doro was—in the older woman's opinion—far behind where she should be. Before the topic could arise again, Doro started with a benign statement. "I hope some sugar cookies will be ready before we leave."

The older woman smiled. "A couple of trays are out of the oven, and we'll have two more." Her good humor disappeared. "We'd rather sell out than not have a lot of baked goods left, especially since we have so many items in our freezer. We bought one mostly because of the Christmas party. Baking some goods ahead eases the burden. Now, it seems like a poor investment."

Freezers were still new, so the couple had probably paid dearly. Doro wanted to say that the committee might buy some items from the Adlers, since Mrs. Frotis was gone, but she needed to consider the deal with the city bakery—and the funds left to spend. "We hate to bother you, but we have a few questions."

Mrs. Adler's frown deepened as she averted her gaze. "About what?"

Evidently, her initial demeanor was a front because Mrs. Adler's tone indicated she knew the answer, but how had she learned about Mrs. Frotis' death? Did she know it was a murder? Doro looked at Ev, whose expression had not changed. Any passersby would think they were in the shop only to make a purchase. She schooled her features to match his demeanor. And she let him respond.

"Could we chat in a more private place?" he asked.

The woman shoved her hands into her apron pockets. "Why not talk right here?" A note of belligerence underscored the words.

Ev's jaw tightened. "Privacy would be better for you, ma'am."

Color drained from the baker's face. "All right." Mrs. Adler turned on her heel and led the way to a cramped office near the back of the store. On the way, she told one of the workers to watch the front counter.

Once inside the small room, she sat behind a desk piled high with papers. Although the baker didn't invite Doro and Ev to be seated, they took the chairs across from her. As Doro pulled out her notepad and pencil, she noticed the older woman scowling at her. To ease the situation, she smiled. "I'm helping Officer Mallow. He has deputy status, along with being our campus security officer."

"I know," Mrs. Adler snapped. "Everyone in town knows, but plenty of us don't see no reason for a deputy. Hardly no crime happens around here, and spending more money is darn foolish."

A muscle jumped in Ev's jaw, and his gaze narrowed. "I'm not being paid any extra by the town or the college, for that matter. I have my regular salary only."

Color swept into Mrs. Adler's round face. "All the same, Wade Lammers oughta be able to handle what little happens around town by hisself."

The last observation created uncertainty in Doro. Maybe Mrs. Adler knew nothing of Mrs. Frotis' murder after all. Or maybe she did and was stalling for time. And where was Mr.

Adler? "The constable is at the scene of an accident outside town."

A harrumph escaped the older woman. "If folks had stuck to horse-and-wagon, there wouldn't be all these crashes. I'm glad we don't got no automobile." She stared at Doro. "Your folks was foolish to give you one. Girls don't need such things. In fact, it's bad for a young lady's innards."

Although Doro had already heard Mrs. Adler's view on un-married girls being jostled around in a vehicle, she felt fiery color burn in her face. She searched her mind for something to say, but Ev stepped into the silence.

"I know you've been at work since early this morning, so I don't want to keep you," the security officer said in a placating voice.

Despite Ev's diplomatic intervention, he appeared to be fighting a grin. Part of Doro wanted to chastise the older woman for discussing her *young lady innards,* but a complaint was apt to lead into modern girls driving men away with their ideas about voting, working, and such. She bit the inside of her lower lip to keep from speaking.

"Running a bakery means long hours," the older woman agreed. "Some folks don't respect our time and effort."

Doro cast a look at Ev, whose attention remained on Mrs. Adler. Was he thinking what she was? That the woman referred to Mrs. Frotis? When Ev glanced at her and lifted his chin a fraction, Doro took it as a sign. She smiled at the baker. "I'm so sorry about Mrs. Frotis dropping our order without notice. None of the rest of the committee knew anything about it until Friday. We tried to change her mind..."

Mrs. Adler scowled. "But you couldn't because she was a mean, vindictive, nasty old woman."

The use of past tense left no lingering doubt about the woman's knowledge. She knew Mrs. Frotis was dead. Did she know it was murder? "She could be very difficult."

The baker rolled her eyes. "You're like your mother. Always putting the best face on everything and everyone."

Although Doro wasn't sure the comment was meant as a compliment, she took it as such. "Thank you. Even though I couldn't change the plan, I should've apologized before today."

One of the other woman's beefy shoulders went up and quickly down. "Maybe you'll be able to use our baked goods now."

The suggestion sent Doro's heart plummeting. If the Adlers thought eliminating the chairwoman would help their business, had they worked together to kill her? Until this moment, she would not have believed it. Now, the idea seemed likely. "The committee will meet soon, I'm sure. I will definitely bring the idea up."

"Good. We got plenty in the freezer, and we're glad to make more items," the woman said. "We deserve to get paid for our trouble."

Doro couldn't argue, so she tried another tack. "We've been looking for Ralphie. I know you often save day-old baked goods for him. Has he been in today?"

Mrs. Adler's features softened. "He's got a sweet tooth. Always has. But, no, I haven't seen hide nor hair of him today."

The woman's change in attitude evoked another question. "We wondered if you saw anything odd early this morning. A stranger roaming around, or someone following Mrs. Frotis. She sometimes stops here if she's out early."

"It takes nerve to come in here after she canceled the order for the party," Mrs. Adler once again spoke in a tone as sharp as a knife.

That tidbit might be meaningful. "So, she was here this morning." When the baker shifted restlessly in her chair, Doro wondered if Mrs. Adler regretted her outburst.

After moments of silence ensued, Ev spoke. "Was she here, ma'am?" Still, no response. "We aren't accusing you of anything, but we need to know where Mrs. Frotis was before going to the auditorium. Finding her killer is important to the town and the college. People deserve peace of mind, and they won't have any while a murderer is on the loose."

The baker opened her mouth but, before she could reply, a male voice boomed through the small office. Doro shifted to see Stuart Adler. Tall and broad, the man filled the door-way. His stern expression and stiff posture telegraphed his displeasure. "You don't have to tell these two nothing, Ma," he barked before focusing on Ev. "Get out."

Ev's immediate response was to rise to his feet. Although he was leaner than the baker, the security officer was the same height, and his features were set in similar unyielding lines. "Sir, I'm here in my role as a special deputy, so I won't be going anyplace until I get answers to our questions."

Adler's attention shifted to Doro. "You ain't no deputy. Why are you here?"

"I'm taking notes," she replied.

The baker stared back at Ev. "You ain't able to do that for yourself?"

A muscle jumped in Ev's jaw as he appeared to grind his teeth. "How we conduct our interviews is none of your concern. Now, sit down." He gestured to an empty chair near the door.

For several moments, Doro thought Adler would refuse. Then, the baker took the seat, albeit grudgingly. He crossed his burly arms over his chest and leaned forward, all the time keeping his attention on Ev.

The interaction surprised Doro for two reasons. She had never seen Mr. Adler be so antagonistic, or Ev act so tough. Although she'd known the security officer for two months, Doro hadn't been able to picture him raiding speakeasies as a Prohibition agent or taking down petty crooks as a beat cop. Now, she could. Authority rang in his voice, and command emanated from every line of his body. Since he stood for a long moment after Adler sat, Ev also radiated strength and power. While Adler didn't appear to be intimidated, he didn't argue more, either.

After he took his seat, Ev turned back to Mrs. Adler, who looked pale and tense. "Ma'am, I assume Mrs. Frotis stopped here this morning. Is that right?"

Doro held her breath, waiting to see if the woman's husband again told her to keep quiet. He did not.

Mrs. Adler folded her hands in her lap. "She stopped before we opened for a sweet roll and coffee."

"I wouldn't have let the woman in," her husband said, "but I was taking cookies over to Professor White's home. His wife wanted them for a tea."

The revelation surprised Doro, because it meant the man admitted to being out and about. She jotted it down and waited for Ev to proceed. When he finished questioning Mrs. Adler, he might pick up on Adler's admission. If he didn't, she would.

The older woman's chin lifted. "I hoped to convince her to buy the items we'd already baked for the party. I explained how much money we'd lose, if she didn't." Despair crept into her voice. "She said it was too late, and we should hire better help because our delivery boy didn't do the entire job last year. He should've laid out the baked goods, but Pa and I went right over when Mrs. Frotis called to complain. We fixed the table, so it looked real purty."

"The old crone enjoyed complaining," her husband put in. "She enjoyed lording her wealth and status over folks, too. She won't be doing no more of that."

Although his lack of sympathy was expected, it saddened Doro. While she had not liked the matron, Doro felt bad for her. And for Mrs. Adler, who looked bereft. "I take it Mrs. Frotis refused to buy any of the goods."

"Refused in no uncertain terms," the other woman agreed. "She took her treat and left in a huff, like I had nerve to even ask."

"That's a shame." Ev injected empathy into his tone as he addressed Mrs. Adler. When he focused on her husband, he showed no softness at all. "What deliveries did you make this morning?"

Mr. Adler glowered. "You suggesting I killed the woman?"

"No, sir," Ev replied. "I'm wondering if you saw her or anyone else in the area."

A hush fell over the office. As she studied the baker, Doro felt certainty jolt through her. He had seen something of importance. She was sure of it. As time passed, she willed him to share what he knew. But what if he was the guilty party? Tension knotted her insides.

"Mr. Adler, you won't do yourself any good by refusing to talk," Ev continued in a calm, but firm, tone. "You're only making yourself look suspicious, especially if others saw you."

As the older man's nostrils flared with a sharp intake of breath, his face paled. Unsure what that meant, Doro waited for his response.

Finally, a long breath left Adler. "I saw her when I was leaving the men's faculty house. She said I needed to get rid of the horse and cart, if I expected to do business with the better folks in town."

The assertion was believable, because Mrs. Frotis often belittled those she considered beneath her, which included a host of folks. Doro glanced at Mrs. Adler, who looked stricken, and her heart turned over. The Adlers did not deserve to be treated so poorly. No one did. Had one, or both, had enough of the matron's highhandedness?

"Was that the extent of your conversation?" Ev inquired.

Adler ran one hand over his lined face before meeting his wife's gaze. "I'm sorry, Ma. I shoulda held my tongue, like you always tell me to do, but she made me mad."

"Oh, Pa," Mrs. Adler responded in a plaintive tone.

Doro shot a glance at Ev, who looked sympathetic but resolute. Was he anticipating a confession? She inched forward to perch on the edge of her chair.

Mr. Adler released a pent-up breath. "I didn't know you tried to get the woman to buy at least some of the original order, so I did. She laughed. She actually laughed. That made me furious, so I followed her and tried to explain how much money we'd lose. The old crone said we shouldn't have baked so much ahead of time, which made me even angrier. There's no way to get it all done on the day of the party, and I told her as much. It's the reason we spent a lot to buy a newfangled freezer." Adler turned to Ev. "You've probably heard I went all the way to the auditorium with her. Then, she slammed the door in my face. I admit I cursed her out, but I didn't hurt the woman."

The last comments came as a surprise. Doro turned to Ev for his reaction, which proved to be guarded.

"You're sure you didn't go inside?" Ev asked.

"Of course, I'm sure. If someone said different, they lied." Adler, sounding panicky and upset, blurted the words out. "I hate the woman, but I'm no killer."

"You must know how she died," Ev suggested.

Adler nodded. "Heard she fell off a ladder. But that could've been an accident."

"Maybe," Ev agreed.

Since they had dismissed that possibility, Doro figured Ev was fishing for more details. So far, they'd learned a little but not nearly enough to make an arrest. To take pressure off the baker, Doro posed a query. "Did you see others near the auditorium?"

Adler's brow furrowed. "It were just getting light. I saw a couple of folks. One was leaving the boys' dormitory. The other looked to be a woman coming from the far end of the parking area on the west end of campus." His gaze went to Doro's cloak, now slung over the back of her chair. "She had a cape thing like yours. Couldn't tell the color."

At the news, Doro's pulse raced. Another woman. One wearing a cape or cloak. One coming from the lot closest to the auditorium. "You didn't recognize her?"

Adler shook his head. "Too dark. She were just a shape amongst all them automobiles."

"What about her height? Tall, short, in-between?" Ev asked.

Briefly, Adler bowed his head. "A few inches taller than Ma."

Although Mrs. Adler was seated, she was a familiar figure to Doro, who knew the woman to be shorter than herself. That meant the figure was about the same height as Retty, Veronica, and Eloise. "Did she go inside after Mrs. Frotis?"

"She did," Mr. Adler replied. "I don't know if or when she left. I needed to get back here, so I took off."

Doro took more notes. She and Ev had plenty to share with Wade and Aggie, whenever the group could meet. Their meeting might have to be postponed due to the vehicle accident.

"What did you do when you left the area?" Ev asked.

"Came back here, since I'd already made my delivery," Adler replied.

"Did you see anyone else out-and-about?" Ev inquired.

"The usual folks," Adler said. "Milk delivery and the iceman, but they wasn't close to the college. Fred Carter was opening the shades at his diner, same time as always. Not many houses had lights on so early."

"All right." Ev got to his feet. "Thanks to both of you. If you think of anything else, or if you see Ralphie, call the constable's office."

After flipping her notepad shut and tucking it into her pocketbook, Doro stood up. Ev helped her don the cloak and, following an exchange of goodbyes, preceded him out of the bakery and on to the sidewalk. Since snow was again falling, she flipped her hood over her head. "We got some extra details."

"We did, and I want to discuss them, but let's get back to the constable's office. Wade may not be there, but Miss Darwine will come soon."

"With luck, Wade is back and there's been a connection with Mrs. Frotis' sister."

Chapter Thirteen

Warmth enveloped Doro as she entered the office ahead of Ev. Although she had wanted to go to the interviews, Doro would gladly spend time inside the station, where two pot-bellied stoves made the place toasty.

"Let me hang up your wrap," Ev said. "Unless you're too cold."

"I'll be fine now," she assured him.

He put his jacket and her cloak on hooks near Wade's desk, while they exchanged greetings with Nola.

"Any news?" Ev asked the girl.

"The mayor called. He and the councilmen are going ahead with the party. I'm so glad. I made a new dress for the occasion. My mother says it's only good for a celebration. Too fancy for church," Nola responded with a smile.

"From what I recall, you're an excellent seamstress," Doro put in.

Color pinked the girl's cheeks. "Thank you. I learned from my granny. She says all womenfolk need to know how to sew before they wed."

Doro cast a glance at Ev, who had no outward reaction. But what did she expect? If he responded at all, it would probably be to agree, which emphasized how different Doro was from most young women. Of course, she did not plan to marry because she had her career. In a few years, she would gain tenure and when her boss retired, she might become the head librarian. That was her goal and had been for years. A husband and children would end any hope of advancing at the college. Or even keeping her current job. The prevailing sentiment was wives and mothers belonged at home. While Doro disagreed, she did not fall into either category and never would. The thought was not as welcome as usual. Since childhood, Doro had known having a career meant foregoing marriage and family, which had not bothered her at all. She was fine on her own and always had been. She silently chastised herself and focused on making a gentle comment. "I'm sure your dress is lovely, and I'm glad about the celebration going forward, too."

"That gives you more to do, doesn't it?" Ev asked.

Worried he might suggest she stop working on the case, Doro offered reassurance. "Some of the women who left the committee may pitch in, and Aggie will, too."

He nodded. "Don't forget about Wade and me."

"Or me," the clerk offered. "I'd be willing to work in the evening or Saturday morning. Some of my girlfriends would, too. We're all looking forward to the party."

"Wonderful," Doro said. She was lucky to live in a town where folks leaned on each other.

"Any word from Wade or from Mrs. Frotis' sister?" Ev asked.

"No, sir," Nola said.

"All right. Wade should be back soon," Ev replied.

"Will the two of you be here for a while?" the girl asked. "I need to pick up a package at the post office."

Ev nodded. "We won't leave soon, so go ahead."

After expressing her gratitude, Nola fetched her coat and hurried out. When she was gone, Doro turned to Ev. "I'm guessing she'd like to share the news about the party with her friends. Some of the girls gather at the diner about this time every Thursday, so she's probably headed there."

A chuckle left him. "Probably so. When my sister was her age, she would've been eager to reveal the news." He gestured toward Wade's desk in the far corner. "Let's sit down and go over what we know."

"I'd like to get my notes in better order before Wade and Aggie arrive. Then, we can get their opinions and set a course for the rest of the investigation."

"Wise planning, Detective Banyon," Ev observed with a grin.

His teasing praise made Doro smile in return. "Reading all those mysteries has been a wonderful education in many ways."

"Added to that, you're intelligent and intuitive," Ev said in a more serious tone.

Doro had no chance to react because the bell above the front door jingled and Wade entered. "Was anyone badly hurt in the accident?" she asked after seeing his tense expression.

"The driver broke his arm, and the passenger has a few bruises along with a black eye and a possible concussion. They're both at Doc's place." Wade glanced around the office. "Where is Nola? Didn't she come in?"

"She got here in short order," Ev replied. "She just went to the post office and will be back soon."

The stress left Wade's features. After taking off his outerwear, he sat behind his desk. "Did you two talk with Miss Vining and the Adlers?"

"We did." Doro pulled out her notepad as she responded. "Do you want to wait for Aggie or go ahead?"

Before Wade could answer, the bell rang again, and Aggie stepped inside. The constable immediately rose and went to help her with her coat.

After Aggie was seated, Ev spoke. "You're right in time. We were about to go over what we know so far."

"Good. I hurried to get here, because I don't want to miss anything." With one hand, Aggie brushed a loose lock of curls from her face.

"Before we go over what Doro and Ev uncovered, I stopped at the Green farm on my way home from the accident scene." Wade massaged his neck. "Around nine o'clock, Ralphie was seen out there. The Greens took the mother dog and one pup, so Ralphie walks out to visit them every so often."

Aggie leaned forward. "The snow has to be deep along the road, especially where it's drifted."

"It is," Wade agreed. "But Zeb Green says Ralphie has come in worse weather."

"Did Zeb talk to him?" Ev asked.

"Nope. Zeb's pa saw Ralphie from a distance and waved. He said Ralphie had no response, which was odd. Usually, the man hangs around, chats, and waits for one of the womenfolk to feed him."

Doro listened with interest. "I wonder why Ralphie took off after seeing the dogs, since he doesn't usually." The possibilities disturbed her and, from the expressions on Wade's and Ev's face, they were equally troubled.

"Acting out of character is always a warning sign," Ev replied.

"It is," Wade agreed, "and it's especially unsettling in Ralphie's case because he's very much a creature of habit and always has been. Plus, he enjoys eating. Taking off before he got fed isn't like him at all."

Wade's observations rang true, which only increased Doro's dread. "I have a bad feeling," she admitted in a hushed tone. "Maybe my imagination is running away with me. You two are lawmen. You have more experience in these matters. How do you feel?"

Following a heavy sigh, Ev turned toward her. "You're not out of line. At least not in my experience, and I'm uneasy, too. What about you, Wade?"

"I'm probably imagining much the same things as Doro. Ralphie's rooms being torn apart is a warning sign. You got great prints, but we have nothing to match them with." Frustration underscored every word. "We don't know if the break-in is related to the murder, although I'm inclined to think it is."

Ev leaned back in his chair and thrust his long legs out in front of him. "I am, too. As things stand now, I'm worried we won't find the killer before Saturday."

"I've got the same concern," Wade put in.

"The mayor didn't say the celebration won't go ahead, if that doesn't happen, did he?" Doro asked.

Wade shook his head. "No, but people are edgy, and I don't blame them. It's my job to find the murderer, and I'm not getting it done."

"It's been less than twelve hours since Doro found the body," Aggie pointed out. "As for fingerprints, in the Corlon case, Doro and Ev got them from some of the suspects without them knowing. Couldn't you do the same now?"

Both men focused on Aggie. Before Doro could support the suggestion, Ev spoke.

"This time, we'd have to go into people's private homes. A judge would likely consider that breaking and entering, so we might be the first ones behind bars," he pointed out. "At the least, the evidence might not be used in court. During the Corlon case, we had access to offices by using keys. Mine."

Disappointment shot through Doro. "I don't know much about legal parameters."

"Viewpoints vary, but I don't want to run afoul of the courts," Ev said.

"Me, either," Wade agreed.

While other lawmen might not be as cautious, Doro respected Ev and Wade for their good sense. How could they obtain prints? Surely, there was a way that wouldn't get them in legal trouble. She planned to consider possibilities but not share them with the men, who were sure to veto creative ideas. When the security officer's gaze lingered on her, she offered a smile. For several moments, he said nothing. Instead, he continued to study her. Ev had said she was intelligent and intuitive, but so was he. Too much so for her peace of mind.

Finally, Ev spoke. "I'm glad you agree. Any of us would take a chance by entering private homes or businesses without permission. Not only would we be breaking the law, we might put ourselves in danger. Serious danger, if the killer caught us."

His statements weren't simple observations. Instead, they were warnings. As Doro thought back to the Corlon case, she recalled Ev being far more heavy-handed. At first, he had forbidden her to get involved. Later, his attitude softened. Now, it seemed somewhere in the middle. In an effort to ease his mind, if not to be completely honest, Doro nodded. "That's all true, which is discouraging. I'm sure the two of you will catch the killer."

"Don't you mean the four of us?" Ev asked.

Thinking she might have overplayed her hand, Doro smiled. "Aggie and I are helping, but you two will keep doing most of the strategizing."

Ev continued to look dubious. "You're the expert on who-dunits. What tactics do the amateur sleuths in your novels use?"

A leading question, to be sure, but Doro would not be led any place she didn't want to go. "They aren't all amateurs. Some are lawmen." The response failed to address his query, because she did not want to admit the fictional detectives often took chances, major chances that skirted the law. On top of that, Ev was an avid mystery reader, so he knew almost as many plot twists and turns as she did.

"That answer is vague." Ev's gaze remained on her.

Which was exactly why she worded it so carefully. Doro didn't want to lie to him, but she didn't want to sit around waiting for the right clues to come along. Not that she planned to make the observation. Wade already felt guilty and worried. Because he was relatively new as the constable, and only had experience as a railroad safety man in his past, Wade was sometimes the butt of criticism or jocularity. Being a hometown boy had its plusses and its minuses. Old buddies teasing him was one of the latter. He had gotten more than his share of joshing after the Corlon case, because she and Ev had taken the investigative lead after Wade's mother had suffered a heart attack and ended up in a Toledo hospital fighting for her life. Although Wade had, and still did, appreciate the help, he must want to be more fully involved this time. She couldn't blame him, but finding the killer had to be their top priority.

"Nothing more to say?" Ev asked.

Doro grinned. "You love whodunits, so you know they're filled with artful misdirections. Some aren't true to life, but some are, aren't they?" Pointing a question at him seemed like a smart move.

Ev pursed his lips. "Most have realistic plot points at their core."

A grin tugged at the corner of Wade's mouth. "Your literary discussion is interesting, but we need to finish our discussion."

While Wade looked like he wanted to laugh, Aggie actually did. "Yes, you can talk books at the party on Saturday night. Or not. Maybe more casual conversation would be nice."

Warmth climbed into Doro's cheeks, and she hastily bowed her head to study her notes. "Right now, our biggest concern is Ralphie's whereabouts. If he's another victim, we need to know."

Aggie and Wade lost their amused expressions before he spoke. "I told Zeb Green I'd get some men together and get out there before dusk. The Greens will join in, as will some neighbors. I saw the mayor on the sidewalk outside, and he's calling some fellows. We'll all meet in his office."

"Great idea," Ev said.

"If Ralphie comes back to town, the Adlers and Mr. Carter at the diner also know to watch for him," Doro added.

Aggie folded her hands in her lap. "Mrs. Otten will alert him to what's happened, although he may know."

The last comment weighed on Doro's mind. Did Ralphie know? Was he the killer, an accomplice, or a victim?

※

A few minutes later, the group broke up. Before leaving, Doro made a trip to the lavatory. When she returned, the men helped the women don their coats. Ev stopped and faced Doro. His expression remained solemn. Unsure how to interpret it, Doro waited for him to speak.

"Both of you have work duties, not to mention preparing for the weekend celebration," he began. "You need to tend to all that."

His words could be taken as observations—or orders. Doro balked at the latter. Not that she planned to argue. The old saying *discretion is the better part of valor* rang in her ears. Deferential discretion seemed wise.

"I have papers to grade," Aggie said. "I can finish them tonight, so tomorrow is open for party planning and helping to investigate."

Wade nodded. "Sounds like a fine plan."

"What if Ralphie goes back to the Frotis house and finds his apartment in shambles?" Aggie asked.

A frown furrowed Wade's forehead. "There's not much we can do about that. When I spoke with Mrs. Otten a couple of hours ago, she planned to leave a note for him in the kitchen and on the garage door before she goes to my ma's boarding-house. The two of them have been friendly from way back, so that'll give them time together before Mrs. Otten leaves town. And the note will let Ralphie know to head there, too. If that happens, Ma will take good care of him."

"But you won't know if he goes there," Aggie pointed out, "since you'll be out searching."

"No, I won't." Frustration echoed in Wade's weary voice.

"Let me contact your mother and ask her to call Doro or me at Wheaton Hall. We can pass the word on to the Greens. I'm sure one of them would let the search party know," Aggie said.

Relief slacked Wade's features. "Thanks. Ev and I need to get going."

"I'd like to find the man, safe and sound. Maybe he can explain why his place was turned upside down," Ev said.

"That's my hope, too," the constable put in.

Doro's mind worked on a plan she had devised while going to the lavatory. With Ev and Wade occupied by the search, they would be out of town for a time. Perhaps hours. During that period, she and Aggie could do some sleuthing of their own, on their own. The thought made her smile.

"You look like the plan appeals to you, too." Ev's countenance had gone from solemn to speculative.

The man was far too perceptive for Doro's liking. "I have papers to grade, too. A whole stack. My students will drop by the library to pick them up before leaving campus. With the party this weekend, I'd like to finish my grading tonight, too." Everything she said was the truth, just not the whole truth.

"Doro has a lot more on her schedule than I do," Aggie observed. "Teaching is my entire job. She's taken on a class as an extra duty."

"Because you love sharing great mysteries with your students," Ev said with a grin.

Since she had told him as much, Doro nodded. "I do, so I don't consider it as extra work. Of course, there's more to do right now, so Aggie and I should be on our way." Doro paused briefly, as if suddenly being hit by inspiration. "Getting the auditorium ready for the party will take a lot of time. Some of those who left the committee might come back to assist us. What do you think, Aggie?"

For a moment, surprise flashed in the other woman's hazel eyes. Then, Doro saw Aggie give a slight nod and knew her friend understood the comment was not incidental.

"I imagine some would," she agreed with a smile. "Maybe we should check with a couple before we head to Wheaton Hall."

Doro allowed a few moments to pass, so it appeared like she was considering the notion. "We could." Another heartbeat went by before she continued with care. "Jennifer Larken used to be on the committee. She left two years ago, but her house is on our way home." And it was close to Eloise Vining's cottage, where Doro also planned to visit. That scheme did not need to be shared with the men, who would have left to organize a search party by the time she and Aggie departed from the Larken home.

"Mrs. Larken is a lovely lady," Wade put in. "I bet she'd jump at the chance to be involved again."

Bless the constable for supporting the idea. Doro beamed at him. "She is sweet." After donning her mittens, she turned to Aggie. "We should get going. That way, we'll still have time to grade papers." Although Doro felt guilt stir within her, she tamped it down. Gathering pertinent evidence came first.

Her friend readily agreed, but before they made their getaway, Ev spoke. "You could telephone her. That might save time."

"Not much," Doro replied with a smile. "Besides, we may need to persuade her to help, and it's easier for both of us to do that in person. We could also stop at Mrs. Lammers' boardinghouse and let Mrs. Otten know about people hunting for Ralphie."

Ev's response was slow to come. "Makes sense. Just be careful. The killer has to know you found the body and may believe you're on to him or her."

Part of Doro softened at his apparent concern, but another part resented being reined in. Or so she saw his observation. "But that person also must realize we haven't solved the case."

"Caution is wise anyhow," Wade suggested in a less dictatorial tone than Ev had used. "We don't want either of you getting hurt." His attention went to Aggie.

"It is," Aggie said. "And we will be careful."

The two men nodded, and the women took their leave.

When they were on the sidewalk and away from the constable's office, Aggie paused and turned to Doro. "Are we really going to see Jennifer Larken?"

Doro could not help but chuckle. "You know me very well."

A wry smile touched Aggie's lips. "I do, and I figure you have some scheme up your sleeve."

"You figure correctly," Doro replied, "but let's talk as we walk. Ev is looking out the front window of the constable's station."

"That's not a bad thing," Aggie said with a laugh.

"It is if he gets suspicious." Doro looped her arm through her friend's elbow and strode toward the Larken residence. "We need more help, so we might as well talk to her. Besides, the men haven't left town yet."

The visit went quickly because the woman was happy to help, now that Mrs. Frotis was gone. Jennifer Larken expressed appropriate sorrow, but she looked to be relieved.

"I hope people aren't as cavalier when I pass," Aggie murmured as the pair left the Larken property.

"You're a long way from passing, and everyone loves and respects you. The same wasn't true of Mrs. Frotis, which is sad. She brought it on herself. Not being murdered," Doro hastened to explain, "but people disliking her."

"I can't argue with that. Since Wade told us about her brother, I've had more sympathy for her. That had to be a horrible experience. I can't even imagine losing mine in such a terrible way. The entire time he served in the trenches, I was half-sick with dread. But to witness the death of a loved one, especially at such a young age." Aggie shuddered. "Awful. Just awful."

For several moments, Doro considered the tragedy. "I keep getting a niggling feeling that it has something to do with her death, but what? Other than her phobia about being on a ladder without support, nothing logical comes to mind."

"It's a clue that she wasn't alone, but I can't come up with how else it might be significant. Sorry." Aggie cleared her throat. "Where to now? We're near the Vining cottage."

"We are," Doro agreed. "Eloise should be invited back to the committee, and we could drop in now and suggest that."

Aggie stopped in her tracks. "Suggest that and what else?"

"Let's keep walking," Doro suggested, partly because her friend's wary gaze unsettled her. "Since it's bitterly cold, we could ask for something hot to drink. We should offer to bring food to her soon. She told Ev and me about having a hard time on her own." Doro shared what the spinster had said about not burning too much wood and her other economies.

"I didn't think about her struggling to make ends meet," Aggie said. "I should have because I'd be in a similar situation without my job. If you and I hadn't met the day Professor Folsing accused me of being negligent, my scholarship would've ended and my dreams of being a teacher along with it."

What her friend said was true, and it was a big reason the two of them had worked hard to clear Aggie's name when she had been blamed for an examination being lost. But Eloise had no one to help her. No one except Veronica, but was she helping the other woman or using her? "I felt terrible when Eloise revealed the extent of her troubles. Pinching every penny is tough enough, but she feels like she's all alone with no one who cares about her. I should've paid more attention after her mother died."

"What about girls from her school days? Isn't she on good terms with any of them?" Aggie asked.

"I've never seen her socialize at all. I suppose it's because they're all married with families. Spinsters often are shunned. At least that's what my grandmother says." Although Bertha Banyon was a doting grandparent, she expressed her fear about Doro being all alone in the future.

"I know," Aggie mumbled, "and I'm afraid I'll experience it firsthand."

"You'll marry," Doro assured her. "If you want to."

"You know I do," Aggie said. "I want children of my own, but I love being a professor. It's a conundrum."

"It is, and it's one that men don't have to consider." Since they were approaching the little lane leading to the Vining cottage, Doro voiced her strategy. "Ev let me take a set of prints at Ralphie's apartment. While he was checking the doorknobs, I took a little of the powder and tape from the kit. Any paper will do."

Again, Aggie halted. "What?" Briefly, she stared at Doro. "You're planning to get Eloise's fingerprints? How? In front of her face?"

"Of course not. If we get her to fix tea for us, you could go to the kitchen to help. Delay her as long as possible, and I'll try to get prints from the table in front of the fireplace. She eats there, so she has to touch it. If we're lucky, I'll get a clear set."

"And if we're not, she'll catch you. Then, what will we do? How will you explain wanting her fingerprints? And what if she calls the constable's office to complain? Then, Wade and Ev will find out what we're doing."

The potential problems did not upset Doro. Her friend could be jittery, especially where risk was concerned. Instead of arguing her points, Doro focused on reassuring Aggie. "I'm the one who lives and breathes murder mysteries. Sometimes, I let my imagination run away with me, as you've pointed out in the past. But you're being imaginative now."

The last statement prompted a slight smile from Aggie. "Both of us like whodunits, but you're much better at solving them."

"Thank you, but I've studied them in depth. Anyhow, I'm sure I can get prints quickly. It isn't much of a risk, or I wouldn't suggest it." Doro spoke in an urgent tone.

Aggie clasped her gloved hands in front of her. "Couldn't we get into trouble?" Anxiety underscored the query. "And what about comparing the prints? How will we do that? It's not like we can ask the men to let us. If we do, they'll find out what we did."

Her friend's concerns were valid, so Doro revealed the rest of her planning. "The fingerprint kit wasn't locked up. When I used the lavatory, I went right past where it's being stored."

A gasp left Aggie. "Oh, Doro. What if Wade and Ev go back there and find the kit gone?"

"They were in a hurry to join the search party, and they won't be taking fingerprints while they hunt for Ralphie." Even though Doro had used this reasoning to herself, it sounded weak when she said it out loud.

Aggie shook her head. "They'll be upset if they find out."

With determination, Doro ignored the niggling fingers of apprehension running up and down her spine. Wade might be troubled by her shenanigans, but Ev would be livid. Perhaps, her actions would spell an end to their budding friendship. If so, Doro had other friends. Many of them, yet not one was like the handsome campus security officer. She shook off all errant thoughts. "If Eloise's prints don't match the ones from Ralphie's apartment, they don't need to find out, do they? We'll get everything put back long before they return."

"What if they match?"

"Then, Ev and Wade should thank us."

"They should, but they probably won't," Aggie muttered before walking on.

It took Doro a moment to regroup. "You're still willing to go along with me."

Aggie kept her gaze straightforward. "You've been right in two previous cases, and I agree about gathering needed evidence. But let's stop at the Lammers boardinghouse first. It's not far out of our way, and we can tell Mrs. Lammers about the search party. Maybe some of her boarders would help."

Doro wondered if her friend's suggestion was a means to delay—and maybe dismiss—their foray to the Vining cottage but, since a brief delay would not impede the plan, she agreed. Whatever they discovered would move the case forward. She only hoped Ev saw it the same way.

Chapter Fourteen

Within a few minutes, Doro and Aggie were on the front porch of the sprawling white frame boardinghouse. After Doro knocked, several moments passed before the door swung open to reveal Wade's mother. A smile wreathed her face. "How lovely to see you girls. Come in out of the cold and let me get you something hot to drink."

After they stepped inside, Doro spoke. "Thank you, but we're in a hurry. We wanted to tell you about the search party for Ralphie. Mrs. Otten will want to know, too."

Mrs. Lammers frowned. "Mrs. Otten isn't here yet. She planned to come after packing, so I figured she'd be back long before now. I called the Frotis place twice, but the operator didn't get an answer. She'll keep trying between other calls and let me know."

Apprehension curled in the pit of Doro's stomach. A glance at Aggie revealed her friend felt the same anxiety. "Did Mrs. Otten mention going elsewhere before coming here?"

The older woman shook her head. "No. She ran errands this morning and told me she didn't have much more to pack, so she expected to be here around five o'clock. I'm worried that she might've fallen."

"Aggie and I can run over there to check on her."

"I'd be grateful if you let me know she's fine," the woman said.

"It's no trouble," Aggie said. "But she isn't very late."

"We'll go right now," Doro added, "and call when we find her."

The landlady nodded. "That'll ease my mind."

When they were on the front sidewalk, Aggie caught Doro's arm. "Maybe we should tell Wade and Ev about Mrs. Otten not answering the telephone. What if the person who vandalized Ralphie's apartment came back?"

As Doro shifted from one foot to the other, she struggled with how to proceed. "She's probably fine."

Aggie shoved her hands into her coat pocket. "That's possible, but what would it hurt to tell them?"

Doro studied her friend's face before providing an answer to her question. "Wade and Ev will want to check the house, if we do," she replied. But resignation reigned. "Since they have the power of the law behind them, I suppose we should. We can still go to the Vining cottage after they find Mrs. Otten and leave to look for Ralphie."

A smile lifted Aggie's lips. "Let's head to the mayor's office, since the search party is gathering there."

"All right." Reluctance slowed Doro's footsteps, but the pair arrived at the town hall within ten minutes. Aggie preceded her into the building, where they found only the mayor's secretary, an older woman of petite stature, behind the desk.

"Hello," she said with a smile. "How can I help the two of you?"

Doro glanced around the room before looking back at the woman. "We wanted to catch Officer Mallow and Constable Lammers before they leave to look for Ralphie."

The secretary's amiable expression became one of concern. "I hope the man is all right. After the incident with Mrs. Frotis this morning, I fear for the worst. Plenty of men turned out to search, and all of them were worried. Real worried."

"Everyone who knows is concerned," Doro said. "But where is the group organizing? In the council room in back?" Since she saw no sign of anyone, Doro figured that was the case.

The secretary shook her head. "No, dear. They left fifteen minutes ago. Others went straight to the Green farm, so they'll organize out there."

"I see," Doro said. What she saw was a chance to snoop around without the lawmen impeding the effort. "Thank you. We'll speak with them later."

Before either the secretary or Aggie could speak, Doro ushered her friend out the door. "I take it you aren't going to call the Green place?"

"They aren't going to spend time in the house," Doro said, "so they wouldn't get the message until they find Ralphie or quit searching for the night, and I don't think it's worth driving out there. Besides, we'd have a fifteen-minute walk to my automobile and a ten-minute drive. By then, they'll be spread out across the fields and woods. It's nearly dark now, so some may have started already."

Aggie pursed her lips but nodded. "You're right."

"We'll be fine," Doro said in reassurance. As the pair headed toward the Frotis home, niggling worry assailed her.

"You're braver than I am," Aggie observed. "One of the suspects lives next to the house. What if she sees us?"

The question brought Doro's worry to the surface. "Veronica has no reason to be at the window staring out. Neither would her help." She paused for a moment. "After we find Mrs. Otten, let's look in Retty Hood's room. I'd like to see if she left anything of interest." Doubt about the woman continued to plague her.

Aggie shot her friend a sidelong glance. "Wade doesn't believe she would kill her sister. Besides, she left for Toledo the morning before the murder. Surely, you don't suspect her. Or do you?"

"Searching her room won't hurt anything." Doro dismissed her latent concern and focused on their immediate worry. "We need to check on Mrs. Otten, but let's be cautious."

"You don't have to ask me twice."

Doro and Aggie continued to the Frotis home. By the time they got there, snow was mixing with sleet. Relief filled Doro when she saw the porch light on. A lamp also glowed in the front parlor window. The killer, no matter who it was, would not be apt to announce his or her presence with a lot of light. Doro mounted the porch steps and used the brass knocker. When no one came, she tried again. "I'm going to see if it's unlocked." She turned the knob, which easily opened, and stepped into the foyer. A Tiffany lamp, setting on the side table, sent warm color through the room and further calmed Doro, although she remained on alert.

"If Mrs. Otten was packing, she'd be in her room, which is in back off the kitchen," Aggie said.

"We'll check there." Doro led the way into the dining room floor but came to a halt. Minimal light filtered in from the foyer, but debris on the floor was easy to see. Chairs were overturned, and linen placemats were scattered around. Two candelabras had fallen off the mantel and several paintings had been yanked off the walls.

Behind Doro, Aggie gasped.

"Someone has vandalized this place, too," she murmured.

Doro slowly turned around to get a complete view of the space. "It's even worse than Ralphie's rooms. The major difference is there are, or were, probably valuable items here."

With one hand, Aggie gestured toward the mahogany buffet situated against the far wall. "The beautiful sterling silver tea and coffee service is gone."

"It is, but I saw it this morning when we walked through the room with Mrs. Otten." She kept her voice muted.

Aggie responded in a whisper. "I did, too, so someone came after that."

"And after Ev and I were here," Doro added.

"What if Mrs. Otten confronted the thief?"

Anxiety reasserted itself inside Doro. What should they do? Part of her wondered about leaving to fetch the lawmen, but they could already be in the fields. How long would it take to find them and get back? Too long with Mrs. Otten's safety in doubt. If the woman required help, Doro and Aggie had to provide it. She pushed open the swinging door to the kitchen and methodically moved forward. Aggie stayed a few steps behind her.

"It's so dark in here," Aggie observed.

The lights suddenly came on. "Not anymore."

As soon as light filled the room, a figure stepped out of the hallway leading to the housekeeper's quarters. Recognition hit Doro like a hammer. "Retty, you startled me." With determination, she kept her tone even, but anxiety clawed at her insides. Her suspicions had not been out of line. Quickly, Doro glanced around the room. Surely, there was something to use as a weapon. An iron skillet rested on the stove a few feet away. If necessary, she could grab it...maybe before Retty moved. Or maybe Doro's vivid imagination was galloping away with her. If only that was true.

Something between a smile and a smirk curved the older woman's lips. "Luckily, you two didn't surprise me. I heard you bang on the front door and clomp inside."

The woman was exaggerating, since she and Aggie had been cautious. But the old hardwood floors squeaked.

Aggie, who had stopped next to Doro, posed the obvious question. "Why didn't you answer if you heard us?"

With her right hand, Retty reached into her coat pocket and extracted a pistol, which she pointed at Doro. "Your presence isn't welcome, so I hoped you'd go away. Since you didn't, you'll suffer the consequences."

Sick, sinking dread knotted Doro's stomach as she realized her misgivings about Retty were valid. She again eyed the skillet. What chance did she have of grabbing it before Retty fired?

Not much. "If you were arguing with Mrs. Frotis, and she fell by accident, Constable Lammers will understand." Not for one moment did Doro find the idea to be logical, but she had to throw up barriers. Distracting Retty might provide an opening to overpower her.

A snort left the older woman. "I've heard you're an amateur sleuth, Doro." Her gaze flickered to Aggie. "And you're one of her partners."

"We're best friends," Aggie replied.

"We are," Doro agreed, "and we both enjoy reading mysteries. But why mention that?" Her words were to buy time because Retty's suspicions were obvious and, so was her guilt. But what could Doro do about it at the moment? Not a lot.

"It's clear you two have dug around," Retty replied. "But I'm sorry you came here. If you had waited another half-hour, I'd have been gone."

The admission was not surprising, but Doro continued to play for time. "What about funeral arrangements for your sister?"

"I'm not staying for that," the older woman said, "and I think you both know why."

Arguing with an accurate statement was futile, so Doro asked a question. "Did you originally come to reconcile with your sister, or was that a lie?"

"Reconcile? No, more like recompense," Retty said in a taut tone.

"Recompense for what?" Aggie asked. "Why would she owe you?"

"People here only got a taste of her selfishness." Anger flared in Retty Hood's gaze. "My sister was always bossy and judgmental. From as far back as I can remember, she knew her way was right, and she'd insist on all of us going along with her. Her tantrums could be frightful, so sometimes our folks gave in. Same with our brother. She's at fault for him dying. Her kitten got stuck on the roof. She badgered our brother until he got a ladder. I was too little to know putting it on muddy ground was dangerous, but Hortie didn't care. Even after he said it was risky. Until he agreed, she pitched a fit."

"I'm sorry," Doro murmured, mostly because she did not know what else to say. The woman was as distraught as if the event had taken place yesterday and not five decades ago.

A humorless guffaw left Retty. "Hortie has said the same thing, more than once over the years. Maybe she really is sorry, but it doesn't do any good. It doesn't bring my brother back." The sardonic expression disappeared and her lips trembled. "Nothing can do that."

"Of course not," Doro agreed. What else should she say? What could she say? Long moments passed before Doro tried another tactic. "How would your sister repay you for your brother dying?"

"She couldn't, but she could've helped me out financially." Several seconds slid by before Retty continued. "My husband fell ill a few years ago. I wanted to bring him here and put him in my brother-in-law's care, so I wrote a letter to Roderick. We'd been corresponding secretly, but somehow Hortie got ahold of that one."

"Did she not give it to her husband?" Aggie asked.

A snort left Retty. "No, but she replied as him. Typed out the note and signed it with a good imitation of his scrawl. She advised me to take Phillip, my husband, to the city. We couldn't even afford to pay our local physician."

"I'm so sorry," Doro murmured.

"I am, too," Aggie added.

"My sister wasn't. When I got here, she let loose with how stupid I'd been to leave home at eighteen and to marry a good-for-nothing musician two years later. That was Hortie's view of him." Retty waved the gun around. "Phillip was very talented, and I didn't mind traveling from town-to-town with him. It was much more exciting than living in this little backwater."

"Wasn't he a vaudeville performer?" Again, the question was meant to delay whatever Retty planned. Doro shifted from one foot to the other. The iron skillet would be within reach in a couple of steps.

A slight smile touched Retty's lips. "He was, but he battled consumption for almost a decade. After a long stay in a sanatorium, he wasn't up to being on the road, so he took a job as a permanent pianist at a theater in Toledo several years ago. Last winter, he caught pneumonia and had to quit. His folks had left us a property near Bowling Green, so we moved there. We have struggled to pay bills since then."

"So, you hoped Mrs. Frotis would lend money to you," Aggie suggested.

Retty's eyes once again glittered with anger. "We deserved to be given money."

"And your sister refused?" Doro asked.

"Of course, she did. And she's got plenty. Helping us wouldn't have put a dent in her coffers," Retty said. "Her suggestion was to sell my house and move here. Since Mrs. Otten is getting old, I could take over as her housekeeper. Can you imagine?" A combination of pain and anger roughened her voice. "She wouldn't give me a dime, but I could be at her beck-and-call for the rest of her life. Roderick wouldn't have liked that. He planned to leave me money, but not my sister. She'd rather it go to charity."

"When did you discover you were no longer in the will?" Doro asked in as calm a voice as she could muster.

"After the meeting on Wednesday," Retty replied. "When I got back here, she was musing about how much help I could be with the party, other events, and in the house. Doing half of the items would've run me off my feet, but she saw me as a servant—an unpaid one."

"Couldn't you sell your house and be free of her?" Aggie inquired.

Retty shook her head. "My husband passed a few months ago, leaving me huge debts. If I sold, I'd have no place to live. If I didn't, I couldn't pay what we owed..." Her voice trailed off.

Doro watched the play of emotions on the other woman's face with increasing dread. Although she could discern what had happened, Doro wanted to hear what Retty would say. "Did you ever go to Toledo this week?"

"No, I stayed at another friend's place out near Lyons. Phillip and I knew her on the vaudeville circuit." Retty smirked.

"How did you know your sister would be at the auditorium early?" Doro asked.

"She expected me to change my plans and help yesterday morning with whatever needed doing," the other woman replied.

"We hadn't intended to work then," Doro pointed out.

A snort left Retty. "You hadn't, but Hortie was going to insist some of the committee *rise and shine*, as she put it. Not that she would've if I'd been here. She said she'd reconsider giving me money, if I got back early. So I did."

Sweat dampened Doro's hands. "To kill her."

"To confront her and demand money," Retty replied. "If she had agreed, she'd still be alive."

"What happened?" Doro asked.

A slight sneer pulled at one corner of Mrs. Hood's mouth. "I'm sure an amateur sleuth like yourself has figured it out now."

Dismay assailed Doro. Retty Hood, with her chattiness and warmth, had fooled all of them at first. "You knew others disliked your sister. People who were here, while you had supposedly left to visit your friend. But we got to the bottom of the case. Aggie, Officer Mallow, Constable Lammers, and me." Not quite true.

A burst of laughter left the other woman. "The lawmen haven't figured it out, or they'd be here with you. Nice try, but they'll find my note when they arrive. Mrs. Otten's note, that is. The story goes that she and Ralphie were upset with my sister about the way they were treated. Mrs. Otten was especially unhappy, since she'd been promised a pension for years. To get even, they stole some of Hortie's jewelry, cash, and sterling silver. Ralphie hid it in his place, but he foolishly told someone."

As Retty unfolded the tale, Doro cringed. While false, it was believable. "You vandalized Ralphie's rooms to make it look like he has something of value. And you put the gold coins in the pillow."

Retty shrugged. "Maybe."

Her tone and expression smacked of sarcasm. "Where are Ralphie and Mrs. Otten?" The handyman had been near the Green farm, but had he returned and fallen victim to Retty?

"Suspects often disappear," Retty said, "but you know that from reading and teaching about mysteries. Ralphie told me all about your career at the college."

The last information surprised her, but the first statement sent fear hurtling through Doro, who focused on the gun. "You didn't shoot your sister. Was it your backup plan? The one you used with Mrs. Otten and Ralphie?"

"You are clever," the older woman observed. "I brought the pistol to scare Hortie, if necessary. But she wasn't scared, and using it in the auditorium where someone might hear the shot wasn't advisable."

"So, you waited until she got on the ladder and knocked it over." Doro spoke with certainty.

Retty shook her head. "She was surprised to see me when I got to the auditorium." A slow smirk moved Retty's mouth. "First, I put the topper on, but it was crooked. I knew she'd hate that, so she got on the ladder herself. Of course, I steadied it until she got about six feet from the floor. Then, it wobbled and wobbled. You should've seen the look on Hortie's face." All the amusement disappeared. "The same expression my brother had when he realized he was about to fall. When I pointed that out, she started pleading with me not to knock the ladder down. Too late."

The last two words reverberated through the kitchen like ricocheting bullets. As the scene formed in Doro's mind, she fought back a roiling tide of nausea. When she finally got her bearings, Doro asked, "Why didn't she take her shoes off?"

"She was going to, but I went up with my high heels on. I goaded her into not being a craven coward." A chortle left her. "And there was this gun." Retty waved the weapon before pointing it back at Doro.

The awful scene became crystal clear in Doro's mind. "What about Mrs. Otten and Ralphie? How did they discover what you'd done?"

"They didn't. Ralphie still isn't aware. Yesterday morning, I left my Model T in the campus parking area. Luckily, it looks like a few dozen others. I saw Ralphie headed for town just before you showed up. Hortie had been ranting about the Parson dogs before she left the house, so I said she planned to fire him if he didn't shoot them. Not that she'd go so far. A lot of bluster but no action from my sister. Anyhow, I suggested he hide out with one of the farmers, while I tried to settle her down. He won't be back until late tomorrow."

"When he'll be implicated in the murder," Aggie murmured.

"That's the plan," Retty agreed.

"There's a search party covering the farms and woods. They may find him, at which time he'll repeat what you said to him," Doro said.

One of Retty's slender shoulders rose and fell. "But will they believe him? Even if they do, I'll be long gone."

Frustration filled Doro. "What about Mrs. Otten? She's supposed to be at Mrs. Lammers' boardinghouse. If we don't call to say we found her, Mrs. Lammers will contact her son." Wade was with the search party, but Retty need not know that.

"Again, it'll be too late, but enough chattering. We need to find a place for you, while I gather my things and go."

Was the woman planning to leave them alive? Doro clung to that hope. "Plenty of places in this house to leave someone bound and gagged." While the idea of being tied up and hidden was troubling, it was better than being killed.

With her free hand, Retty reached into her pocket and extracted two lengths of rope. "I came prepared."

"So, you aren't going to kill us," Aggie murmured.

Her friend's ashen face and quavering voice made Doro wish she could offer reassurance, but what could she say? With uneasiness, she waited to hear Retty's reply.

"Not unless you give me trouble."

The words were spoken in an implacable voice that carried weight, enough weight for Doro to remain circumspect. "Neither of us will do that."

"No, we won't," Aggie agreed.

"Good. Now, Doro, put your hands behind your back. Aggie, tie your friend well with no funny stuff. Any of that, and I'll shoot her."

The harsh tone convinced Doro of Retty's intent. With a sigh, she followed orders. Once the bindings were in place, she focused on their captor. "How can I tie up Aggie with my hands behind my back?"

"You don't need to do that," the older woman replied. "Aggie will cooperate because she knows I won't hesitate to shoot you, don't you, dear?"

Aggie nodded. "Of course."

"Then, turnaround and walk backward toward me." When Aggie hesitated, Retty barked another order. "Now."

Aggie, keeping her attention on her friend, did as directed. Doro tried to look confident, or at least calm. She was neither. After the rope was secured, Retty gave Aggie a little shove. "Again, don't try anything, if you know what's good for you and for your pal."

"We'll cooperate," Doro assured her. What choice did they have? With their hands bound behind them, they couldn't grab a makeshift weapon. As long as they were both alive, someone—maybe Ev and Wade—would come looking for them. Mrs. Lammers would get in touch with the lawmen when Aggie and Doro did not call or return. The pair would come as soon as they knew.

"You mentioned calling the boardinghouse," Retty said. "We should do that before going to the storm cellar. One of you will make the call. Don't try to alert the operator or Mrs. Lammers. Just say you found Mrs. Otten, and she's spending the night here after all. Add that you two are going home and to bed because you're exhausted. Got it?"

The friends murmured their agreement.

As they walked to the telephone room, Doro searched her mind for what to do. Attacking someone with a pistol was apt to end with both Aggie and herself dead. She fought to keep a shudder from ripping through her.

After Retty picked up the candlestick base and earpiece, she put both to Doro's head, while keeping the gun close at hand. The operator came on the line, and Doro asked to be connected to the Lammers boardinghouse. Sweat dampened Doro's clothing while they waited. The next minutes seemed more like hours. Doro conveyed the story to Mrs. Lammers.

The landlady's relief echoed down the line. When she ended the conversation by saying, "You girls get your rest. I'll tell Wade not to bother you tonight."

If Retty hadn't shaken her head repeatedly, Doro would have said it wouldn't be a bother. Unwilling to risk it with her best friend's life on the line, she thanked Mrs. Lammers. As soon as the call ended, Retty put the telephone down and pointed the gun at Aggie's head. "Head to the cellar and remember, no funny business."

Since the gun spoke more loudly than the command, the two friends followed orders. They returned to the kitchen before descending the stairs into the dank, dark cellar.

When they reached the bottom, a weak voice called out. "Who's there?"

As Doro came to a halt next to her friend, she squinted to see the figure better. "Mrs. Otten?" A combination of relief and uneasiness hit her. "Are you all right?"

"Better now that you're here," the housekeeper mumbled.

"Enough," Retty barked. "Sit down on the floor, you two. Again, no tricks or I'll shoot the old lady."

With her hands tied behind her, Doro found getting settled tricky. Beside her, Aggie seemed to have the same problem.

"Miss Retty, don't do this," Mrs. Otten urged. "You'll get in more trouble."

"Too late to consider that," Retty replied. "Once I leave here, I'll be fine."

"I wouldn't be so sure. I didn't see your vehicle here earlier. Maybe it's not distinctive, but Officer Mallow and Constable Lammers can easily track you," Doro pointed out.

"I'm taking my sister's vehicle, which is far more powerful. I'll get to a train station in no time. From there, I'll catch a train. Not sure to where, but Phillip and I still have friends on the vaudeville circuit. I'll join some of them. Dye my hair, change my name. It's not impossible to disappear, and I won't be the only one in the group keeping away from the law." Retty grabbed three rags from the nearby bench and tied one in each of the women's mouths. "Your rescuers won't get here soon, but I don't want you attracting attention before then."

Doro threw her head from side-to-side to no avail. The nasty gag was tightened as she fought against it. Glances at Aggie and Mrs. Otten revealed the other two women had the good sense not to struggle. With some luck, one of them might be able to speak.

After Retty disappeared up the stairs and her footsteps faded above their heads, Mrs. Otten did just that. "My gag isn't too tight, although I doubt if I can get it off. Should I scream? I tried that earlier, but Miss Retty said to shut up or she'd shoot me and anyone who might come along." Although her voice was dampened, she was audible.

Doro's efforts to talk were futile, since the cloth filled her mouth. Aggie had better success, although her voice was muffled. "I don't think you should yet. We don't know if she's still in the house. Let's give it a few minutes."

"All right," Mrs. Otten agreed.

Unable to sit and do nothing, Doro pulled at the ropes, but they were tight. Although the cellar was chilly, Doro felt sweat trickle down her back. As the minutes ticked away, her frustration grew. She was not loosening the bindings, but they were digging into her flesh.

Finally, Aggie spoke again. "Mrs. Otten, are your hands tied behind you?"

"Thank heaven, no," the older woman said in a prayer-like voice that remained hoarse from her gag. "When Miss Retty went to bind me, I moaned. Rheumatism. I've had it for years, which she recalled, so she tied my wrists in front of me. Of course, I exaggerated a little. Told her I'd never be able to move enough to wriggle out of the ropes. I may be able to do that and get the cloth out of my mouth, too. It's not shoved in far."

Hope spiraled through Doro.

"Go ahead and try," Aggie urged.

Mrs. Otten's silhouette was not clear, but Doro saw her squirming. The sound of heavy breathing ended with her voice, now firmer. "The gag is out. Let me see if I can do the same for you two, but give me time. I've been down here for a while, and this old body is stiff and sore."

"Take all the time you need. We aren't going anyplace," Aggie told her with a lilt of humor.

Within a few minutes, Doro breathed a sigh of relief. "Thank you." After Aggie offered her gratitude, Doro went on. "We've got to get out of here somehow, because no one is likely to look for us until tomorrow." And what if Retty changed her mind and came back to kill them?

"True, since the men already think we went straight to Wheaton Hall from town. When Mrs. Lammers tells them we're going to bed early, they won't search for us."

"But there must be something we can do." Doro shifted toward Mrs. Otten. "Do you think you can get the ropes off without causing yourself too much pain?"

"I'll be in more hurt if I have to spend the night down here. The chair isn't comfortable, and the chilly dampness won't do me no good, either," the housekeeper said.

"We'll try too," Doro said. "My bindings are really tight, though."

"So, are mine," Aggie observed.

"You couldn't play on Retty's sympathies like I did," the housekeeper added.

Once again, the woman's form twisted and turned like a fancy dancer. Doro bit back the urge to ask if she was making progress. Putting pressure on Mrs. Otten would be too much. After what seemed like an eternity, the housekeeper stopped wriggling. "The ropes are loose enough that I can use my hands and arms. Now, let me see if I can find the old clippers that used to be down here."

"That would be easier than trying to untie these heavy knots," Doro said.

Mrs. Otten moved slowly toward a battered table in one corner. "They're still here."

"Thank goodness," Doro murmured.

Within a few minutes, both Doro and Aggie were free. After they tossed the ropes aside, Doro turned to Mrs. Otten. "We can help you upstairs, but we need to be quiet and cautious. I haven't heard the car leave and, since it was sitting near the house, I'm sure we would."

"I agree," Aggie added.

"I'll be silent as the grave," the housekeeper said.

Everything considered, that was a poor comparison, but Doro helped the older woman toward the steps.

Getting Mrs. Otten up the stairs proved to be a challenge. When the housekeeper was seated at the kitchen table, Doro murmured, "I'm going to see if the car is gone." After peeking out the windows, she sighed. "Still there."

"Before you two came, Miss Retty said she was going to take Mrs. Frotis' jewelry, so she may be upstairs. Maybe we should get away from here and telephone for help," Mrs. Otten, her eyes wide with fear, said.

"I don't want her to get away," Doro said. More than that, she wanted to see the woman get her comeuppance. Besides, who was in town to help them? No one.

"We can't confront an armed person," Aggie pointed out. "That would be foolhardy."

While she wanted neither her friend nor the housekeeper to be in danger, Doro yearned to catch Retty before she made a clean getaway. "I'm not planning to confront her, but who knows how late the search party will stay out? Precious time will be lost if we walk to the boardinghouse and call the Green farm from there. Hours could be wasted."

Aggie shifted from one foot to the other. "And we can't stay here waiting for her to come back and check on us before she leaves."

A shudder ripped through Mrs. Otten. "No, we can't."

Doro rushed to offer reassurance. "Don't worry, we won't." But what should they do? She was saved from pondering the question when the sound of footsteps crossing the dining room reached them. When the noise stopped, the opening and closing of drawers followed. Retty was banging them hard, which was a blessing. Her racket would surely blot out their whispers. Doro turned to Mrs. Otten. "Go to your suite and close the door. Wait for us to come. All right?"

"What are you going to do?" the older woman asked.

After a moment's hesitation, Doro revealed her plan. "I bet Retty checks on us before she leaves. Aggie and I will need to hide some place. There's a door right across from the cellar stairs. What's behind it?"

"The pantry," the housekeeper replied. "Plenty of room for the both of you. Just be careful. Miss Retty has changed a lot. No sweetness left in her." Sadness filled the woman's voice.

"We will," the two younger women said almost simultaneously.

"See that you do." Mrs. Otten turned to disappear into the hallway to her suite.

When the older woman was gone, Aggie spoke. "Since Retty Hood is armed, and we aren't, what's your plan?"

"Let's get in the pantry and see what we can use as weapons," Doro suggested. Going back to the kitchen for a skillet was too risky.

Aggie followed Doro to the spacious room and closed the door behind them. The single light bulb illuminated the space to reveal a plethora of staples, along with baking dishes, utensils, pots, pans, and bottles. "The rolling pin might work, especially if you plan to pop out behind her. But there's only one."

"I'll take that." Doro took another survey of the room. "Maybe you should get the cast-iron pot. It wouldn't be as easy to wield, but it's better than trying to fend her off with a bowl."

A nervous giggle escaped Aggie. "Probably so."

Doro faced her friend. "I'd like to say we've been in worse straits, but that wouldn't be true. Things were a little tricky when we investigated the lost exam, though."

"Less tricky than now, but we don't have a lot of choices. I don't want Retty to get away, either. Or to reconsider leaving us alive."

"Right. We need to turn out the light and wait quietly." After Aggie nodded, she pulled the string, and the room went dark.

"What will we do if she doesn't come to look in the cellar?" Aggie inquired in a whisper.

"We'll have to head to the Lammers boardinghouse, call the Green farm, drive out that way, and hope to get Ev and Wade in short order." But it would be a long, not a short, time to accomplish all that. Doro crossed her fingers and waited.

"Be careful, Doro. She'll struggle with you. If she gets leverage, she might pull the gun or toss you down the steps."

"I'll be very cautious," Doro promised, because neither of those scenarios appealed to her.

Only five minutes had passed when footsteps echoed on the kitchen's hard floor. Doro held her breath. When the sound moved closer, she slowly released it. She put one hand on the doorknob and gripped the rolling pin more tightly in the other. Aggie, standing across from her, moved the pot in front of her.

As soon as the footsteps stopped outside the pantry, Doro threw open the door. In the semi-darkness, she could only barely make out Retty's form. The woman, carrying a large bag that was likely filled with her sister's valuables, had the cellar door partly open, so Doro darted forward and swung the rolling pin at Retty, who gasped and shifted. The blow landed, but not hard enough to fell the woman. What happened next was a blur of rolling pin and iron pan, but Retty ended up on the floor, while her gun clattered a few feet away. She fought like a wildcat, but Doro and Aggie subdued her. Once the killer was down, the two friends held her arms.

Nearly breathless, Doro said, "We've got to tie her up."

"Can you hold her down alone?" Aggie asked, doubt in her voice.

"I doubt it," Doro replied. "Why don't you sit on her legs? That should help."

"Let me go," Retty screeched as she fought back harder.

"I'll get some rope. We got more in the broom closet," Mrs. Otten, who was now standing behind Doro, said. Within moments, she was back. She moved surprisingly fast for an arthritic sexagenarian.

Doro took the rope from her with gratitude. Getting Retty bound was not easy, but Doro and Aggie accomplished the task. With one hand, Doro brushed a lock of hair off her forehead. "You came in the nick of time, Mrs. Otten."

"I was listening at my door, in case you girls needed help." She lifted the gun. "I found this."

When Mrs. Otten held it out, Doro took the weapon.

"What next?" the housekeeper asked.

While the three women talked, their prisoner thrashed around and cursed them. Screeching sounds left her.

"I can't listen to much more shrieking, so we need to gag her," Aggie said.

Her friend's vehemence surprised Doro, but she agreed. "Good idea. Then, the three of us can go to Mrs. Lammers' boardinghouse."

"There are rags in the pantry. I'll get one." The housekeeper performed the task in only a moment.

Retty Hood continued to carp, but her words were soon shut off when Doro applied the gag. "You're lucky we're using a clean cloth, not filthy ones like you put in our mouths." The nasty taste from the dirty rag remained on Doro's tongue.

"That's right," Aggie agreed.

Doro turned to the housekeeper. "If Aggie and I help, can you walk to the boardinghouse?"

"I'm not sure," the older woman admitted. "Maybe we could go next door. Mrs. Parson has always been nice to me. She might give us a ride."

The idea did not sit well with Doro, but Veronica was no longer a valid suspect. Because Mrs. Otten looked spent, Doro reluctantly agreed. "All right."

Within a few minutes, the trio was on the front porch of the Parson home. A knock led to Mr. Fulton answering. The tall man scanned the group. "What brings the bunch of you over here?"

After giving only the bare bones of the situation and Retty Hood's machinations, Doro finished with, "We need a ride to Mrs. Lammers' boardinghouse."

Dismay filled Mr. Fulton's gaze, but he had no chance to speak since his wife, who now stood at his side, expressed her own consternation. "Mrs. Hood killed her sister, and she's tied up in the house?"

"That's right," Mrs. Otten said. "We'd be so grateful if you two could help. Perhaps, Mrs. Parson would drive us over."

The married couple exchanged a long look before stepping back. "Come in out of the cold. She's away, but my husband will take you, and I'll call Mrs. Lammers, so she knows you're coming."

"Thank you," Aggie said.

Although Doro added her gratitude, she wondered where Veronica was. Had she dismissed the woman as a suspect too soon? Or could she be another victim? Apprehension stalked Doro as she and Aggie helped Mrs. Otten into the Fultons' vehicle and got in herself.

꒜

When they arrived at the boardinghouse, Mrs. Lammers opened the door before the group exited Mr. Fulton's vehicle. While he assisted Mrs. Otten, whose arthritis was now taking a toll, Doro and Aggie went to the porch.

"My lands," the landlady said, "come in, come in."

As Doro and Aggie waited in the foyer, Mrs. Otten came in behind them. Mrs. Lammers immediately ushered her into the parlor and to a seat next to the fireplace. The housekeeper murmured her thanks when her hostess laid a wool blanket over her.

"I have hot water on the stove, so I'll make tea right off. Since Mrs. Fulton telephoned to alert me, I already put in a call to the Greens' farm. Irma is going out to tell the men what's gone on here. Word will get passed to my boy and Officer Mallow," she said.

"Thank you," Doro replied in a weak voice. Now that they were out of danger, her energy was slipping away.

Mrs. Lammers nodded. "I'm so glad you're all safe." She looked from Doro to Aggie. "You two sit by the fire, too."

Blessed warmth embraced Doro as she took the suggestion, and she sighed with gratitude. When Mrs. Lammers returned with tea and cookies, she served the trio before sitting down with them and clasping her hands in her lap. "I should call Doc Silven and have him check you, Mrs. Otten."

The housekeeper shook her head. "I'll be fine once I'm warm again. Being in the cellar got me stiff and sore. That's all."

"If you're sure," the landlady said. After Mrs. Otten nodded, the other woman turned to Doro. "I'm sorry. I didn't realize you were being forced to say everything was all right when you called."

"You had no way of knowing." Doro drank half of her tea before setting the cup aside. The refreshments rejuvenated her enough to pose a question. "Does Mrs. Green think she can find Ev and Wade?" Doro had mixed feelings. Ev would be upset with her for not going home, as she had told him. Not that he was her boss. Nor should his opinion matter.

"She plans to," Mrs. Lammers replied.

Twenty minutes later, the telephone rang. Mrs. Lammers hurried to answer and returned with news. "Wade and Officer Mallow are on their way. They'll go to the Frotis house first, but they'd like all of you to wait here."

Anxiety held Doro mute, but Aggie had no such compunction. "They didn't find Ralphie?"

"I'm afraid not," the landlady said. "Some of the other men are still looking. We'll hear right away, if he's located."

"I hope he is," Mrs. Otten said. "He was terribly upset early today, and the last few months have been hard on him."

"He must be hiding some place," Aggie said, "due to what Retty Hood told him."

"The men will find him eventually," Mrs. Lammers said.

Time hung like a leaden weight as they continued to wait for Ev and Wade. After what seemed like forever, but could only have been thirty minutes, the telephone rang. Mrs. Lammers again hurried to answer. When she got back, Doro perched on the edge of her chair. "Was it Wade?"

After sitting down, Mrs. Lammers nodded. "He and Officer Mallow went to the house and arrested Mrs. Hood. They're all at the constable's station now. The men don't want to leave her alone there, so they'd like the two of you to go over." She looked from Doro to Aggie as she spoke. "That way, they can write a report tonight. You can use my vehicle. Wade will bring it back later."

With reluctance, Doro stood up. "All right." After she and Aggie donned their outerwear, they got into the vehicle and took off.

"You don't seem eager to go," Aggie mused.

"Are you?" Doro asked.

"Not exactly, although I doubt Wade will be as upset about our—uh—activities as Ev."

Since the comment was undoubtedly true, Doro released a pent-up breath. "It doesn't matter what Ev thinks. We didn't usurp his authority, since we weren't on campus."

A chuckle left Aggie. "He's also a deputy constable."

"If Wade doesn't find fault with us, and you're right that he won't," Doro replied, "that's the main point."

"We'll see," Aggie remarked.

Since brazening out her actions was the only option, Doro drove on in silence.

In an act of pure cowardice, Doro let Aggie go into the station ahead of her. A furtive glance revealed Ev and Wade behind the counter.

The constable spoke first. "Let's all sit down. You two look exhausted."

"It's been quite an evening," Aggie murmured.

"That's one way to put it." Ev looked at Doro. "I thought you and Aggie were heading to Wheaton Hall to grade papers."

His tone was odd, but Doro couldn't tell if he was upset, angry, or a combination of the two. The set of his features did not reveal his mindset, either. Out of the corner of her eye, she saw Wade take Aggie's elbow and guide her to a chair beside the woodstove in the middle of the room. Doro felt wobbly enough that she hesitated to walk over. Instead, she leaned against the counter. "Yes, well..." Her voice sounded as weak as she felt. The endless day's events had evidently taken a toll, because the room swam around her. Abruptly, she felt her hand tucked into the crook of Ev's arm.

"Come on. I'll help you over to a chair before you fall flat on your face," Ev murmured.

Doro wanted to deny needing support but found speaking impossible. Within a moment, she was seated and warmth from the fire encompassed her. Ev released his hold, but Aggie reached out.

"Are you all right?" her friend asked. "You're white as a sheet and your hands are like ice."

Slowly, the fog receded. As it did, Doro was able to respond. "Somewhere along the way, I lost my mittens." But she had been chilled most of the day. The trip in Mrs. Lammers' open vehicle had added to Doro's frozen condition.

Ev crossed to where his uniform jacket hung on the hall tree. When he came back, he laid mittens in her lap. "They were in the Frotises' cellar. Maybe you should put them on."

When she met his gaze, Doro saw some emotion there. Was it concern? How long would it last after she admitted to lying? "Thanks, but I'll be fine now. Besides, I should take notes."

"I can do that," he replied before grabbing a pad and a pencil and taking the vacant seat beside her.

After Wade settled in the only empty chair, he cleared his throat. "I hate to make the two of you go over what happened after you left here, but we need details for the report. I've already called the county sheriff. Mrs. Hood will stay here until the sheriff sends someone for her. Maybe tomorrow."

For the next half-hour, Aggie and Doro shared what had happened after they left the men, without saying they had planned to get Eloise Vining's fingerprints. Ev and Wade asked pertinent questions. Both were understanding and patient. As they wrapped up, the constable expressed his thanks. Ev aired what could have been considered an observation or a criticism.

"You're fortunate that Mrs. Hood isn't a skilled criminal. She didn't secure the three of you very well," he pointed out. "Not well at all."

"None of us saw her as a strong suspect," Doro, feeling more like herself, shot back.

His silver eyes filled with gray storm clouds. "We discussed her antipathy toward her sister, and that she might need money, which she did. She just shared that with Wade and me. She also admitted to vandalizing Ralphie's apartment."

The knot in Doro's insides loosened. "Good. That simplifies things."

"To a degree. We'll still need to get her prints," Ev said.

The knot was back, and now it rose in Doro's throat to make speaking impossible. Long moments passed before Ev continued.

"Wade and I looked for the kit, but it wasn't in the usual place," the security officer commented.

Aggie, her face pale and her eyes wide, shifted toward Doro. Again, silence reigned.

"The kit wasn't locked up," Ev said. "You two knew where it was, but I don't suppose you're aware of what happened to it."

Resignation overtook Doro as she reluctantly met Ev's steady gaze. "I took it."

His jaw went rigid. "Why?"

Honesty was the only policy, so Doro blurted out the truth about her plan to nab Eloise's prints. "It seemed like a good idea, and you two couldn't do it." She glanced from Ev to Wade.

The constable shook his head. "No, we couldn't." The reply smacked more of disappointment than disgust.

"And what if Miss Vining had been the killer and caught you getting fingerprints in her home?" Ev asked. "Do you think she would've let you go?"

"I doubt if she would've hurt us. Besides, it would've been two against one." Doro could not keep the defensiveness out of her voice.

Ev's nostrils flared again and again as he took several deep breaths. "You were supposed to be talking to possible volunteers before returning to your apartments, so you blatantly lied to us. Which means you knew we wouldn't approve."

Anger flared inside Doro. "I don't need your approval. I'm not a child."

"No, so you ought to know better. But you shouldn't have gone to the Frotis house without alerting us, either," Ev shot back.

"We stopped at the mayor's office to tell you, but everyone had left. We didn't want to take time to drive to the Green farm and hope to locate the search party, so we went to check on Mrs. Otten," Doro said. "I knew it was risky, but we couldn't leave her there not knowing if she was hurt."

Ev continued to pin her with his steely gaze, but Wade intervened. "I'd like the kit back."

Doro withdrew it from her bag, which the men had retrieved after arresting Retty, and handed the kit to the constable without comment. What was there to say? One of them, Doro's money was on Ev, had probably peeked into her purse and seen the kit.

An uneasy silence fell over the group. After several moments, Aggie spoke. "Unless the two of you need more information, Doro and I should get back to our apartments. The term isn't over, and we're both going to work on party preparations, along with our regular work over the next couple of days."

"Anything else we need to clarify can wait until tomorrow afternoon," Wade said as he went to collect the women's outerwear. "One of us should stay here, but the other can drive you."

"I'll wait here," Ev offered before helping Doro with her wrap.

After he assisted her before hurriedly stepping away, she murmured her thanks. When he said nothing in return, Doro followed his gaze, which was focused on her chafed wrists.

"She tied you tight," Ev muttered.

Doro nodded, but did not reply. If she added how much they hurt, he would have more ammunition with which to scold her—and she felt sure he would. Censure radiated from him. She yanked the sleeves of her cloak down, so the red marks were no longer visible.

Wade lightly touched Aggie's arm. "Yours are raw, too, Aggie. Maybe we should stop at Doc Silven's place."

"I have salve at home," Aggie replied, "but I appreciate the thought."

"Both of you better use it," Ev said in a taut tone. "Infection can be bad, although not as nasty as being shot would've been."

The caustic comment made both Aggie and Wade go silent.

Doro felt the wedge between herself and Ev widening, but she did not regret what she'd done. The killer was in custody. With more luck, Ralphie would be found safe and soon.

Chapter Fifteen

The next morning, a knock on her door sent Doro to answer. Her friend, smiling brightly, was in the hallway.

"Wade called and asked if we could stop at his office at one o'clock. He wants to wrap things up," Aggie said.

"Good. That gives me more time to do nothing. Final decorating won't take place until tomorrow morning." Doro retraced her steps and collapsed into a chair. "Join me. A bit of a sit feels wonderful."

Aggie frowned. "You're planning to do nothing for three hours?"

Her friend's question rang with disapproval. But why? "Yesterday was beyond long. It was interminable. I rose before dawn and didn't get home until nearly midnight. *Forever Thursday* is how I see it. After that, is relaxing a bad idea?"

"Not usually," Aggie replied, but her expression did not lighten.

Curiosity dogged Doro as she considered her friend's comments and countenance. "But I shouldn't relax now?"

"You can do whatever you want," Aggie replied. "However, I'm going to bake cookies. Your family sugar cookie recipe." The smile returned.

"We have treats from two bakeries for tomorrow night's celebration," Doro pointed out. "We don't need more." The committee—with several members back—had purchased everything the Adlers had already made, and it had honored the order with the city bakery.

Aggie folded her hands in her lap and glanced down at them. "The cookies aren't for tomorrow. They're for today."

"Today," Doro echoed. "Why?"

Red suffused Aggie's cheeks. "They're for the meeting, and for anyone who comes to the constable's office over the next couple of days. A holiday treat is always welcome."

"You want me to help." Lack of enthusiasm flattened Doro's tone.

Aggie rose from her chair. "We can bake them in the kitchen downstairs. It's more suitable for big batches than our little kitchenettes. Besides, it'll be fun."

Doro reluctantly got up. Helping her friend was more important than a long rest. "Do you have the ingredients?"

"I do, and I have the recipe from your grandmother. I'm a little nervous about the part that says *enough flour to pat cookies out*." Aggie frowned. "I haven't made them before, so I don't know what that means. A cup? Two? Three? More?"

Her friend's confusion was understandable. The old recipe had baffled Doro when she first read it as a child. "About three cups is right for one batch. I haven't made the recipe in years, but I recall needing to adjust it a bit from time-to-time. My grandmother and mother usually started with two-and-a-half cups before adding, as necessary. You're a talented baker, so you'll get a feel for it in no time."

"I'll appreciate your experience," Aggie said, "because I want them to be perfect."

Doro did not ask why, but the town constable could be the reason.

⁕

Three hours later, the two women entered the constable's station. Aggie, toting a large basket filled with cookies and a flask of coffee, let Doro hold the door for her. Wade, who was standing behind the counter, came to the entrance as soon as he saw the pair.

"What do you have here?" he asked, relieving Aggie of her burden. He took an appreciative sniff. "Something that smells wonderful."

"Cookies and coffee," she replied. "Doro and I felt like baking, so we made her family sugar cookie recipe."

Wade glanced at Doro. "I loved those as a kid. Your grandmother always sent a box to us, and your mother followed suit later. I mentioned it to Aggie a while back."

His last remark revealed the reason for her friend's insistence about baking the sweet treats. Aggie was dedicated to her career, but not as much as Doro. Perhaps, her friend was returning the constable's regard. "We did a taste test, and I think they're as good as in the past. That's mostly due to Aggie, who is a talented cook."

Delicate color swept into Aggie's cheeks. "We brought coffee, too."

"Good." Ev joined the group by the door and helped both women remove their coats. "Wade always has a pot on, but it's not the best."

A harrumph left the constable. "This week, you've wanted something to keep you going, and it did, didn't it?"

"Most folks make a fresh pot when they want a pick-me-up," Ev replied. "They don't keep reheating the same coffee."

Doro could not repress a grimace. "Ours is fresh-brewed."

Ev slanted her a glance. "Thanks."

The single word held no emotion. Was his gratitude grudging? She probably owed him an apology for lying, but giving it with an audience present went against the grain. When Wade ushered the group to the corner where his desk sat, Doro went along without saying more. She let Aggie put out the refreshments and accept the compliments.

"These are delicious," Wade said after finishing two cookies.

"They are," Ev agreed after eating one and reaching for another.

"And you made plenty," Wade observed.

"You can take some home for your children," Aggie suggested, "and keep some here for people who drop in."

"Good ideas," Wade replied.

Ev cleared his throat. "Let's go over the last details of the case."

Once again, his voice sounded terse. After pulling out her notepad and pencil, Doro spoke. "We talked about Retty Hood's arrest already. I don't suppose you've heard when the trial is."

"Not yet," Wade said. "A date will be set in the next couple of weeks, but the district attorney wants our report by Monday."

"With the celebration tomorrow, you'll need to work today and Sunday," Aggie pointed out.

"We can get most of it finished today," Ev said. "Doro, would you read over what we discussed last night?"

"Of course." She quickly reviewed her notes. "Is anything wrong?"

"No, you got everything, which is amazing after what you two went through." The compliment came from Wade.

Silence followed. After several moments passed without Ev speaking, Doro focused on the constable. "It all ended well, and no one was hurt."

"A lucky happenstance," Ev muttered.

Wade cleared his throat. "We learned more from Retty, and we found her car. It's the same as a number of others in town, which made it easy for her to conceal it the other morning. Plus, she switched plates with old Mr. Smith, who never noticed."

"Did she ever leave town?" Aggie asked. "She said she went to a friend's place near Lyons."

"We talked to the friend, who confirmed the story. The woman knew nothing about the murder, though," Ev replied. "Mrs. Hood hid out in the garage after Ralphie left for the farms. She vandalized his apartment and went through the woods to where she left her vehicle. It was near the tree line at the far end of the parking area. When she returned late yesterday, she parked in the Frotis garage."

"If we'd checked, we would've seen the car," Doro observed.

"But why would you have looked?" Wade asked. "You were concerned about Mrs. Otten."

"We definitely were," Aggie agreed, "but Doro mentioned Mrs. Hood on our way to the house."

Ev shifted toward her. "You talked about her as a suspect before."

His observation held an accusatory edge. "Yes, but we still needed to check on Mrs. Otten." Couldn't he understand the urgency? Doro turned to Wade. "Did she give other details about the crime?"

"Retty came back and surprised Mrs. Frotis at the auditorium," Wade said. "She stopped short of saying she planned to kill Mrs. Frotis, but it seems likely, since she had a gun."

Fresh dismay hit Doro before she shared what Retty had revealed about forcing her sister to get on the ladder in high heels. She finished with, "By then, Retty planned to kill her, although she didn't want to use the gun for fear of attracting attention."

"She didn't tell us that part," Ev said. "We'll make sure it's in the report."

Wade nodded. "Unless you two know more, that's all the news regarding her." The women shook their heads, so he continued. "We didn't discuss Ralphie, since he was located after you two went home."

Aggie and Doro had gotten word earlier but not details. "Did you talk with him?" Doro asked.

Wade nodded. "We both did. He confirmed seeing Mrs. Hood after Mrs. Frotis left for the auditorium. He wasn't sure of the time, but Ralphie said she was sneaking around the back of the property. When they crossed paths, she mentioned forgetting something—but not exactly what. Even though Ralphie isn't a sharp thinker, he knew that was odd. He asked Retty where her sister was, which got her upset. She said he better keep quiet and lie low, because her sister wanted him to harm the Parson dogs. That rattled him, so he took off like she suggested."

Aggie put both hands to her mouth. "He must've gotten scared."

"He was still shaken last night," Wade agreed. "Even after we said Retty was behind bars, Ralphie was uneasy. It took some convincing to calm him down. Ev and I went with him to his rooms, which shook him up again."

"Poor man," Aggie murmured.

After a long swallow of coffee, Wade responded. "Evidently, Retty was good to him when she lived with young doc and Mrs. Frotis. Ralphie's having trouble accepting her threats and actions."

"You told him about her admitting to vandalizing his place," Doro suggested.

"We did, since it's better to tell the truth," Ev said.

Although he had not directly addressed her, Doro felt the sting of criticism. While she wanted to defend herself, what defense was there? Dishonesty was wrong, and she knew it. Usually, she lived it. But not when she had misled Ev and Wade. Ambivalent feelings tore at Doro. She and Aggie had solved the case, although not in the way they had planned.

"He would've been guessing who did it, which would be worse for him," Wade added, oblivious to Ev's pointed condemnation.

"It would," Aggie agreed. "When you called earlier, you said he's staying at your mother's boardinghouse for now. Is he comfortable there?"

"Ma and Mrs. Otten were fussing over him when I stopped an hour ago," Wade replied. "Since one of Ma's boarders isn't coming back to school next term, she has an empty room that she's willing to let Ralphie use indefinitely. In the meantime, Ev has talked to President Adams about a job at the college."

The news had Doro forgetting the rift between her and Ev, so she turned to him. "What he did he say?"

"He'll speak with the janitors about hiring Ralphie to work part-time. There won't be housing with the job yet, but maybe down the road," Ev said.

Relief filled Doro. "I'm so glad. Ralphie will have spending money and a home, which is important."

"Very much so," Ev agreed.

The chill in his voice kept Doro's enthusiasm in check. Wade wasn't upset with Doro and Aggie for not admitting to her plans. Why was Ev? Once again, she recalled his stiff, starched manner at their initial meeting in October. Since then, he had loosened up, or so she had thought. "Have you heard any more from Veronica? Or her lawyer?"

Low laughter left Wade. "Her attorney called just before you two arrived. Evidently, she wasn't as quick to call him with news of an arrest as she was when you and Ev questioned her. He was glad we caught the killer and planned to let her know...although

I figure she already knew." The constable glanced at Ev. "You recognized the attorney's name."

Doro glanced at Ev in time to see him scowl. The silence following Wade's observation increased her curiosity. "Is he a friend?"

Ev's gaze met hers. "No. I only know of him." Several seconds ticked away before he went on. "He's represented bootleggers and speakeasy owners in court."

Surprise and certainty collided. "Rumors have circulated around town about Mr. Parson being involved in rumrunning," Doro observed. "He was never charged with the crime, but maybe he feared that happening, so he hired a lawyer."

"That seems to be the case," Wade said.

"Do you think Veronica is involved?" Aggie asked.

"She goes to Toledo often enough," Doro put in. "She was probably there last night."

Wade held his hand up, palms out. "I don't know, and Ev isn't sure, either."

All three turned to the former Prohibition agent, who kept his attention on the constable. "I'm fairly certain she isn't hauling booze through this area, but the trips to the city make me wonder," Ev said.

Recollections seeped into the corners of Doro's mind. "You said she was interested in your time as a federal agent."

Ev looked directly at Doro. "Now, we may know why. If she's involved in bootlegging, she'd like to find out if I still report to the bureau."

"You told us you don't," Doro pointed out.

"Because it's the truth," he hurried to say.

Truth. There was the word again. Doro bit her tongue to keep from responding with a sharp retort, but resentment filled her.

As the uncomfortable silence spread out, Aggie stood up and grabbed the flask. "Maybe I should make more coffee."

"It's not necessary," Ev said. "Let's get through the other details. I have to make a pass around campus and get Tee out."

"Thanks, Aggie." Wade's tone was softer, as was his expression. "If Ev has to leave, we should wrap up."

Ev had the good grace to look embarrassed. "Yes, thanks, Aggie. It was kind of you to bake cookies and make coffee, which was excellent."

"Doro brewed the coffee, and she helped a lot with the baking," Aggie said with a smile.

Color darkened Ev's lean cheeks but, as he turned to Doro, his gaze focused on a point over her right shoulder. "Thanks."

His grudging gratitude irked Doro more, but she ground out, "You're most welcome." Then, she looked back at her notepad. "So, whether or not Veronica is committing crimes remains to be seen."

"As long as she's not doing it in Michaw, I can't investigate her," Wade said. "Although I'd report any information to the Prohibition Bureau."

Since Doro figured Ev would do as much, and maybe already had, she went on. "Let's hope she's not involved at all." She tapped her pencil on the notepad. "Any other information you want me to put down for your report?"

"No," Wade replied. "Retty admitted about everything. I didn't want to believe she was capable of killing her sister, but she was."

"What about services for Mrs. Frotis? Have you heard anything?" Doro asked.

"Doc Silven said she left her request with him. She'll be buried in the Frotis family plot at the town cemetery. No service is planned, but interment is scheduled for Monday," Wade said.

"I'll go," Doro said. "Someone should be there."

Aggie offered a soft smile. "I can go with you."

"Nice of you two," Wade said. "I'll be there, as well. If Ev will watch the office. Nola has asked for the day off." He grimaced. "She told me she plans to move to the city after the first of the year, so I'll be putting out a Help Wanted sign."

"You may not need to do that," Doro commented, "but we can discuss details after this weekend." While Colleen was not an experienced clerk, Nola wasn't, either.

"All right," Wade said.

Ev rose to his feet. "I'll see all of you tomorrow evening." Then, he donned his jacket and left without a backward glance.

Doro turned to Wade. "I'm sorry about taking your fingerprinting kit, and I was the one who did it. I had to convince Aggie to come along."

"It didn't take a lot of persuasion," her friend said.

A rueful grin curved Wade's mouth. "You both took a chance, but I agree Eloise wasn't likely to attack you. You tried to find us at the mayor's office, and I understand wanting to check on Mrs. Otten."

"But Ev doesn't," Doro murmured.

"He's got a unique set of experiences behind him—as a city cop and as a federal agent. He's seen a lot more violence than I have and, even though Michaw is a quiet place, he views everything through an old prism." Wade paused for a moment. "Retty said she didn't plan to kill any of you, and I believe her. Ev doesn't, but I knew her way back, which makes a difference. That being said, I hope the two of you won't run headlong into potential danger in the future. I don't want you getting hurt." He addressed both young women but focused his attention on Aggie.

"We'll be cautious, if we ever investigate again," Aggie assured him.

"Of course," Doro agreed, but she thought neither Aggie nor Wade heard her.

Chapter Sixteen

The next day passed in a whirl of activity. With a prisoner in the jail, Ev and Wade took turns staying at the office until the county sheriff transported Retty to Toledo. After that, both helped with the final preparations for the party, but Ev avoided Doro. Clearly, he was still upset with her.

As they left the auditorium, Wade offered to pick up Aggie and Doro that evening. Since she wanted her friend and the constable to have time alone, Doro made sure she was not quite ready when he arrived to fetch them. Aggie looked suspicious but did not argue. Possibly, a positive sign.

Before leaving her apartment ten minutes later, Doro donned her velvet wrap. The elegant outerwear was a gift from her mother, who had shipped it from Colorado. The color, gunmetal gray, was perfect with her shimmering chiffon tea dress. Delicate flowers, embroidered in silver thread, cascaded down one side of the burgundy gown—a long-sleeved, drop-waist frock—giving it a festive flair without being showy or suggestive. While poised as a librarian and professor, Doro felt anxious attending social events. Although she focused on her career, Doro hated never having an escort. Maybe she should have gone with Aggie and Wade. Too late. She was on her own, by choice.

Walking the short distance from Wheaton Hall to the auditorium, Doro wondered if Ev was coming. While she didn't owe him an explanation for her actions, Doro felt uneasy and uncomfortable. Why, she did not take time to examine.

Laughter, chatter, and music reached her as she entered the building. The main double-doors to the inner space stood open, giving her a good view of the partygoers. She had seen many folks earlier when the sleigh rides went on. Everyone seemed pleased about the party going forward and the rides being reinstated. Since the Ressigers had volunteered, at the last minute, to take part again, Doro—grateful they had stepped forward—gave them credit, as she did with all the others who had pitched in over the past two days. Without them, the annual celebration would have been a bare bones event. With them, it was better than ever. Next year, the other activities might be added again. What fun that would be. She was still standing near the outer entrance when a voice broke into her thoughts.

"Good evening." Ev's baritone flowed over her like warm honey, but silver ice was in his eyes.

Reminding herself she did not need Ev's goodwill, Doro lifted her chin. "Good evening, Officer Mallow."

One dark eyebrow raised a fraction. "We're no longer on a first name basis?"

Warmth rose in Doro's face, and she was glad the doorway was not brightly lit. "It slipped out." A weak and foolish response.

"I see."

Was a note of amusement in his voice? Did it matter? She wasn't the one who had been distant and dismissive for two days. But she was the one who had not been forthright. "Enjoy the party."

When Doro started past him, Ev laid a hand on her arm. "Are you leaving already?"

She pulled out of his light grasp. "No, I'm just getting here."

Ev's hand fell to his side. "Since you still have your wrap on, could we talk? Outside?"

The question caught her off-guard. "Why?" she blurted out.

He ran a hand over his face. "I have a couple of things to discuss."

Doro opened her mouth to say he had avoided her earlier but resisted. "All right." After exiting the building, Doro walked toward the benches placed a few yards away and sat down.

Ev joined her. For a moment, he gazed into the distance. "I owe you an apology."

Surprise rippled through her as she turned to study his profile. "For what?" Would he apologize for his recent shunning of her? He should.

He turned toward her. "For berating you the other night."

Confusion joined surprise. "You didn't berate me." Not exactly.

"I was upset that you went out looking for clues instead of going home," he pointed out, "and I said as much. You knew the danger when you went to the Frotis house. I didn't need to mention the possibility of getting shot."

"That hardly ranks as berating me," she replied. But his demeanor had stung.

"Maybe not, but you're a grown woman who doesn't need to follow my wishes. I wanted you to go home, but I had no right to be upset when you didn't."

His statements baffled her. "You're a lawman. The campus security officer and a deputy constable. You have every right to tell people to stay out of your investigations." She did not add that his right hadn't swayed her. Nor would it.

Ev leaned forward, braced his elbows on his knees, and clasped his hands in front of him. "I wasn't speaking professionally," he admitted in a hushed voice. "I was speaking personally."

Doro's pulse pounded riotously. How personally? "I see," repeating what he had said moments earlier.

He cast her a sidelong glance. "You're an independent, modern young woman. A career girl, too. I admire you for all that, and for your skill as an amateur sleuth."

"Thank you," she murmured when he did not continue. "I sense there's more."

A chuckle rumbled out of him as he sat back against the bench. "As avid mystery readers, we know that book detectives frequently take chances to solve crimes. Sometimes, they get into a pickle. Since they must survive to catch the crooks, they're never killed. Or even seriously harmed." He exhaled long and low. "But you came close to being hurt or worse. Mrs. Hood could've shot all of you. I'm still not sure why she didn't. Wade believes her, and I should, too, I guess. It's just that..." His voice trailed off.

"It's because you've seen more violence and expect the worst to happen." Doro spoke with Wade's observations in mind.

He released a pent-up breath. "I have to get used to living in a small town, but bad things can happen any place. Keep that in mind, all right?"

His words had Doro bouncing between dismay and gratitude. Her reply met the former. "Aggie and I were worried about Mrs. Otten, which is why we went to the house. Mrs. Hood might not have tied us up well, but she was clever."

"It helped that her vehicle looks exactly like a lot of others on campus." He drove his fingers through his hair. "That was lucky, but it's a popular vehicle."

"It is. Unlike my Essex. She's unique and beautiful." Doro let a note of humor enter her voice and was rewarded when Ev chuckled.

"She's special."

Doro clasped her hands and stared down at them. Ev had apologized, but so should she. "I'm sorry I misled you and Wade by saying we were going back to Wheaton Hall. I had no intention of doing that, although Aggie did. I convinced her to go with me to get fingerprints, but we went to the boardinghouse first." A series of emotions played across his face, but Doro could not discern exactly what he was feeling. Why did she have to be so socially inept? School and work were her world and had been for most of her life. She always had been happy. She still was. But she liked Ev and wanted to be back on good terms with him. That need not involve courting. As she studied his face,

Doro saw the inner turmoil revealed. What would he say? He didn't seem to know himself.

Ev cleared his voice and glanced away. "We've gotten to be friends over the past couple of months. At least, I think we have."

"We have," she agreed, although his comment veered into a new direction. "And we share Tee." Doro aimed for a lighthearted note.

"We do." His voice seemed flat, and his features schooled. "I don't want my hovering to spoil that, but friends worry about friends."

Several uses of the word *friends* sent a powerful message, and Doro felt foolish for worrying about the man asking her to step out, let alone court. "They do." Had she injected enough enthusiasm? To ensure she had, Doro emphasized the point. "They certainly do."

He nodded. "I hope we're still friends, despite the last couple of days."

A hush fell, while Doro debated whether to reassure him or to ask why he had avoided talking with her. Doro folded her gloved hands together and stared down at them. "You helped with party preparation. You chatted with almost everyone, but not me. That didn't seem friendly." She was pleased with the tone and tenor of her statements.

"It wasn't. I overreacted, I guess. My sister has accused me of being too protective many times, and I haven't overcome it completely. She believes, like you do, that women are as capable as men. I agree with her. It's a big reason I supported her attending college and getting a job after graduation."

"You've never said what your sister does," Doro commented.

"She was a teacher," he replied, "but she had to give it up when she got married. Sally was terribly upset, but it's the policy at most schools."

"It is," Doro agreed. "Even at the college. No married ladies can work here."

"Mrs. Jones said that'll change. Michaw is such a progressive school."

When had he discussed the topic with her mother's friend, who was also the president's secretary? And why? A heavy breath escaped Doro. "In most ways, it is. But the Board of Trustees is at odds with regard to making a change, despite President Adams favoring it. Right now, they're almost evenly divided at five against and four in favor. If he can't sway them, I'm afraid it won't happen for a while. Maybe years. He's only back temporarily, and the next head administrator may not want to rock the boat for a time, no matter how he feels about working wives."

"Could you work at another college?"

The question surprised her. "I don't plan to wed. I never have."

Even in the faint light, his dismayed expression was obvious. "You don't ever want to get married and have a family?"

Although Doro had heard the question from many people, Ev voicing it bothered her. Immediately, she went on the defensive. "There's nothing wrong with me wanting a career."

"Of course not," he said. "But most folks, men and women, want a home and children."

The old resentment rose inside her and spilled over. "Men can have everything. Women can't. We have to choose. I've wanted to be a librarian and professor since I was a little girl. When I told people, most of them said I couldn't do that while being a wife and mother."

"You decided not to get married when you were a child?" Again, surprise was in his tone.

"Not as a child, but in high school." Back then, the boys had not liked her excelling in class and getting better grades. Several of her mother's friends had commented on what they termed *the problem*. "*The problem is Doro winning the class essay contest every year.*" And "*The problem is Doro getting the highest scores in mathematics.*" The remarks began with the problem and ended with...*that's why no one asks her to dance, or escorts her to a party* and so on. It had not taken Doro long to choose what made her comfortable—books and studying—over what made her anxious—socializing.

"You must've disappointed a lot of boys with that decision."

Since Ev sounded sincere, Doro answered honestly. "Not really, since boys didn't chase after me." Heaven knew, she hadn't pursued them.

"That's hard to believe. You're pretty and smart."

His compliment touched her, but Doro maintained her composure. "Thank you, but I was a tomboy, too. Boys don't like girls who can best them in school and in sports. At least I could out-skate and outrun them until they shot past me in height and weight. By then, they were interested in girls who dressed up and stayed clean."

A chuckle left him. "Your mother didn't make you bathe?"

The injection of humor pricked at her defenses. "Of course, she did. I was dirty a lot because I liked to dig for arrowheads and fossils. There are lots of both around here. And I played ball with the boys until they wouldn't let me anymore."

"Their loss," he murmured. After several seconds, Ev spoke again. "But, unlike those kids, I don't want to lose your friendship."

"You haven't," she replied. "And you won't."

"Good. Going forward, I'll try to avoid fretting over what you do. Not that we're apt to have another murder to solve soon."

"Or ever. Two homicides in three months is shocking enough, especially when Michaw never had a murder before October."

"It's unlikely to ever experience another one. Or any sort of major crime, so you'll be back to studying mysteries with your students, not investigating them with Wade, Aggie, and me."

"You're most likely right." Doro failed to keep a wistful note out of her voice.

"You sound disappointed."

"Maybe a little." A shiver rippled through her. "I've had enough fresh air." And enough time battling conflicting emotions.

"Let's go inside," he suggested. "If you don't mind dancing with a friend, I'd enjoy getting on the floor. The music sounds wonderful."

They had danced at a Halloween party in October, and Doro had enjoyed it—probably more than she should have. Being in Ev's arms had been a treat. Since the only time that would happen was at a party, she would savor the occasions because they would never be more than dancing partners and sleuthing teammates, which was fine.

Once back inside, Ev helped Doro remove her wrap and stood back. "You look lovely."

Heat scorched her cheeks. "Thank you." When he took off his coat, she smiled. "You're not wearing your uniform." Instead, he was clad in a gunmetal gray suit with a fitted wool jacket. His pristine white shirt was set off with a burgundy tie. If they had discussed matching colors, the two of them could not have done better.

"I'm not working, and I don't have much chance to wear my good suit," he admitted.

"You look very nice," she observed, although *nice* was far too tepid. He was devastatingly handsome.

"Thank you." Ev offered his arm to Doro. "Let's not waste the music."

"We have a phonograph for the first time," she replied, stating the obvious.

"Wasn't that one of your suggestions?" he asked.

She nodded. "It was one of three. Electric lights on the tree were another." Doro's gaze moved to the tall tree at the far end of the auditorium. "I love their sparkle."

"Pretty," Ev murmured as he glanced from the towering Fraser fir to Doro. "Very pretty. Let's dance?"

"Yes, let's."

Ev's answer was to lead her on to the dance floor. When he took her into his arms, she rested one hand in his and the other on his shoulder. Despite layers of fabric, and a suitable distance between them, Doro felt his warmth, and inhaled the subtle scent of sandalwood. Over his shoulder, she gazed at the sparkling lights on the tree before scanning the other decorations. Evergreen boughs, red bows, and baskets of pine cones added festive touches. So did mistletoe, her third idea, in every archway. The sprigs, sporting red ribbon, looked lovely. And inviting. Heat spread into her cheeks just as Ev gazed down at her.

"Getting too hot?" he asked in a soft murmur. "Some of us set up benches outside."

Doro's attention went to the wall of windows at the far end of the room. Lanterns and seating dotted the space, as did a lattice archway festooned with evergreen boughs and an enormous bunch of mistletoe. To get to the benches, couples would pass under the kissing bough. Was Ev suggesting they get more fresh air? "I see," she murmured.

"We could take a break."

Doro did not say they had only danced a few moments. Instead, she agreed. "That sounds lovely."

A grin lit his handsome face, and as he swirled her closer to the exit, Doro could not keep from beaming in return.

Author's Notes

At one time, there actually was a Mitchaw, Ohio (sometimes called Mitchaw Corners). It was the birthplace of many of my relatives, including my dad. At its height, Mitchaw was an unincorporated village surrounded by farms. Like many other small, rural communities, it has disappeared as a separate entity. Now, it is part of Sylvania Township, and subdivisions have replaced most farms.

The town never had a college, nor was it as large and bustling as the Michaw in the Doro books. That is a big reason I dropped the "t" to change the spelling. However, Sylvania is a very real city. It is my hometown and where I still live. Since the 1920s, when this book is set, it has gone from a small village of around 2000 to a small city of 19,000. The township's population is approximately 50,000.

About the Author

D.S. Lang started making up stories to entertain herself as an only child, and she is still making them up. Now, she puts them in writing! She pens historical mysteries set in post-Great War, small town America. The books feature amateur women sleuths dedicated to catching bad gals and guys.

She holds Bachelor's and Master's degrees in Education from the University of Toledo. Among her jobs have been teacher (junior high, high school, and college), program manager, mentor, tutor, and golf shop manager.

In her free time, D.S. enjoys swimming, reading, spending time with family and friends, and walking with her dog, Izzy.

FAMILY FAVORITE COOKIES

In the book, Doro and Aggie use an old Banyon family recipe to bake cookies. In reality, I found this one handwritten in an old recipe book of my mom's. I have not made them in many years, but I remember these treats as being delicious. My friend Joyce, a terrific baker, has a similar recipe and she helped jog my memory about the amount of flour. We only had the cookies for holidays, so they are a special memory!

1 cup brown sugar

1 cup white sugar

1 cup butter

2 eggs

Cream above ingredients well.

1 cup buttermilk

1 tsp baking soda

1 tsp baking powder

2 tsp vanilla

1/2 tsp salt

1 tsp nutmeg

Add the above to creamed mixture.

Add enough flour to spoon cookies into your hand and pat out. (This is tricky!)

Bake @375-400 degrees for 10 minutes, watching carefully

Thank you!

Thank you for reading The Murdered Matron! I hope you enjoyed it. If you have time, please rate or review it. Comments from readers are helpful and appreciated. I am on Goodreads and BookBub. Most retailers also accept reviews.

https://www.goodreads.com/author/show/21325652.D_S_Lang

https://partners.bookbub.com/authors/6026727/edit

For more information, please go to my website or Facebook page.

https://www.dslangbooks.com

https://www.facebook.com/profile.php?id=100064024056297

You can sign up for my newsletter on my website. I share other authors' work, news about my books, a peek into the writing life, historical tidbits, and more. Your email will never be shared, and you unsubscribe at any time!

Doro Banyon Historical Mystery series

The Doro Banyon series has a cozier tone than the Arabella Stewart books. History and mystery still mesh as amateur sleuth Doro solves whodunits with a team of colorful characters in smalltown America during the 1920s. Travel back in time to a college campus and crack cases with them!

Prequel-The Lost Exam

Book 1-The Catalogued Corpse

Book 2-<u>The Murdered Matron</u> (December 2023)

The prequel is not available for sale, but it is free to my newsletter subscribers. You can sign up at: https://www.dslangbooks.com

Arabella Stewart Historical Mystery series

The Arabella Stewart Historical Mystery series is set in small-town Ohio after the Great War. Bella returns home from serving as a U.S. Army Signal Corps operator to find her family resort and hometown in dire straits, and the murder of a neighbor adds to the trouble. Much to the dismay of Constable Jax Hastings, an Army veteran, Bella turns amateur sleuth to solve the case. As the series continues, Bella and Jax vanquish the shadows of the war, while solving a series of whodunits with a team of colorful characters. If you love history and mystery mixed with touches of humor and drama, this series is for you!

Book One-<u>A Precarious Homecoming</u>

Book Two-<u>A Lingering Shadow</u>
Book Three-<u>A Lethal Arrogance</u>
Book Four-<u>A Baffling Absence</u>
Book Five-<u>A Fatal Reunion</u>
Book Six-<u>A Surreptitious Undertaking</u>
Book Seven-<u>A Treacherous Accusation</u>
Book Eight-<u>An Uncertain Ceremony</u>

www.ingramcontent.com/pod-product-compliance
Lightning Source LLC
Chambersburg PA
CBHW052021020726
47501CB00004B/1180